BETWEEN
THE
LINES

BETWEEN THE LINES

S.J. BUTLER

ACCENT

First published in 2020 by Headline Accent
An imprint of HEADLINE PUBLISHING GROUP

1

Cataloguing in Publication Data is available from the British Library

ISBN 978 1 7861 5770 6

Typeset in 10.5/13pt Bembo Std by Jouve (UK), Milton Keynes

Printed and bound in Great Britain by Clays Ltd, Elcograf S.p.A.

HEADLINE PUBLISHING GROUP
An Hachette UK Company
Carmelite House
50 Victoria Embankment
London EC4Y 0DZ

www.headline.co.uk
www.hachette.co.uk

For Teresa and Louis

Part One

CLIFFS: downward, land to sea (a good start); earth that is suddenly sliced, falling to rocks and beach; a hanging jut, eroded by time; a mound, worn mercilessly by the elements (bit dramatic); where you arrive at the edge; a place to just stand and stare (poignant); a vantage point; somewhere to sway in the breeze and reflect; a drop which you arrive at if you walk from one side of an island to the other; where you abruptly cease and can't go on no more; land that suddenly comes to an end; a point of . . .

And I don't want to think any more so I stop myself.

Chapter One

'It's a point of no return,' he said to himself.

Briefly closing his eyes, the man on the cliff shifted uneasily from toe to toe as if engaged in an awkward slow dance. His hands, thrust deep in the pockets of an ankle-length overcoat, fingered the cold assortment of stray coins, kneading them in his palms until warm, then letting them drop like winnings from a one-armed bandit. He stood restless, preoccupied and at the same time confused by what lay before him, as he struggled to link shapes, clouds, and terra firma. Slowly, he lifted his binoculars from his chest; rubbing the scar above his left eye he pulled the glasses close, wincing at the suddenness of hard metal on skin. Each time the wind blew in from the sea he could feel the salt setting on his pockmarked cheeks, puffed up like scarred boulders. Nervously checking his watch he returned to the tubular vision of his glasses, from left to right and back again, his shaking hands the only giveaway that they were being operated by someone not used to watching and waiting for something to happen.

Pushing his hair to one side he now surveyed further up the worn trail towards the headland which gave the appearance of a piece of embroidery, knitted together by the odd chalk vein or sodden patch of grass. Like an unwanted blemish on a newly washed white sheet, a man with a dog spilled into his line of vision, rambling down the path five metres from the edge, the dog zig-zagging around his master, frantically sniffing every cranny in its path. The owner, a stooped elderly man with a tartan cap, barked instructions to the spaniel, who continued to make imaginary triangles as he went – the words lost on the rising wind as if bellowed from the mouth of a silent movie star.

Tiring of the man and dog, he switched his attention to the ocean, expecting to see a ship or maybe a submarine, but saw only a vast restless greyness which threatened the white cliff face with slow rhythmic slaps, each clap reminding those safely above of the violence of the waves below. Hearing a far-off cry, he anxiously swung towards where two children, a boy and a girl, appeared to sprint towards the edge only to suddenly stop as if commanded to do so. To the right their mother sprung into view, running and waving her arms wildly; her red cheeks and cross expression a symptom of the anguish within as she grabbed both toddlers roughly by their mittened hands, marching them away and no doubt explaining the dangers of running towards the fall of a cliff.

He stayed with the woman for some time, admiring the light lines around her eyes. Her flushed beauty making him want to watch her more. Lowering his glasses, the mother and her children became mere dots on a rain-drenched landscape; lost in time; now further away in a distant parallel world they drifted slowly out of sight as they disappeared down the coastal path towards the car park.

Alone, the man on the cliff swayed like a meditating Buddha, caught at times on the wind which threatened more than it blew. Allowing his weight to be held, his billowing long coat a sprung sail, he felt as if he were floating on air as the gulls above showed him how it was done, gliding up and down on the currents of air, their cries ringing in his ears like the songs of sirens. Looking down at his six-foot-two block of a body, his gaze arrived at his scuffed, muddy, brown brogues and focused on the light scratches around the tips and the oil stain on the right toe he could never get out.

'What you looking at?' asked Steve from Accounts who'd shuffled over with two pints of lager, locked together like a rack of snooker balls.

'Me shoes; look,' motioned Kev, nodding downwards, 'the burger dripped all over me new brogues.'

4

'You'll never get that out.'

'What?'

They looked at each other for a moment, their words lost, muddled and competing with the booming disco coming from the front of the riverboat.

'Me shoes,' he managed again, staggering forward as a strong current of the Thames decided to ripple and lurch in another direction.

'Hold on a minute.' Steve expertly placed the pints down on a spare table. 'Just a second,' he said holding down the bile in the pit of his stomach as best he could. He didn't make it though, puking up in the bin besides the gents as the rest of the partygoers from an assortment of companies cheered him loudly as they punched the air in between singing a chorus of 'Don't Look Back in Anger'.

Kevin Parker, reasonably competent literary agent, was out celebrating his colleague Rachel Winkler's successful book launch: debut novelist Emma Brockenhurst had got a glowing mention on Richard and Judy's Book of the Week slot with *Spider in the Garden*.

'How's your list going?' Rachel had asked him earlier in the evening, when everything was relatively normal and each had had a complimentary white wine plonked into their hands as they stepped from the gang plank.

'Fine,' he'd answered unconvincingly. The list was a disaster: two plodding crime novels, a debut thriller and a book of jokes by a clapped-out old comedian who was making something of a comeback due to the resurgence in un-PC comedy. He always thought it strange how they'd both started out as literary agents around the same time: Rachel coming straight from university with a First in English, while he'd come the same route with a 2.1, before slogging it out in the lower echelons of publishing, working in circulation, eventually gaining a position at the venerated Hargreaves & Bennett Literary Agency.

Now, while his colleagues' writers were winning awards, he was still struggling, picking up the pieces and playing catch-up. Sonia Allen's *The Wave of Time* had been his best success so far, and sadly his only dinner party story. He desperately needed something *fresh and intensely absorbing* (his boss's words, not his).

Fuck the YA route, thought Kev, as one of the company directors threw some glowing comment Rachel's way. Anything but Young Adult Fiction; why, he didn't know exactly, but he detested the genre, even if it did sell well as Rachel had demonstrated time and time again.

'That's better.' It was Steve again. 'Drink up,' he said handing Kev a whiskey which he'd somehow acquired in between throwing up and returning from the gents.

There was something very normal and uncomplicated about Steve that Kev liked, or rather, that reminded him of his old comprehensive. Sadly, apart from his mum and dad, he only met confident, well-educated literary types nowadays, who were far detached from the world he used to know. He was also drawn to Steve's hook nose, Buddy Holly glasses, and nasal whine which was used to good effect if he wanted to entertain or annoy those around him. Kev was sure the other agents thought it strange that he preferred to hang out after work with Steve from Accounts rather than Rachel or Josh from Notting Hill.

'Oh, hi, Josh,' sighed Kev. Annoyingly always on a high, Josh had just crept up behind Kev and flicked his ear.

'How did you know it was me?'

'I'd know that limp flick anywhere,' he managed, slurring the last part as he turned and flung his arm around Josh's shoulder, dragging him in for a hug.

'Anyone would think it was your party,' remarked Josh smiling and showing a very white, straight set of teeth in a perfectly square chiselled jaw as he managed to slip Kev's drunken grip.

'Some might say he's just a geezer who loves to party, hey, Kev?' whined Steve pushing up his glasses which kept slipping over the bridge of his nose as his head bobbed to the music.

Barely acknowledging Steve, Josh continued. 'Do you know who I met today?'

'Go on,' said Kev, knocking back another shot which had materialised in front of him.

'Holly Watkins Lockhart,' he announced proudly before clicking his fingers and making the shape of a gun as he shot off an imaginary round of bullets.

'Wow, Holly,' mimicked Kev winking at Steve. 'Isn't she . . .' What had happened? Ah, there they are, he almost said, as the words began to form in the pint glass of his mind. 'Isn't she a commissioning editor at . . .'

'Penguin,' interrupted Josh, red-faced, the affirmation he'd wanted drastically sucked from his clutches by a few fading brain cells in Kev's frontal lobe.

'Look at me shoes,' he began again his back fully arched as he struggled to touch his toes.

'Burger juice,' added Steve.

'Yeah, bastard burger . . .'

'Juice,' helped out Josh smarmily before making a quick beeline for the company director who'd been gushing at Rachel.

'Tosser!' said Steve as Josh sidled off.

'Ah, he's alright, he's just . . .'

'A tosser.'

'Yeah, a tosser.'

For a while that was all he could remember. Though he vaguely remembered spending some time in the gents, where he'd met Josh again who'd offered him a line of coke. Whether he'd taken it or not, he couldn't think, but he was sure there was now a numb bitter taste at the back of his throat.

12.01 a.m. 'Murder on the Dancefloor' by Sophie Ellis-Bextor. The jacket was off, neatly folded in a safe place, as was his waistcoat. Spinning, lost in the music, he tried to make sense of his surroundings. Steve, he'd last seen sitting with Cathy (also from Accounts) looking as if they were having a serious heart-to-heart. This, he was sure, had something to do with her running mascara. Things suddenly seemed slower than usual as he pumped out his arms and moved in time to the beat as best he could. It was as if he was everywhere, gliding like a bird over the dance floor. As Steve had remarked before, *Kev could dance himself sober*. It was something he'd done from a very young age.

Back when his mum and dad went dancing in Streatham they always took Kev and his sister Alice along. Though nothing like his sloppy repertoire of moves now, back then they'd copied as best they could the moves of The Temptations, The Drifters, and The Four Tops – dancing was a bit more stylish back then. Now, he threw himself around the floor until that time when what you felt, said and did and what you thought you may hear others say was of little consequence. The faces (mostly happy), bodies, muscles flexing, joints springing, sweat pumping, twisting, moving within the haze of drink. Slow it down and it's really not much fun at all: ritualised, hardly spontaneous fun.

'Dance, brother, dance!' he shouted wondering where the words had sprung from as he smiled gormlessly at another face he didn't know.

The pulsating beat was now pouring into his ears from the pounding speakers he'd got too close to, while the brightly coloured light provided an almost hypnotic, Morse-code flashing dance. *Whose tongue is this in my head?* he thought, landing in another place across the dance floor. *Whose hips am I holding on to?* he wondered as he became suddenly disentangled from the warm curve of a pencil skirt. The music was now a wall of noise booming in his ears, as another pair of arms sprung like roots around his neck; a new smell; a different perfume; her hair splayed, bouncing and hitting him in the face as they jumped and clutched and finally collapsed in each other's arms as the song ended. Then another tongue in the back of his throat (or was it the same one?) along with the bitter taste and gurgling whiskey fumes.

Back in the dark spot, in the corner of the dance floor with his brown pin-striped jacket, a young woman sits on his lap as he cradles her bottom and someone flicks his ear. The yearning, the feeling that he's between the sheets but he's not, as his hands move up and down, rubbing, trying to colour in the curves and make sense of the warm body which feels as if it's attached to him like a limpet on a rock. The sensation; the need; the frustration; the constant desire for; the desperation; the fumble for the unattainable. He's there for some time, lost, hopelessly drunk, stranded as if a beached whale on a lonely shore, scarred, his lips lacerated by sticky red lipstick and a longing for home.

1.15: They're all gone; lost in a bad dream; dispensed with; left spinning in a throbbing skull somewhere on the lonely river. Alone outside on the deck the distant thud of the speakers are just audible above the soft slurps of the Thames as the boat ducks under Waterloo Bridge for the tenth time. Pint of water in hand and trying to quell the taste of vomit in his throat, Kev pulled up the collar of his jacket and marvelled at the ink black river and sky which had merged into one, only separated by the embankment of lights and looming, lit buildings on either side appearing as if leaning in like lurking riverside branches and reeds. The blues and greys in between the architecture blurred by the fuzzy bulbs decorating the Queen Elizabeth Hall rising into the night sky as if mixed on a French Impressionist's palette.

'Penny?' The word rang clear and would have leapt into the sky if it had been a starry night. Turning, Kev could just make out the silhouette of a woman, her hair tied into a high bun, smoking a cigarette. Whatever she was wearing it gave the impression of edgy elegance in a vintage 1950s style. Moving out of the shadow, the woman squinted before opening her eyes to reveal their wide, chocolate brown opulence. She was dark; petite; mysterious-looking with a Parisian aura about her.

'For your thoughts,' she said.

'Ah, just sobering up,' shrugged Kev, trying to appear casual while still admiring her.

'Are you with the marketing company?' she asked, moving closer and standing by his side as he leaned against a warm steel hatch which had some kind of boiler humming under it.

'No, the Literary Agency; there's only a few of us – celebrating a colleague's success,' he said glancing down at his shoes. 'And you?'

'The Design Company: Blue Larsson. We're the ones where the women have pale faces and red lipstick and the men wear glasses with the top buttons of their check shirts done up tight,' she said, consciously pushing her hip to one side and taking a deep drag on her cigarette.

'Is that a pen in your hair?' It had been bothering him ever since she'd moved into the light. If it was a pen, it was a look he liked: that arty student or silently moving effortlessly between tables, professional waitress look.

'It's a pencil,' she laughed as the creases around her eyes danced and then disappeared as her muscles relaxed. 'I like to draw.'

'An artist?' he said scratching his stubbly chin. 'I mean – you draw.'

'Yes, I draw,' she giggled.

'What do you draw?' A game of verbal ping-pong seemed a good idea. In his experience a lot of good conversations started out this way.

'Eyes.'

'Eyes?'

'Yes, I love eyes. I do large charcoal drawings. If I see a pair I like, I sketch them, then upsize them later.'

'Big art?'

'Yes, big art. And if I have my camera I just zoom in like this,' she added, making a tube shape with her hand, putting it up to her eye and pushing her head closer to his as he laughed.

He thought about asking her if she wanted to draw his, but knew it would sound a bit predictable. Anyway, he was still doing his best James Dean: back to the wall and right foot up against it, coolly supporting him. He was quietly flirting without being too obvious.

'So you're an art school graduate?' he said, aware that others were slowly making their way out onto the deck, their conversations lost on the night air.

'Yeah, a bit of a giveaway isn't it?'

'Don't they just spend their grant money and form indie bands?' he said before realising how old-fashioned the comment sounded.

'Kind of thing my dad would say.'

He liked her; knew instantly that she was different, had a uniqueness that couldn't be bottled or imitated convincingly. Some people just had that beauty about them: that verve and mindset which made them pieces of self-contained, ever changing art.

Hoping she had an exotic or French-sounding name, he asked her.

'Eve Blake,' she answered, holding out her pale hand. He liked the name, it suited her. Great if her dad was a William like mine, he thought, as he felt the warmth of her touch and a tingling sensation in his stomach which he was sure wasn't reflux.

'And you?' she asked.

'Oh, Kevin Parker; Kev.' He always introduced himself this way, as if his Christian name was somehow offensive.

'Kev Parker: Literary Agent.' She said it slowly and deliberately.

'No, no one well-known,' he quickly added anticipating her next question.

'Oh,' she said, 'you thought I was going to ask you about your writers?'

'Weren't you?' he said, feeling a bit foolish and less cool than before as his foot suddenly slipped down the wall and made him wobble on the spot.

'No; though it was probably going to be my next one.'

'Well, to answer your next question then: Sonia Allen.'

'Oh, yeah, *The Wave of Time*,' she replied excitedly.

'You read it?'

'No.'

They laughed.

'Is that a scar above your eye?' she asked suddenly as, as if on cue, another passing riverboat illuminated his face, honking its horn as it tore by.

Instantly conscious, lit for all to see, he put his hand up and stroked his chin.

'I like it. Can I touch it?' she asked, rolling up her fingers into a lens shape again.

'Sure,' he said.

As she ran her finger over the smooth laceration he felt a cold pleasant ache above his brow and behind his socket, like he'd just swallowed ice cream and got a brain-freeze. He didn't for a minute think it strange that she would ask such a thing.

'How'd you get it?' She was inquisitive in a friendly, good cop kind of way – the type you'd readily spill your guts to.

'Fight in school over a girl named Jane.'

'Chivalrous.'

'Stupid – scarred for life for a girl who cared for someone else.'

'Unrequited love.'

'Something like that.' He smiled, noting something else crossing her brow as if her mind appeared to come to a decision about the next thing she was about to say. 'You like to dance then?' she said cautiously. 'I saw you dancing. I watched you for some time,' she blurted.

'Right,' he said simply, with the vague inclination that she probably saw more than he would have liked. After all he had been that dancing fool: the drunken two-step, fox-trot-dog.

'The other women: they seemed to like you – a lot,' she said with a mischievous smile, but the lowering of her eyelids as if in prayer on the final word seemed to reveal more.

He'd been trying to link it all together before she'd appeared on the deck. There had definitely been two women he'd snogged. Cringingly, he remembered snippets of dirty dancing and a slow dance which had perhaps a little too much bum-squeezing, and then the elusive, yet-to-be-comprehended fumble in the shadows which he couldn't place.

'Yeah, bit embarrassing, that part of the evening.' He felt like saying sorry; was even guilty that she'd been a voyeur of his drunken escapades. He felt a sudden compulsion to say more. 'Sometimes I just drink too much.' He couldn't say anything else on the matter. It was hard enough talking to a stranger about the intricacies of being drunk.

'We all let rip now and again,' she said, coming to his rescue. 'Even me.'

He knew she was humouring him. How could someone who wore flats, who fashioned a pencil in her bun, grope her way around a dance floor?

12

'Here,' he said, taking off his jacket and draping it over her shoulders. He couldn't think of anything else to do or say. Seen it done in so many films before that it seemed only natural that the action should complement the scene. As if acting in the same movie, she moved in close, nestling her head on his chest. Thinking of their conversation, he hesitated for a second before wrapping his arm around her shoulder as they passed one last time under the now very familiar Waterloo Bridge.

Chapter Two

Kev let his body take the full force of the wind as it made him take two lurching steps forward. He remembered doing the same thing with Alice when they were both bored teenagers, grudgingly accompanying their parents on various camping holidays to Whitby and Scarborough. It was Dad's, Bill's, idea: 'See how long you can stand on one leg for,' he'd bellow above the crashing waves of Robin Hood's Bay. Sometimes it was two legs, depending on the force of the wind; Margaret, his wife, always in the throes of unwrapping sandwiches or pouring hot sweet tea from a tartan flask, urging them on, knowing that a few minutes more swaying in the wind would stop them from killing each other. Thinking back, it seemed as if he were always standing on a cliff.

The wind died. Just as it had when he stood on the East Cliff at Whitby all those years ago, he thought, both events placed side by side in time. It was as odd then as it was now, the gusting wind just ran temporarily out of puff.

When it returned the gulls could be heard again, no doubt rein-vigorated after the lull, squawking at an imaginary foe that appeared to surround them. The light had changed, the sky almost pure white and the sea more blue than grey. Many of the flocks of seabirds were heading back out to sea, recharged and ready to fish. Further out, he saw his first fishing boat bobbing up and down, heading towards land, relieved no doubt that the bad weather which had threatened had disembarked for the shores of Calais.

Retracing his steps he clambered back up the headland. Reaching higher ground he sat down on what must have once been a stone stile or the beginnings of an ancient animal pen. From here he could see the tip of the ridge where, if you reached the top, you'd be stunned by the sudden image of the lighthouse below looming into view, rising like a concrete leek from the water.

Nothing showing, he scanned back down the cliff edge to where it appeared more rugged, like a line of jigsaw pieces that didn't quite fit properly. At the point where the V-shaped clump of white chalk and stone jutted out on its own, as if separated from the cliff, sat a green-fleeced figure holding a camera with a long lens. His heart thumping, he anxiously adjusted his glasses until the image became clearer and intimate. A woman, mid-forties, a huge mop of frizzy hair standing on end, was sitting precariously close to the edge; the heel of her hiking boot dangling over the ledge; underneath it there appeared to be a hairline crack in the cliff face. The gulls forming above her head seemed angry at the intrusion and were letting their feelings be known as they screeched and dived around her. Whatever she was looking at wasn't wildlife – birds, dogs and human beings the only warm-blooded creatures patrolling the contours of the downs. She could easily have been a statue gazing out to sea, oblivious to the excruciating din above her.

When you watch someone for long enough they become portraits. Instinctively, Kev framed the figure before him, incorporating the birds while trying to capture the atmosphere of steely concentration being steadily played out. Rapidly following her line of vision he landed on the source of the composition: a man in his mid-thirties, hands thrust deep into the pockets of his trousers, stood frozen two or three metres from the edge. The stretch between photographer and subject could only have been twelve feet at the most; and although within talking distance, nothing was said. Looking at the man's lack of coat or jumper, he felt a shiver down his back as he stood and contemplated calling out to them both, and ruining what he hoped wasn't a woman eagerly awaiting a photo of a man jumping to his death. Straining his eyes, trying to see more, he felt the compulsion to run towards them, perhaps to scream and put an end to the sinister possibilities pouring into his mind. It was how animals viewed one another, he reasoned, as again he nervously switched back and forth from the photographer to the man in the hope they'd both give up whatever intentions they had.

Another figure had arrived on the stage. A man in his seventies, wearing a red fleece and black trousers and shoes, was talking earnestly to the young man, appearing to gesture to him to follow him back up the headland. There had been little movement on the young man's part as he barely turned round, continuing his interest in what lay beyond out at sea. Moving closer, the older man now stood beside the younger one, reaching into his pocket for cigarettes and offering one which the young man took casually, as if they were both standing at the bar of a quaint country pub. After a few seconds they both turned and began to stroll slowly back up the incline to the safety of the greener grass.

The photographer was now standing. Quite a tall woman, dressed in one of those generic bird-watching body warmers over a bottle green fleece, she began unscrewing the lens of her camera and placing it in a yellow rucksack. Suddenly she threw her arms in the air and made an exaggerated face in the direction of the two men. Zooming in on the old man, he noticed that he too was mirroring the woman's actions, throwing his arms behind him as he crossly called back at her, stopping in his tracks from time to time to make an angry point. Watching the two men, they could easily have been father and son as they appeared to joke and exchange pleasantries as they arrived at a parked Land Rover. The older man handed the other a card and patted him on the back, then took a call on his mobile. They both got into the car and carefully drove away.

'What time is it?' yawned Kev, rolling over onto his back as the sunlight pierced his eyes and a cold draught from an open window slapped his face.

'Eight,' she said brightly. Eve was adjusting the curtains she'd just pulled apart. Fully dressed, it was clear her morning had started some hours before and that by busying herself in the bedroom, having already made a clean sweep of the flat, her ulterior motive was to get him up.

'But it's Saturday,' he moaned, throwing his hands up to his face.

'And it's Christmas Eve.'

'Oh, yeah,' he replied, rubbing his eyes and adjusting them to what would be a perfect Chelsea morning if she'd only lived just over the bridge from the now very trendy Battersea.

Duster in hand, she vigorously polished her dressing table mirror above which the arching figure of Iggy Pop, his chest scarred and smeared with blood, stared down, his mind someplace else than the Roundhouse in which the photograph was taken. On the odd occasion Kev stayed over he always made a conscious effort not to look Iggy's way. It was as if he saw everything; particularly the sex.

'Remember,' she said, polish can in hand, 'we're meeting my parents today.'

It was as if the manic cleaning was somehow synonymous with her family. Well, everyone's nervous upon introducing a new boyfriend or girlfriend to their family, he thought. Somehow he'd managed to duck his part of the bargain and was putting it off to the end of the year: New Year's Eve to be precise.

'*Three months and two days*,' she'd kept reminding him. It was her on-going joke. After their first week of meeting, every time they met for a date she'd announce the exact amount of time they'd been seeing each other. He liked her humour, it was mischievous as well as playful; the considerable difference in height between them (her 5'3 and his 6'2) meant that he was naturally the butt of most of her jokes, as was the nature of her initial sighting of him on the ship. Upon meeting her friends he'd be introduced as '*the groper from the dance floor*' she had been telling them about. She liked to see him squirm when she relayed the finer details of how they first met. He didn't mind. It kind of acted as a humbling release for him from a sequence of events he wished had never taken place. She would usually make the quip that they were '*warming him up for her*,' or that '*she'd saved him from a life of drunken debauchery and hell, Amen.*' Always the

Amen at the end – he'd noticed he too began to place it at the end of his own sentences. *Amen.*

'Are you anxious?' he asked, pulling on his white T-shirt before slumping back into the plump, puffed pillows and avoiding eye contact with Iggy.

'About?' she answered a little sharply, her eyes darting across to the poster as if the voice of the arching figure had spoken.

'The first family dinner with me at the table, Amen.'

She smiled. 'Still mimicking me, huh?' she said flicking his stray toe with her cloth as he made an exaggerated *Ow!* 'Why would I be anxious about meeting my own family,' she continued, her hands placed firmly on her hips as she stood in a now familiar comic pose, the light from the high window pouring down the right side of her body. He felt like saying *Amen* again at what was like an apparition, the moles on her pale skin and particularly the one on her left cheek like a spot of paint on the tip of a Flemish artist's brush. 'Well, there is the Kev issue to contend with I suppose,' she added as the dimples in her cheeks rose and she laughed out loud. 'Just remember to keep on smiling.'

'Is your sister going to be there?'

The mere mention of Sarah seemed to signal a change in atmosphere as the vein in her neck decided to temporarily twitch and throb. 'Yes,' she managed, her smile wiped from her face.

'You never mention her,' he said even though he sensed he'd hit a nerve or two. He wasn't being cruel, he was just interested, always fascinated when someone's mask slipped, revealing some inner angst or secret.

'You'll meet her soon enough,' was all she said, firmly drawing an imaginary line underneath it as she polished even more rigorously than before.

They spent the rest of the morning reading the weekend papers, drinking coffee, and breaking fresh croissants in a very nice bourgeois way as Radio 4 oozed in the background, the soft voices of the presenters relaxing their weekday bones.

Midday and it was time to get going. The plan was to have lunch

18

with Eve's parents, get in and out ASAP; allowing the early evening to themselves, before both returning to their own families for festivities. Eve had already promised her mum she'd make Christmas Midnight Mass which had been an unbroken tradition as far back as she could remember. She and Sarah were always there, even when they weren't speaking to one another.

The trip to Clapham Common had been a short one. In fact it was such a lovely morning they'd decided to walk through Lavender Hill and take one of the many straight, tree-lined streets which led to the Common. Reaching the concrete mounds where the old gun emplacement and air-raid shelters used to be during the war, they walked on past the grandstand and the wooden tea room which was surprisingly still open, with wrapped-up old men sitting outside playing chess at rickety metal tables which dug into their ribs every time they bent over to make a move. When they reached the pond on the north side they decided to sit at a bench overlooking a small island in the middle of it before crossing over the road to where her parents lived.

He wanted to say it there and then, the thing he hadn't managed to get beyond his tonsils yet; the three words she'd been waiting three months and three days to hear. Looking at her now, the blood-red lipstick and dark mascara, the collar of her mauve woolly overcoat pulled tightly up around her ears, and that concentrated gaze which seemed to be studying swans but could easily have been writing the first page of a novel. Why? He didn't know. He just put it off. Instead the idea entered his head that somehow New Year's Eve would be the right time – the symbolism of Auld Lang Syne. It sent shivers up his spine, seeing them both standing, cold by the magical, glittery Thames, at midnight and him whispering those words that always sounded strange and corny no matter how you said them.

In fact it wasn't the swans she'd been staring at, but a duck attempting to get to its feet beyond, on the icy island. Every time it tried to lift its tattered body, it slumped to the ground. The bird desperately repeated the whole process again, tragically refusing to give up. Staring at it now, Eve knew that the poor creature would keep trying to mend itself through the night and into the early morning when, finally defeated by exhaustion and hunger, it would probably heroically die.

'Why the tears?' he asked, wiping a wet trickle that now slowed, then turned like a stream down his own hand as if trying to escape being dried.

'It's nothing,' she said, forcing a smile and briefly squeezing his hand. 'We'd better get going,' she added as they both rose and headed for the main road.

Feeling the dampness on his fingertips he secretly licked them, the saltiness somehow willing him to follow suit and sob like a child. Searching for her warm hand he pursued the tears no more.

What would have been a lush leafy avenue in summer was now a bare lifeless habitat of balding hedges and ominously closed garden gates; the whole street deserted, disregarded for a season as its occupants hid in their middle-class Shangri-Las, selfishly content and satisfied. Turning the corner of Cherry Orchard Road, that was how he felt: it was an almost apocalyptic and stifling view of Eve's childhood surroundings.

Barely a word spoken between them, they reached an impressive Victorian ivy-covered red brick house which could easily have been a scene from a Christmas card. The intensity of Eve's grip as they opened the noisy black gate affirmed the dread he'd already felt. They'd both instinctively slowed down as Eve announced that they were there.

'Eve!' Her smaller, rather frail-looking mother embraced and stroked her elder daughter, then stood back to look at her as if it had been years since they'd last met.

'Mum, this is Kev, who I was telling you about.' It wasn't the usual 'groper on the dance floor' introduction he was used to.

'Your new friend,' her mum said innocently as they all lingered in the hallway and the grandfather clock in the front room began to *bong!*

'Kev, this is Vera.'

'Nice to meet you,' Kev said, taking her cold outstretched hand

and shaking it a little too firmly as she appeared to wince at the solid grip.

'Very tall,' remarked Vera, slowly retrieving her limp paw and gently patting her daughter's elbow.

'Are we just going to stand here?' said Eve, guiding her mother by the waist towards the dining room where she knew her father eagerly loitered.

'Dad!' she cried, hugging him and giving him a peck on the cheek. He visibly jumped at the impact of the kiss. 'This is Kev.'

'Good to meet you,' said Kev, deciding to change his original greeting from *nice* to *good* and considerably dropping the pressure of his handshake to medium.

Squinting from behind his half-moon reading glasses, before taking them off as if he were about to make a point on a late-night arts debate, Doug opened his eyes wide as if Kev's sudden entrance had affronted him in some way.

'Is that short for Kevin?' he asked his daughter instead of Kev.

'What do you think, Dad?' she said smiling. 'Of course it is.'

Thinking he'd get in on the jokey nature of Eve's retort, Kev rolled his eyes to heaven, perhaps misplacing Eve's which had threatened to do the same but remained straight and satirical. This he soon regretted, noting that Vera had caught him and that her expression had gone from warm and smiling to cold and sullen.

'Yes, the name's Kevin,' he recovered, nearly adding his surname but deciding that it sounded a bit schoolboyish, though Doug must have been on the same frequency as he asked if his surname was Parker.

'Yes; Parker,' he replied. Why did he suddenly feel like a child in a room full of adults? It seemed to take an unnecessary amount of time and effort to establish that he really was, indeed, Kevin Parker.

Hanging back a little he observed the Blake family gradually falling into their natural blocks; their mannerisms and communication now more casual as it swung before him like a hypnotist's watch, their figures of speech and the way they all seemed to emphasise their W's and E's, which sounded strange when they all spoke in succession. It was only when they brought him into the conversation and the pauses opened up that the droning *W*s and *E*s ceased.

How was she a mix of this nervous mother and laid-back father, he wondered, noticing how her mother laughed out of context and appeared to constantly get the wrong end of the stick every time her husband made a dry, flippant comment which didn't require the attention she would give it. Judging by the wry smiles on Eve's and Doug's faces, the family dynamic seemed to point towards a loving acknowledgement that Mum will naturally tie herself in knots and that father and daughter were constantly in on the joke.

'Sarah's not here yet,' announced Vera as they at last sat down around the table. Eve just nodded while Doug appeared to sigh to himself as he pushed his glasses back up his nose.

'So you're a literary agent then?' asked Doug, aware that his wife's words had given a cloak of silence to the air.

Now on familiar ground, Kev, more confident than before, reeled off the usual: Sonia Allen, *The Wave of Time*, which they had both surprisingly heard of, and the once-famous comedian Ollie David's book of non-PC jokes, which they all agreed people just didn't get any more.

'You'll have to draw his eyes, Eve,' said Doug, who Kev noticed had the same mischievous glint in his eye as his daughter. 'He might find a bestseller one day!' he added, his gaze darting towards the Turner print above the fireplace, as if it could easily have been Iggy Pop.

'Do you still draw eyes?' asked Vera, who suddenly appeared downcast again. 'She drew mine once,' she told Kev, 'made me look like Petula Clark.'

'Really?' replied Kev, reaching for the red wine Doug had poured.

'Well, I suppose I did a bit when I was younger.'

'I was more the James Mason type,' added Doug. He winked at Kev as if he was now in a club of which Doug and Eve were the founding members.

'Downtown!' sang Vera.

'Been on the sherry already?' laughed Doug, throwing another wink Kev's way. Not wanting to offend Vera again, Kev politely smiled back at his new partner in crime.

Watched closely by Eve, he was acutely aware that she was studying his interactions with both her parents with interest – and it seemed approval – as they now appeared to warm to him after a shaky start.

'He seems nice.' He thought he saw Vera whispering the words to Eve when she moved in close, as if imparting some important news.

'I never know what they're on about,' said Doug, making a 'yakking' shape with thumb and fingers. 'Secret stuff!' He looked nervously at his watch.

'It's a lovely house you have,' said Kev after a lapse in conversation.

Doug smiled and his wife nodded her head in agreement, while Eve shifted uneasily in her seat. It was like he'd just spoken a foreign language and they had merely gone through the motions of pretending to understand him.

The doorbell rang and seemed to toll for ever, although it was only three times. You would have thought they were all in the cast of a spaghetti western.

'That'll be Sarah,' announced Vera, jumping to her feet and appearing to throw a sly glance at Eve. 'I'll start dishing up if you get the door,' she said to Doug, who exhaled deeply and rose despondently.

Now alone with Eve, Kev gazed across at her for some kind of recognition, but found none. It seemed she was mentally preparing herself for her sister's entrance. He wanted to say something, maybe a soothing word or a witty comment, but it didn't come. Was this how he'd be if she really needed him? A mute, waiting for time to pass in the hope he wouldn't have to act?

The door opened and Doug walked back in and sat down, Eve watching him carefully all the way. He picked up a serviette and flapped it open like a sail, straightening it before pressing it across his thighs. 'She's just talking to Mum,' he said simply, picking up his wine glass.

From the kitchen they could hear laughter. It was as if a very excitable girl was flipping a pancake for the first time. 'She's happy about something,' stated Doug, before asking Kev if he'd ever considered writing himself.

'Not really,' he managed. The truth was that he, like everyone else, wanted to write, but having been in the business for so long, he'd just seen so many good stories slip away because they were just not commercially viable. Only the really lucky ones made it; better still if you had the contacts, which he certainly had. But to get there with the help of a friend was something he wasn't prepared to do.

'So, you're like me: more a reader of good literature. The classics,' Doug said.

Not really, Kev thought as he nodded in agreement anyway. He preferred novels which had a bit of humour and a clear voice; simple and definitely not convoluted or pompous. His favourite at the moment was Tony Parsons, though he was an avid Iain Banks and Pat Barker fan. He liked honest, no-nonsense writing.

All the time, Eve remained silent, sitting rigid as if danger was imminent. She'd barely looked his way since the doorbell had sounded.

'Sarah's here.' Vera's voice rang out like a tolling dinner bell in a Littlehampton guest house.

Where? wondered Kev, as Vera struggled with a tray of food.

Eve bit her lip and managed a limp smile in Kev's direction.

'*Hi!*' Poking her head around the frame of the door, half in, half out, she could easily have been appearing from behind a pantomime curtain.

Staged, thought Kev instantly as the exaggerated, almost Aussie *Hi!* seemed to have longevity all of its own.

Although not a twin, Eve's sister would have been a pretty good double. The only things telling them apart were Sarah's height – she was at least two inches taller – her blue eyes, her dyed blonde, straightened hair, and of course her over-exuberant disposition.

'Hi, Eve,' she said, her eyes doing a quick twice-over at Kev, before returning her attention to her sister.

'Sarah,' she smiled back, 'your hair's lovely. Where did you get it done?'

This was a side of Eve that he'd never seen before. He knew she was just fobbing Sarah off with some mindless chit-chat.

'Simon's on the high street,' Sarah beamed back, glad at her sister's supposed interest.

'Really suits you.' The smile slid from her face as soon as she'd delivered the final word.

Kev was no psychologist, though he had been tempted once to take a young therapist as a client having liked her book *The Lost Art of Mindless Chit-Chat*. Having read extracts from the self-help monologue, he was now sure he knew passive-aggressive behaviour when it was at the dinner table.

'So,' Sarah gushed taking the vacant place next to Kev at the table, 'who's this?'

She was a type he'd met before, the kind who intentionally or otherwise makes you feel important and liked instantly.

'Kev; Sarah; Sarah; Kev.' A stolid introduction delivered without either sister making eye contact, though he was sure they had both made a connection with the Turner, a foot above his head.

'Wow, your new boyfriend,' Sarah said deliberately as she patted him on the arm.

Eve's steady gaze was temporarily broken as her eyes followed the touch, and she appeared to swallow hard a couple of times before the glint in her eye returned. 'Yeah, a bit better than the old one,' she managed.

She was back, thought Kev. Perhaps she'd start the groper on the dance floor routine, though as Doug offered him a seeded roll from the wicker basket, he thought it unlikely.

'He's a writer,' said Vera, placing a plate of roast beef in front of him.

'A literary agent, Mum,' corrected Eve, managing a smile in Kev's direction.

'Wow! A literary agent,' mouthed Sarah, her eyes even wider than before.

That book on mindless chit-chat would certainly be useful now, he thought as he effortlessly ran through his now familiar repertoire of literary achievements, and the near-misses of an unremarkable agent, littered throughout by Sarah's '*Oh, that's so cool*' and '*OMG!*'

'What about you; what are you doing now?' cut in Eve who knew that Kev was winding up the routine when he'd reached *The Wave of Time* and how it was nearly a bestseller.

'Oh, photography.'

'Photography?' mirrored Eve with a hint of sarcasm. 'You're a photographer, now?'

'Well, not exactly; mainly lighting, you know?' said Sarah. 'In the studio: mood setting; aperture and all that,' she added dismissively, waving her hand as if wanting to move rapidly on to something else.

'So, you're seeing a photographer,' Eve stated triumphantly.

'Well, yes,' stuttered her sister, 'I was just going to say . . .' The bubbles which had followed her into the room had burst. As a shadow of anger spread across her face she started again: 'I was just going to say that I've met an American called Guy.'

'Well, you couldn't say that you've met a guy named Guy,' interjected Eve, who was clearly relishing seeing her sister squirm and fumble.

'No, of course not, silly! And anyway, Guy's a freelance photographer. He's got me into the studio. So,' she smiled, 'that's what I'm doing now and who I've met.'

'Wow!' mocked Eve, who it seemed was enjoying herself. 'A new man and a new job all in one sweep; good for you, girl!'

'Yeah, in one sweep,' Sarah repeated, not recognising the irony or the spite seeping from her sister's lips.

'That's great, Sarah,' said Doug deliberately. 'It's always good to try new things.'

He was obviously used to quelling rebellions and insurrections, thought Kev, noting that Doug's words had dampened Eve's vindictiveness as she followed suit and agreed with her father's sentiments. The conversation moved on to other less threatening topics such as the crazed masses of Christmas shoppers and Vera's opinion on the reluctance of the young to give up their mobile phones.

'Do you remember that game you used to play as children?' Everyone turned expectantly towards Vera, who appeared startled by their attention.

'Go on,' encouraged Doug, putting out a faint smile for anyone that caught his eye.

'What was it? Oh, yes, Eve was the strict teacher and Sarah – you were the naughty schoolgirl.'

'They used to nearly kill one another,' added Doug. Kev nodded in acknowledgement.

'Oh yeah, you always insisted on being the teacher,' stated Sarah.

'That was only because you didn't want to shout at anyone,' replied Eve.

'I don't remember that?' Sarah said, her face reddening.

'See,' said Doug, 'could never agree on anything.'

The two sisters briefly smiled at this, as if both of them were twelve or so and merely nodding in embarrassment at another family story from the archives.

Dinner finished, Kev was sure they were on the home straight. With no sign of a dessert or the intention of one arriving he wondered if he should offer to help clear away.

'Mum, I'll help you,' insisted Eve as Vera began clearing away. 'You stay there and talk to Dad,' she instructed Kev who'd risen to help.

Sarah, who'd already answered a few calls during dinner, organising her busy seasonal schedule, was now talking to Guy about their imminent trip to Oslo. The mention of the young overusing their mobile phones by Vera was hopelessly lost on her as she cradled her lifeline to her ear.

'She's a good kid, Eve,' said Doug, 'Sarah as well,' he added as she excitedly accentuated *Oh my God*. 'But Eve's special, quite complex really – our first child,' he sighed, checking on the Turner again. 'You know she's fond of you, don't you?'

27

It was unexpected and of course Kev had guessed that she was, but he didn't know it was so obvious or that her father had any inside intel. Before he could answer, Doug continued.

'I've seen that look many times. Me and her mum,' he laughed. 'And of course the odd dopey boyfriend.'

'Right,' answered Kev, unsure if the conversation they were having warranted more from him. He knew that what they had put together in three months and three days was special, but he hadn't realised it as much as he thought until Doug brought it to his attention.

'Kev,' Doug suddenly whispered, almost making him jump. 'I'm afraid I'm going to have to leave you for a bit on your own. I have this digestion problem – age-related,' he added, rising awkwardly. 'Here, sit there, make yourself at home,' he said, gesturing towards the sofa by the piano. 'See you in a mo.' He moved gingerly to the door.

Trying his hardest to remain focused on the turbulence of the sea and the light which stretched the horizon like an elastic band, the blues and greys of the Turner struggled to contain Kev's gaze as his eyes darted surreptitiously towards the figure who crossed and uncrossed her legs every time she began a new sentence. It was a habit he was sure all men struggled with: the compulsion to look at a woman when you knew you really shouldn't.

'OK, yeah, will do – see you later, bye,' came the infectious voice from across the room. Shifting his eyes Kev focused on the Turner again. 'Sorry about that,' said Sarah, plonking herself down next to Kev on the sofa. 'Where've all the family gone?' she asked looking around her. 'Left you to me, huh?' she giggled, crossing her leg towards him and tapping his knee with her hand. He visibly jumped.

'Looks like it,' he answered, suddenly feeling immensely vulnerable and knowing why he wished Doug hadn't abandoned him.

'Sorry.' She'd accidentally stroked his shin with the side of her shoe as her leg jigged manically up and down. The mere touch had sent him shifting slightly towards the arm of the couch. 'You mad about Eve, then?' she asked. He couldn't be sure, but her eyes appeared to dilate a bit as she tongued the corner of her mouth, her stare intense as if she was about to begin a story.

'Yeah, I like her a lot,' he replied as if answering a question in a job interview.

'You know she hates me, don't you, or should I say *dislikes*.'

'Why does she dislike you?' he asked, attracted to her and wishing he wasn't: the flick of her straight fringe every time she spoke, and those startling blue eyes that made you feel needed and worthy when she flashed them at you.

'She'll tell you in time – I suppose,' she said, uncrossing her leg, scooping her feet up onto the sofa, and bringing her knees up to her chin as she kicked her shoes off. 'I still love her, though,' she said and as if on cue the door opened and Eve frostily walked in.

The horror, the horror, the only quote from *Heart of Darkness* he could remember, as a student thrown into every essay he'd written on man's inhumanity to man, now showed on her face as she interpreted the scene before her as she intended it to be seen.

'You finished?' she snarled, glaring daggers at Sarah.

'Oh, Eve, not that again – come on, it's Christmas.'

'*Hi!* It's Christmas, everyone. Let's party!' she mocked.

'Eve, I never . . .'

'Stop! Right there,' demanded Eve, placing her hand out in front of her. 'You've no right to say it! Don't you dare say it!' she spat, her eyes blazing and hands visibly shaking.

Biting a nail, Sarah shook her head as if her mind was made up. 'Happy Christmas,' she said, rising and coldly brushing past her sister and slamming out the door.

'Give me that wine,' Eve said as if Kev were a barman, before draining the glass completely dry. 'She do her touchy-touchy, oh I'm sorry routine, did she?' Her eyes were red with rage.

What was the right answer? he wondered. 'Yes, she did – briefly,' he added, thinking that the end part was somehow necessary.

'Briefly,' she laughed, pouring herself another wine, 'oh, Kev – fucking briefly, really?'

He was sure he'd never heard her swear before. It just didn't

29

sound right. 'She accidentally stroked my leg – that's all,' he managed.

'Just say nothing, Kev. It's nothing to do with you,' she said at last, placing the glass on the table. 'Sorry I snapped at you. Me and my sister,' she continued, 'we just can't be around each other for long.'

'What happened between you–?'

'Just leave it, Kev, I don't want to talk about it,' she said solemnly. 'Let's just have a few hours to ourselves before bloody Christmas begins.'

The depressing tick of the clock said it all, reminding them that in the time it took to complete a family meal the atmosphere had turned sour as the unavoidable family conundrum had reached its inevitable climax. Sighing deeply, it was as if Eve was exhaling time itself.

She must have arrived at the part where the storm had blown itself out, as her smile slowly began to return. It was as if he'd seen her dimples for the first time, and her chocolate button eyes were now free of the tempest and rage of earlier as they shone through her dark mascara. 'I'm sorry,' she said, pecking him on the cheek and trying not to laugh at the absurdity of it all. 'It's fine,' she added as he went to embrace her.

'You sure?'

'Sure,' she said retreating back into another passing thought.

'What shall we do?' he asked desperate to leave.

'About?' She was still somewhere in the family matrix.

'Shall we just go back to the Common; maybe go to the Wind-mill for a drink?'

'Oh, that's what shall we do,' she said, now smiling again. 'Sounds good; I like the Windmill.'

'Then you don't have far to walk,' he reasoned.

'Back here?' she laughed. 'Oh, you are funny, Kev.'

'Where's Sarah?' Vera had a distressed look on her face as she entered the dining room. 'She's just said that she has to leave early.'

'That's Sarah, always in a rush,' Eve managed.

'Bye, Mum!' the shout came. Sarah, having said her quick goodbyes to Doug, had already banged the front door behind her.

'I didn't even get a hug,' Vera said accusingly, looking at Eve, who blushed.

'Said she's got to meet that new boyfriend of hers, but she'll be back for Mass,' stated Doug who'd seemingly recovered from his *digestive problems*, but was still walking gingerly.

'Oh, about the Mass, Mum—' began Eve.

'It's alright,' interrupted Doug, 'we know you probably want to see as much of Kevin as you can before Christmas Day.' The wink and sigh which followed a furtive glance at the Turner and then at Eve transmitted that he knew the real reason.

It was a good idea of Eve's to suggest they watch *ET*. She'd instantly reached for the *Radio Times* just as her mother was about to quiz her a little bit more about Sarah's sudden departure.

'You'll enjoy it, Vera,' stated Doug, 'it's about that little alien who is left behind by his family. Do you remember?' he said, pointing at his wife. '"*ET go home*".'

'Well, alright,' she managed, still looking at her daughter for a late explanation. 'I suppose it might be fun.'

The film used up the best part of three hours what with Doug pausing it a few times to go to the toilet and Vera's insistence on making some tea. 'It's called Blake family half-time,' chuckled Doug.

'Perhaps Kevin would like to use the toilet?' Vera asked Eve as they all laughed.

'Oh, do you have to go so soon?' Vera said as they all crowded around the front door. 'I mean there's still more cake.'

'She'll be back soon enough,' said Doug, who winked at Kev for what was probably the umpteenth time that night.

'Well, thanks, Vera, Doug,' said Kev clasping both their hands and this time getting an equal measure from both their grips.

'Look after our little girl, won't you?'

Doug's final words followed them out the door after a lengthy performance of goodbyes on the doorstep in which Vera managed to say that she wished her daughters got on a little better and Doug naturally made a joke of it, saying they wouldn't be as colourful and entertaining as they were if they did.

Outside and away from grasps and hugs they sighed and waved goodbye.

Chapter Three

The grey of the English Channel, painted with white spumy lines and rippling waves, spread across the horizon, lit by rogue rays of sparkly sunlight which gave the impression that there were little slits cut into the sky where they peeped through. Inland, the wind had changed direction and was blowing in hard and cold from the unforgiving North Sea. Swooping gulls were diving for fish, appearing as if dancing on the blue fuzzy dividing line of sea and sky, far out where the light spread across their feeding grounds as they hunted, following the rays downwards like missiles towards the smaller fish that had risen to the warmer surface.

Marvelling at the far-off glittering horizon, Kev's cold aching bones were briefly warmed by the vision before him as he caught a distant memory, of salty sunshine and the smell of suntan lotion smothered over his young back as his sister patted upturned buckets with the back of a red spade a few feet in front of him. The sounds of summer and the fun of the beach flooding his head as his mother naturally poured coffee from a flask into a plastic cup by his side, the aroma warm and aromatic like the hot inviting grains of sand between his toes.

He had to have coffee, he decided, looking out to sea at the changing weather. The sky now appeared as if a dimmer switch was being slowly turned down as the distant rays of light began to fade and gulls began returning to the safety of the rocks. Nervously he made another check of the headland and the nearer cliff's edge, ignoring the small scout troop which had gradually got closer.

Well-behaved and drilled they hardly deserved his attention as they were led by a tall, upright, sullen scout master who appeared to be counting and measuring the steps he and his group were taking.

'Marcus, keep up,' was all he heard from them as they merely slipped by, almost unnoticed apart from their navy and yellow scarves, marked and buttoned with pride by leather woggles.

Returning his binoculars to his chest Kev rubbed his eyes. They felt as if they'd been forced back into his skull.

'Ornnnn! Ornnnn!'

A shadow; then light and then another looming shadow. The dark bow of a warship, blue steel, smudged by light greys, guns primed ominously, aiming east at some imaginary enemy, steered ahead half a mile from the shore.

'Lads, not too close to the edge,' corrected the scoutmaster. They could easily have been providing a guard of honour as they lined the cliff and gazed out at the destroyer.

Why? He didn't know, but the sheer spectacle made him want to cry: the unexpected surprise, the suddenness of an omnipotent force thrusting itself into view. The vision had melted him; no, crushed him into insignificance. For several minutes he felt numb and totally lost, gazing out to sea and willing its return.

Kev was eerily alone; the scouts almost gone as was the last glimpse of the warship heading south into the steady grey like fog, steaming and mysteriously disappearing off the face of the earth, slowly slipping away like the last act of death. The whole sequence made him long for his mum and dad: a deep sadness, one that arrives unexpectedly when you're a child and you think your parents will live for ever, and then you realise they could be gone tomorrow. He felt a deep remorse; could not rid himself of the aura of loss that was somehow entwined in the landscape before him.

'Coffee,' he said to himself, smacking his cold hands together. Sounds like coffin, he thought, as he caught the last shadow of the grey menace on the dismal line in the distance.

*

'So Josh is the guy you share an office with?' laughed Eve, trying to keep up with the story above the din of a very packed and excited Windmill pub.

'Yeah, the posh bloke.'

The wine from earlier had caught up with him and scrambled his mind somewhere between Eve's parents and his third pint of Guinness.

'And you asked him what?'

The noise was unbearable, a babble of exaggerated festive frivolity, as customers drank considerably more just because they felt they had to. As Sarah had screeched earlier – *it's Christmas.*

'Who?'

'Josh.'

'Oh, yeah. I asked him one day who he supported; you know, meaning football.'

'Right and what did he say?'

'He said that out of the two girls he'd got pregnant so far, only one had kept the baby and that to his knowledge had never asked for any help – meaning child support.'

'Arsehole!'

'Oh, yeah – goes without saying,' he smiled, pleased to have the story ironed out.

'Sorry about earlier,' she said. She had at last taken to speaking directly into his ear as she nestled into his shoulder. They hugged the bar rail and the line of customers appeared to sway one way or the other every time someone pushed in to try and order a drink. 'She slept with my first serious boyfriend, you know,' she whispered suddenly, as if in confession, and dropped her head onto his shoulder as if relieved that she'd at last got it out.

'I'm sorry,' he started, placing his finger under her chin.

'That was the one before you; the rest she just flirted with; but the one who I felt I'd like to play happy girlfriend and boyfriend with, she screwed on my birthday,' she added with a hopeless giggle. 'Can you believe it?'

'Jesus, no wonder you don't get along.'

'Walked in on them: her on top, her cute arse grinding up and down, towering above his contorted stupid face as she shagged the fuck out of him.'

'Christ!' he said, placing his arm around her shoulder.

'Didn't even know I'd seen them. Just silently closed the door behind me like a church mouse nibbling at a crumb, hoping it hadn't been seen.'

'So she doesn't know you know?'

'Oh, I told her alright. She was hysterical. Can you believe it? I'm wronged and she's crying and falling about the place like *she's* just walked in on *me*. And then she was weird for the rest of the year.'

'And now?'

'Oh, we just go through the motions; for Mum and Dad's bene-fit.' She seemed suddenly lost, her words frozen. 'Well, that's it: that's the Sarah story,' she concluded, making her hands into the shape of an open book and then shutting it with a clap.

He wanted to quiz her more, but judging by the intent of her sudden clap, he knew that stillness was preferred to exploration and inquisitiveness.

They said little, and time seemed to slow; the air around them in the crowded bar appeared looser; Eve's heaving breast now more relaxed and less evident as she took a long satisfying swig of a rum and coke, almost serene that she'd shed the words that had been stuck in her throat for years. With the fourth pint on its way the mood had lifted as they both now temporarily gave up the nastiness of living in the real world. Carol singers were doing the rounds and a Salvation Army band had done an impromptu performance of 'O Little Town of Bethle-hem'. Eve even managed the odd joke remarking that she had every faith in Kev's fidelity, having witnessed his moves first hand.

'You will always be my groper on the dance floor,' she giggled now feeling the effects of the alcohol.

'Thanks,' he said as his mind briefly wandered.

A tall woman; confident; elegantly dressed, places her hands on her hips, shouting above the music. What is she saying? It seems important and then it's all gone as if a plug has been pulled and the lights have gone out.

'You OK? You seem suddenly lost.'

'No, I'm fine, just a thought,' he said smiling.

'About?'

'Oh, nothing.'

'Nothing sounds good,' she laughed.

Taking a large gulp of his beer, a song on the jukebox nudged him back to a happier time and he started singing 'Saturday Night at the Movies' and she joined in until they both forgot the words.

The moment was right, he thought. Maybe he should just say that he loved her? But his mind was still stubbornly made up. It had to be New Year's.

Kissing him tenderly on the lips she held him tight, like a frightened cat stuck up a tree, clutching at him with all her tiny might. She loves me, he assumed, as the same expression he'd seen at the park bench earlier that day reappeared and her grip suddenly loosened as she pulled away.

'Next Christmas it will be fifteen months and three days,' she said, her playful smile returning as she lightly pumped his forearm with her fist.

He wanted to say that it would be harder to do the maths in the coming years but for some reason he said clumsily, 'We'll have to get this one out of the way first.'

After a while they both reluctantly noted the time, as the barman called last orders and the overflow began to dwindle. Everyone made their high-spirited goodbyes as the doors were unceremoniously flung open to the cold night.

'So it looks like goodbye.'

'Yes,' Kev said, smiling because it sounded so corny and yet very human.

Outside they hung on for as long as they could, both aware that the last tube was on its way and Kev had to be on it.

'I can walk with you,' he said, glancing at his watch. 'I could get a cab.'

'Don't be silly; not on Christmas Eve. I only live beyond the pond,' she laughed, pointing towards her parents' road. 'Go on, you'll miss it,' she urged him giving him a gentle shove as his fingers hung from her grip, as if they were relay runners exchanging batons. 'Run, run!' she called out to him, giggling girlishly.

Turning as he made for the direction of the tube station, he was sure that he saw her lips move as if mouthing the three words he'd failed to, before she too turned on her heel and walked towards her parents' home.

'I'll call you tomorrow, or call me at my parents,' he shouted out as she raised her hand. 'Merry Christmas.' He nearly tripped on an upturned paving slab, his lungs filling with cold air as he was dazzled by the bright lights from the hurrying cars which sparkled like baubles in the distance.

'Merry Christmas!' cried a voice from the opposite direction as a car honked its horn in a celebratory kind of way.

Chapter Four

The café back at the car park was in fact a pub. Kev was sure he'd seen a Full English Breakfast sign outside, and ice-cream advertising, when the taxi dropped him off earlier that morning. But it was a dirty, depressing saloon bar that beckoned him to enter. Timidly opening the door, an annoying bell dinked above his head as a warm, damp odour filled his nostrils: a mixture of airless central heating and derelict moisture – the kind of smell that lingered in a bedsit on a rainy day. Looking around him he noted the familiar surroundings of a dank yet functioning English pub: torn red seats, matching grimy carpet, and fruit machine encapsulated by a mixture of mock Tudor/Georgian/Victorian wood panelling, mouldings, and arches, from which hung an assortment of Toby jugs, their scary doll-like faces appearing to follow your every movement. A rarely played jukebox by the bleach-smelling gents gave the impression of perhaps better times, as did the various photographs adorning the walls of past patrons, huddled together in celebratory poses, proudly clasping cups and medals. A dilapidated pool table with many an initial carved into its black plastic panelled sides suggested an air of casual violence. *Bob is a cunt* and *Millwall Fucking FC* no doubt daubed by visiting tribes who for some reason had an unwelcome fascination with the place. Nodding in the direction of the sole barman – an expressionless young man with a wisp of a moustache; his face dotted with acne scars and a hairline which had already receded – Kev wondered if he'd be acknowledged at all.

'Afternoon,' he said almost startled by the sound of his own voice.

'Mid-morning,' replied the young man sardonically, raising his eyes from the tabloid spread across the bar as he appeared to coldly wink at the sole customer in the bar. Following the young man's glance he saw the old man with the tartan cap he'd seen earlier, his dog panting heavily at his feet.

'It's brightening,' said the old man to no one in particular, all the time taking small sips from his half-pint pot of bitter.

Ordering a coffee, Kev hoped it wasn't instant but knew it would be, and served in a cold, chipped, white mug. It was Nescafé, and a white mug with *I Love New York* emblazoned on the front. He made for the far side of the bar, as far from the others as he could, and passed the old man, who he was sure was going to make a remark about bird-watching as his eyes darted temporarily to the binocular case, before reverting back to the drink in front of him.

'Supposed to be a good weekend,' was all he said, and the barman managed a grunt.

Relieved the old man wasn't going to engage him in conversation, Kev sat gazing out at the broken-glass-strewn car park and the sea that lay beyond.

'Jim,' announced the barman as the dink above the door sounded another entry.

'Any jumpers?' asked the old man, barely looking up as the white-haired man in the red fleece popped his head around the door.

Briefly scanning the bar as if searching for somebody, Jim dismissed the comment as if it was somehow offensive and asked if anyone had seen a young man in a green T-shirt, to which they all slowly shook their heads. Jim left in a rush and soon climbed back into his Range Rover and drove back up the headland. He came to the conclusion that the place definitely lived up to its reputation as a suicide hotspot.

'I don't know how he does it. Watching the cliffs day and night for jumpers,' rasped the old man.

'Do-gooders, they have to do something,' said the barman, folding his newspaper and reaching for and straightening the beer mat in front of him.

Just then the boy in the green T-shirt shuffled across the car park and sat down on the bench facing the sea; his pale, bare arms disfigured by DIY tattoos and cuts and scratches. He intermittently scratched them with a pair of restless, *Love* and *Hate* scribbled hands. He was now joined by a young woman of no more than seventeen, her hair stretched tight back across her scalp and tightly secured into a pony-tail. Her gaunt features and high cheekbones masked what was left of girl-like beauty. Sharing a cigarette, they resembled tragic lovers, no doubt torn apart or lumped together by drugs and abuse. Tenderly, the girl clasped the boy's head in her hands and kissed him lovingly on the forehead as the boy hung his head and began to cry, uncontrollably banging his fists on his lap as he desperately kicked out. Gathering the boy in her arms, they both appeared to fade as the returning cloud darkened their pale silhouettes. A sudden freak shower of rain made them scamper for cover.

'Good morning; I've got you a nice cup of tea. Sit up, so you don't spill it,' said Margaret Parker, a smile beaming across her face at the sight of her son who moaned at the light creeping into the room through a chink in the curtains.

'Morning, Mum,' he yawned, 'or should I say Merry Christmas?' Kev managed, sitting up in bed.

The room hadn't changed much since he was ten, when his dad had bought football pattern wallpaper and put together an MDF work table-come-desk which folded up when you'd finished with it. His dad said it was revolutionary for its time and that if he paid attention he'd be able to make things for his own son when he was older. The Airfix Spitfire still dangling from the same piece of cotton from the ceiling made him smile. And there was his mum bending over him with a morning cuppa as she'd always done, the sounds of his father in the distance always happy ones, whether whistling tunes no one knew or noisily banging around, or *pottering around* as his mother would say.

In truth the house had changed very little from when his parents had first walked through the door. Margaret and William Parker had moved to London during the early sixties, Bill finding work as an electrician at the Battersea Power Station. Margaret had instantly taken to London life and would let her Northern accent be punctuated with learnt London phrases and slang. Mainly things like *it's a bit parky, isn't it?* or sometimes *ain't it?* depending on whom she was speaking to. Bill on the other hand disliked the capital, missed the community feel back home in Manchester. If the truth be known he hated cockneys; particularly the non-trades employees at the power station who never tired of relentlessly mimicking the way he spoke – *alright, chuck.*

'Your dad's getting everything ready,' said Margaret softly, her light green eyes twinkling and as beautiful as ever, deep in her wrinkled yet still firm face.

Kev knew exactly what his dad was like: an industrious buzzing bee with a helping hand for anyone. Even if his own son was fast approaching middle age and his only daughter lived in Canada, Christmas morning was no different to any other, Bill making sure the presents were under the lit tree and the traditional fry-up was sizzling in the kitchen ready for the house to come alive with a magic he had created.

'I'll be in in a moment, Mum,' he said as she pulled the door to.

Swinging his legs round he let the cold floor try and restore any life he still had. The hangover ringing in his head made him feel as if pressure was being applied by a vice every time he attempted to open his eyes fully. As the morning slowly got clearer, Eve was there in his thoughts. As he took his first gulp of sweet tea, he saw her wave him goodbye again as he had stumbled off into the night drizzle.

The distant ring of the telephone in the hall was no surprise to anyone. Even if the time difference was an inconvenience his sister Alice always managed the customary Christmas-morning call.

'I'll get it,' he heard his dad call out, always eager to speak to his little princess and his grandchildren Sam and Megan. 'Merry Christmas,' his dad cried out, the unsullied Mancunian accent making Kev feel warm inside as he felt the serenity of being a child within the bosom of a loving family. He loved his dad's soft tone and the way he sounded as if he were telling a children's story no matter what he was saying.

'Oh,' his father said flatly, followed by a confused 'Who?' and mystified 'What?'

Moving to the ajar door, Kev quickly put on his trousers and spied his father down the corridor scratching the crown of his bald head as if trying to solve some mathematical equation. He seemed shorter, he thought, more hunched over than before – though age had been good to him. He could never remember his father being sick and to his knowledge ever attending a hospital appointment.

'Kev?' queried Bill. 'Yes, Kev's here,' he confirmed now holding the receiver away from his ear as if it was hot.

'It's OK, Dad; it's Eve,' said Kev, walking towards his fazed father.

'It's for you, son,' stated his dad solemnly, no doubt sad that it wasn't Alice calling.

Why was there a long throbbing silence when he excitedly uttered her name? A tense gap; a period of anxiety where the only sounds were the faint carols playing from his dad's wireless in the next room.

'Eve?' he repeated.

'Kev.'

It wasn't Eve's voice; distinctively similar, but not hers. 'Who is this?' he said, fiddling with the cord of the receiver.

'It's Sarah.'

That was all he needed: Eve's scurrilous, over-sexed sister phoning him. 'How did you get my number?' he asked sternly, as a barrier to the weirdness she might have in store for him. Her next two words were simple words he'd heard a thousand times on the TV to good dramatic effect. They were no different now, thrown like a hand grenade into a bunker.

'Eve's dead.'

'Merry Christmas,' Eve cried. Kev's black shape slowly fuzzed and then disappeared into the damp night as she turned to the blur of car lights slowly circling the Common. She wasn't sad that he hadn't heard her, only annoyed with herself for not turning around sooner. Anyway, at least she'd missed Mass, she reasoned, almost making the sign of the cross across her chest. A day with her family and a brief Merry Christmas to her sister and she'd be gone. Sighing to herself, she knew it had been a strange night and felt relieved it was over. She was torn: she couldn't stop being anti-Sarah, that was hardly going to change overnight, but she regretted that Kev had had to experience her hostility and perhaps irrational behaviour. But Jesus, she had the right to be mad – didn't she?

Pushing it all aside, she focused on the future and the fantasy that she'd been indulging in: that Kev would find his bestseller, then they'd marry and move to a very trendy suburb of North London and start a family. Oh, and she almost forgot: the townhouse would have a roof garden with an artist's studio perched proudly on top of it. Smiling to herself as she turned into her parents' road, she whispered to herself *three months and three days, ongoing*. Just as she turned the corner, she heard the sound of acceleration; saw the bright, full beam of headlights, a Ford Focus. The chaotic certainty of carnage; the crack; the grind; the smash; bump; screech; then the urgency of the getaway vehicle. Lastly, the sudden silence of it all as the driver disappeared from sight.

She'd died instantly from the shock of the impact, the doctors said later, as the car had hit her head-on as it turned, knocking her to the side and twirling her body as she flew at speed into the path of an oncoming Fiat Panda. She'd hit the side of her head as her neck broke and heart stopped. Instant; violent; no last gasps; no life flashing before your eyes; no lingering moments before the white light – just the end of life.

'Kev, Kev; are you there?'

He could barely answer after the last detail of how she died: a watered-down police statement of events in which a hit and run had resulted in the death of a young woman. The probability that her

44

life had been taken by a boy racer or drunk driver, a wrong person in the wrong place scenario, had little bearing on the helplessness and sheer horror of what he felt.

Why didn't you walk her home? You should have got a cab, said the accusing voice in his head. *You should have said you loved her.*

Chapter Five

Kev trudged solemnly back up towards his position beyond the lighthouse. Taking the worn chalky path he was aware that he was one among many, as the sun came out and more people appeared from wherever they had been sheltering earlier. Hikers, families, and lone walkers littered the landscape like eager ants. The woman with the camera was back. He'd seen her at the car park, briefly talking to the desperate young lovers who'd also returned before he'd left. Surely she hadn't been fishing around; asking the right questions and setting up a possible photo jump? She appeared to shrug her shoulders as the teenage girl mouthed what looked like a silent expletive and pointed her finger angrily. Why? He didn't know exactly, but he'd handed the couple a ten-pound note upon leaving the pub, placing it like the Eucharist in the girl's unsuspecting hand. Judging by their expressions they'd been shocked at the gesture of compassion: the boy laughing to himself, as if either kindness itself was a cheap joke or he recognised a mere expression of middle-class guilt.

Words lost, mumbled on the wind like unclear definitions from a sodden dictionary. Nouns, verbs, and mere guttural sounds merged and flew around the various people who now headed for the cliffs as the rain stopped.

'They are too many people around. We might be seen.' Their words caught on the breeze, a man and a woman in matching blue windcheaters and tracksuits, holding a rucksack between them, were deep in conversation as they rushed ahead of him. Judging by their accents and dress they appeared to be holidaymakers. Straining to hear more, he caught only the odd jumbled-up sentence.

'It doesn't really matter, does it?' stated the man with a strained expression. 'I mean we're all going . . .' He suddenly stopped right there, in his words and in his tracks; his partner, her large mournful eyes and Spanish looks, had said it all: that no one could or would witness whatever it was they had to do. Determined, they upped their pace again and quickly put some distance between themselves and the throng.

Looking at his watch and then at the accelerating couple Kev decided he still had time and out of curiosity followed them as they took a different chalk path which brought them to higher ground.

Shit, why now, he thought looking at the caller ID on his mobile, which was humming like a demented bee. He'd better answer it.

'Mum; everything OK?' Kev asked a little out of breath as he almost tripped over a loose stone on the path. 'No, I'm sure it's not tomorrow,' he said. He had again caught sight of the couple who had disappeared over the crest of the cliff. Facing each other, close to the edge, they now both slowly reached down, the man gently unzipping the bag as the woman reached inside.

'Mum, really, I made a note of it: it's the twentieth not the seventeenth.'

Holding what looked like a dead baby in her arms, the woman rocked it gently, the man craning his neck to kiss its forehead.

'I'll call you later.' Rubbing his eyes Kev watched them, not fully comprehending what was really before him. As if showing their baby the lighthouse beyond and mouthing *lighthouse; yes, lighthouse*, the couple then kissed and cradled their child once more before walking towards the edge and jumping.

'No!' he screamed, losing his step and temporarily falling to his knees. 'A baby, for Christ's sake!' he shouted as he slowly got to his feet. Caught by a freak burst of wind, he had to stop himself from stumbling again as he wobbled as if on a circus tightrope. Narrowing his eyes as if trying to erase what he'd just seen, he felt an overwhelming sadness. His thoughts swung heavily like a pendulum as the couple, infant in arms, and Eve flickered through his head like a faulty light bulb. Steadying himself, he took a deep breath of sea air. Swallowing hard to suppress the vomit stirring in the pit of his stomach, he pulled up the collar of his coat – the action itself a stab at normality.

Kev looked once more to check that he hadn't imagined it; played it back in his mind in the hope that they'd reappear and he'd be able to somehow prevent it from happening. Closing his eyes and then opening them again, there was no one before him.

Of course he was going to the funeral, he'd snapped when his mother had asked him, more out of concern than anything. It had seemed like weeks rather than days since Eve's death. He'd met with her distressed parents and sister to give his condolences, but it was all a fog, one he blindly slept through: numb and monosyllabic, shaking hands with a family he barely knew. He couldn't shake off the feeling that he was somehow an outsider, an interloper – the new boyfriend of only three months and three days they'd only met once before, for Christ's sake. How could he intrude? His own mother and father had clumsily reminded him that he hadn't been seeing her that long, for the sake of his own mental state. They were only looking out for him, but it had only made things worse, confusing him and making him question how much grief he should publicly express – he was not worthy of Eve or her family.

Doug was devastated by the death of his first-born, so much so that he'd gone into information overdrive, acting as the press officer of the tragedy, embracing his new role to mask and smother the extreme pain he was experiencing. 'The police have nothing yet. They haven't found the reported silver Ford Focus. They suspect it's a hit and run; always hard to follow up,' he kept saying to anyone and everyone who entered the same dining room he had sat in with Eve and her new boyfriend only a few days earlier. Vera appeared much older, her eyes now sunken, red-rimmed, and lost some place in the darkness of her soul, reluctant to peep out at the reality of it all.

As for Sarah, she'd only looked up once when Kev entered the room, immediately turning her eyes to her lap where her gaze rested, no doubt stuck some place in her own private hell of regrets. Why? He didn't know, but he thought her posture and countenance a little contrived. Perhaps Eve was at his shoulder, he thought, saying: *look at her milking the drama of it all, playing the grieving, misunderstood sister. She couldn't keep her knickers on when I was alive.* When she'd squeezed his hand when he offered his sympathies, he'd shivered and couldn't help think of the foot which had stroked his leg on the couch and excitement he'd guiltily repressed.

All he knew that day was that he wanted to be as far away as possible from the grief. He wanted to drink; he wanted to dance. He knew the desire to dance was an odd one, but he'd always done it since he was a kid. As a teenager he'd danced away his insecurities to the sounds of the seventies: of the O'Jays, The Temptations, Barry White and Hot Chocolate – songs not of his era but of his mum and dad's; the place he'd felt most happy and safe.

That evening, along with a bottle of Teachers, he'd danced around his childhood bedroom to the soulful sadness of Otis Redding until he'd crashed, crumpled up unapologetically drunk and emotional on his single bed – the poster of Bruce Lee on the wall above gazing sternly down at him as his heart broke into tiny pieces and flowed on his tears to *The Dock of the Bay*.

The night before the funeral, he'd met Steve and naturally got drunk, or just topped up what was already there. He'd grieved enough and needed the constant fuzzy anesthetised drip of alcohol; wanted the chaos and confusion that inebriation demanded.

'To Eve,' he slurred, knocking back another tequila and not bothering with the salt and lime. He was back in his trademark brown three-piece striped suit and tieless white shirt, unshaven, red-eyed and mad. He hadn't worn it since the riverboat party, the stain on his brown brogue as greasy as it had been then.

'To Eve,' returned Steve solemnly, his glasses now stuck together with a plaster. Apparently the girl from Accounts had sat on them. Though the rumour was that she'd hit him having found out he'd been in contact with his old girlfriend Stacey and had lashed out in a jealous rage at a friend's wedding.

'Jesus! Turn it off, will ya!'

'Shhh, you'll get us thrown out.'

'Fucking Robbie Williams shite,' insisted Kev, unaware that a group of women on a hen night were frowning his way having selected a trilogy of hits from the walled jukebox.

'Sorry, sorry!' he called out with a wave of his hand. 'Maybe we should go over?' he bumbled reaching for his pint and going to get up.

'Probably should stay here, mate,' said Steve reassuringly holding out an arm. He knew what could happen with hen parties, and his friend was in no fit state to get entangled in a *what goes on tour stays on tour* girls' night out.

'Just ran her over and drove away.' He'd said the same line a few times within the course of the evening, not in an engaging way (he didn't want a reply), it was a drunken mantra he just would slip into, remembering the detail and not being able to move beyond it.

'I know,' said Steve, who was more worried that Kev was going to start dancing or, worse still, join the women.

The Duke's Head was a typical City pub: loud and crowded with tipsy office workers with loosened ties, unbuttoned blouses: the burst for freedom brigade, an atmosphere that spelled disaster for anyone who started drinking at six and continued on an empty stomach until closing.

'Brilliant; love this: Roxy Music, 'Dance Away'.' He was up before Steve could catch him, jacket off, shuffling across the floor toe to heel, almost twisting: a sole dancer, a spectacle on his own; for some a novelty, but for most a laughing stock. 'Come on Steve, come dance with me.'

Steve was soon up, reluctantly, positioning himself close by the jukebox where he kept lookout. Shit, he thought as two women from the hen party joined Kev who was doing his best Bryan Ferry. Both wearing pink *girls on tour* T-shirts, a tall redhead and a busty, plump brunette who appeared to be constantly biting her top lip were soon being twirled around by Kev's fingers. Steve could smell the potential for trouble as Kev began to swing the girls around, attempting a jive-come line-dance series of moves. A group of young, pissed City boys were leering at the women and laughing at an oblivious Kev, who was lost on some dance floor with his wide four-buttoned flares, like his dad and bell-bottomed, blue-eye-shadowed mum.

'Careful, you twat!' Kev had waltzed himself into the path of the lad with the broadest rugby shoulders and spilt half his pint.

'I might be a twat, but I'm not a fucking rugby ape,' said Kev, continuing his dance.

So what if he hits me, was his fleeting thought on the matter. No more than what he deserved. If anything he wanted to be struck as hard as possible between the eyes.

Sensing the danger, Steve was soon by his side. 'Come on, Kev – let's go,' he said grabbing him by the arm.

'I'm not frightened of a troupe of Swing Low, Sweet Chariot fucks,' he said, loud enough for them to hear before slipping free of Steve's grip.

'That's it, go off home with Buddy Holly,' one of them piped in as they all laughed.

Throwing the first punch was always going to be tricky. Firstly, it had to be on target and directed forcibly. Kev missed the bulbous head in front of him by six inches, and he found himself crashing to the floor where he gashed the side of his face on the hard, beer-soaked wooden boards.

'Fuck!' he shouted, instinctively curling up into the foetal position expecting a kicking.

To Steve's relief the head barman was on to the situation. 'Move on, lads.'

'You OK?' asked Steve, kneeling by his friend's head.

'She's dead,' he said before bursting into tears and sobbing like a child. 'She's dead, Steve, she's dead.'

Chapter Six

The red fleece had caught the corner of his eye, tearing past him like a blood clot to the brain. Turning away from the cliff face, mobile phone in hand, the old man shook his head. Up close he almost appeared to be blind, his eyes fixed and unblinking as if a thin layer of glue was stuck across his pupils.

'Didn't see anything odd in it; just two young people carrying a rucksack,' he said breathlessly.

'They had a dead baby, you know?' It didn't sound right because he'd never said anything like it before. The words betrayed his humanity and made him blush.

'I know. I saw it too. Must have wanted to join the child,' the old man said, his right eye turning as if on a swivel in another direction as if spurred into action by a scurrying field mouse.

It was all so matter of fact, he thought scratching his belly. People just jumping to their deaths, contemplating the most violent of ends, and those like himself and the man in the red fleece talking about it almost casually, as if it was the most natural thing in the world to do. He'd been in shock when they'd jumped, but now he only felt numb.

'What happens now?' Kev enquired coldly, checking his watch and shifting uneasily.

The old man's eyes twinkled, caught by the shifting light off the sea. Although withered, his skin hanging from his aging cheekbones, he oozed vibrancy and life. 'You're going to have to wait, I'm afraid,' said the man almost reading his mind.

'But you saw what I saw,' he pleaded.

'I know, and that's why you have to wait: confirm we saw the same thing.'

He knew he was stuck and that the old man had relayed the same information thousands of times before. What if he missed what he was looking for? Maybe it was happening. He had to get going.

'Why are you here?' said the old man. 'I've seen you a few times this morning; are you looking for someone?'

'Someone?'

'Yes; up and down the headland. I see everything and of course you probably know what I do, considering you were in the pub earlier.'

'Saving people,' Kev said simply.

'I try. I do my best,' replied the man running his age-spotted hands through his white wavy hair.

'They are dead, aren't they?' he asked, just because it had crossed his mind that they may still be alive.

'No one survives that jump,' said the man expertly. 'Not when the tide's out, jagged rocks like razors everywhere. Splits them in two I'm afraid and it's too high at this point. They all know that.'

'Look, I need to get away. I have to watch things,' Kev stated clumsily.

'Things? What things?'

'I won't know until I see it.'

'Oh, those kind of things,' he said as if he knew his whole story, beginning, middle and end.

'That's why I can't stay; you understand that?' he added optimistically.

The old man knew too well what watching entailed, just look at the couple he'd missed jump, failing to interpret their body-language. 'Look, give me your mobile number,' he said after some consideration. 'If we need you, I'll call you; I'll say you had to meet somebody urgently or something.'

'I really appreciate it,' Kev said, going to shake the old man's hand which the other missed completely, his expression suddenly distant as if a painful memory had spiked his side.

Turning his back to the sea, the old man made the dreaded call to the police as the wind began to blow again, accompanying the solemnity of the words he spoke; the sea gently sloshing against the rocks and the broken bodies below as he ended the call.

Wincing at the images circling his mind of the couple and baby taking their last tentative steps and saying their goodbyes, he was tempted to walk towards the edge and gaze down at the dead. 'Here,' Kev said at last, handing back the pen and pad the old man had given him. 'My number.'

The old man took it and placed it in his pocket. 'I hope you find what you are looking for,' he said as he stared back at the sea. 'You might have to wait for a long time,' he added. 'Things move very slowly up here – like the clouds.' He pointed upwards as he said this, to where the clouds appeared to fold in on themselves like white cotton sheets, rolling in across the horizon. 'They've been forming for some time, since just before they jumped, and now they're almost here.'

Was that how he'd been roaming about all day, like a cloud in its infancy, waiting and then blown in, exposed for all to see? Was that what he was waiting for: the change in form, the movement of light; the looming sky, slowly revealing a mystery; an unseen blot on the landscape that he might, just might, overlook? Feeling the cold in his bones and the worry on his brow he moved swiftly back up the worn chalk trail and beyond where he'd been that morning, hoping and praying that he'd soon be able to leave the shitty, sodden cliff.

'Godspeed!' shouted the old man after him. 'May the Lord be with . . .' The 'you' lost on the wind.

'And may the Lord be with you,' enunciated the priest.

'And also with you,' the congregation obediently replied.

Kev had had no idea that Eve's family were such devout Catholics and felt even more alienated than he'd already imagined, stared down at from the *Stations of the Cross*, by the Lord at the various stages of his suffering; Jesus being ridiculed by Roman soldiers, his cross heavy on his back, being the nearest to him.

He'd sat alone to the left of her family, awkwardly among friends and distant family members.

'How did you know Eve?' the woman next to him, an old school friend of hers, had asked.

'I was her boyfriend,' he'd answered, as three months and three days flashed before his eyes. She told him what a special person Eve was and how deeply sorry that he'd lost her. When she asked how long they'd been together he'd felt embarrassed. He wanted to lie and say five years and three months. The gaze of the Lord had put paid to that as he told her the truth and the woman appeared to quickly lose interest in him.

Trying to avoid as many people as he could he stared straight ahead, only for Doug to catch his eye just as the priest had finished and was filling the air with incense. They were a pall-bearer short. Shit, he thought as Doug gave him the signal to join him and his brothers at the casket. It was as if the whole congregation followed his hungover walk to the coffin of his Eve. Although the suit he was wearing was a new one and he'd shaved, the still-fresh gash on the side of his face and dark rings under his eyes told a different story. He resembled a dressed-up drunk or a criminal attending court rather than the well-presented literary agent Eve had brought home with her a little over three weeks ago.

Being taller than Doug and his brothers, and Eve's two uncles from her mother's side, Kev naturally took the full weight of the coffin, so the cedar tore into his shoulder and made him stoop and wince with every solemn step as he followed the way of the Lord, who had fallen for the second time on the wall above him. From the deck of a Thames disco boat to carrying her in a box beside his head, it was the strangest reality he'd ever known. He tried to imagine her above: her tiny body shrouded in white cotton as he tried (though it was fading fast) to see her as she was the first time they'd met, but he couldn't, he just felt the deep pain in his soul and the pulsating one now tearing into his shoulder and back. At the graveside he'd turned his face away as the coffin was lowered and tried his hardest not to listen to the priest's final words. Instead he tried counting from one to a hundred in French, but only got to sixty-six as he became aware

of the tears and gasps of loss as Eve's family huddled and collapsed into each other's arms as Eve disappeared into the ground.

'How you bearing up?'

Wasn't I supposed to say that? thought Kev as he held Doug's out-stretched hand after the graveside drama was over. 'You'll come to the pub, won't you? There's a few sandwiches and some soup, I think.' Doug was back in information overdrive, secure in the knowledge that a cacophony of words would temporarily quash his spiralling darkness.

Of all places: not the Windmill. He'd frowned, though he was sure Doug had missed it; strange kind of marker, a point of reference where his brief relationship ended within weeks. The smell was the same: yeasty beer, crisps, and the distinct odour of bleach coming from the gents. He stood ordering drinks at the same spot where he'd held Eve in his arms on Christmas Eve. And he'd never made that connection either – Christmas Eve and Eve – until then. The points of symmetry and coincidence clogged the mind and made his presence there odd, strange, and chillingly surreal.

'Kev.'

The voice: clear like a bell; like Eve's, but not hers. He held it possessively in his heart for as long as he could, remaining turned towards the barman; he hung lifeless, lost in their love, in the residue of their last embrace at the bar.

'Sarah,' he replied, choosing a brief eye to eye before focusing on his chosen object, a generic photograph of the Queen Mother pull-ing a pint of Young's bitter.

'Come and join us – the family,' she added, presumably noting his hesitation.

He said nothing, only jumped at the momentary tip of his elbow as she led him towards Doug and Vera.

'Have a sandwich.' Eve's mum had caught the bug from her hus-band, busying herself and fussing. He was sure she hadn't recognised him, her eyes only flickering with recognition when Sarah called his name again and brought him over towards the seated assortment of cousins, uncles, and college and work friends of Eve's.

'Oh, the groper on the dance floor.' He searched the room for the murmur. As clear as day. He was sure he'd heard it. Maybe it was because it was the way Eve had introduced him so many times before? There were certainly one or two faces he recognised, maybe colleagues of Eve's, but surely not at a funeral – hardly appropriate. Quickly, gathering his wandering thoughts, he allowed himself to be convinced that it was somehow Eve having one last laugh at his expense.

Sitting down next to an aging aunt of Doug's, he was relieved that the conversation was centring around the weather and her obvious preoccupation with the UK leaving the European Union. How quickly things turn to normal so soon after the dead had been boxed, stamped and posted, Kev thought. All around, the chatter flowed: views on cremation vs burial, Chelsea's resurgence at the top of the league and whether it was safe to eat meat any more. Where was Eve? he wondered. Had she moved on so quickly; become ephemeral, erased from her own story?

Animals observe other animals; eye contact is often brief, yet purposeful. It was one of those momentary and somehow meaning-ful gazes that had worried him. He didn't have the entire picture processed, quickly re-aligning his eyes from a woman who'd clearly been watching him. One of those strange moments when the person realises they've been caught and they act as if you're no longer there. Before wondering whether it actually happened at all, he retrieved a piercing glance instantly hidden from view by half-moon eyelids as soon as he'd spotted them; a blink and the image was gone.

'What happened to your face?' Sarah was now seated at his side having brought Aunty May a cup of sweet tea not too much milk.

'Fell over.'

'Sorry,' she tapped his shin with her black ankle-strapped shoes. Maybe she was just not spatially aware, he thought, dismissing the presupposition that she had done it intentionally the first time they'd met. 'Nasty graze,' she noted, now turned in towards him. 'Guy couldn't make it.' She began fiddling with her earring.

Like before, he couldn't escape the chemical in his brain that told him that an attractive woman was within his line of vision. He hated the fact and despised himself that, sitting here at his girlfriend's funeral, he should have such a thought about her sister's overt sexual presence.

'But do you know what? I think my sister would have loved him.'

Christ, Eve's got a mention, he thought, even if it was in line with Sarah's *me, me, me* mantra. *'My sister'*: how fucking contrived. He wanted to stop her right there, but she was like a hideously beautiful magnet: as horrible as she was tantalizing.

'Guy's your boyfriend?' He knew as much, but just wanted to say it anyway.

'Yes, you remember: at the dinner table with—'

'Eve.' He wanted to say it before her. It was his way of trying to rid himself of the guilt he was feeling as he felt a twinge in his groin.

'It was a shame, you know,' she began, lowering her eyes, 'the way it turned out with me and Eve. She probably told you everything?'

It didn't seem right: why was she acting as if her shagging was so important, today of all days? Why couldn't she just leave it alone? Was she really so shallow?

'I heard,' he managed, indifferently enough for Eve to have approved.

'I really regret it; especially now,' she added mournfully, wiping a stray tear from her cheek. 'None of us are perfect, are we?' Those wet eyes, wide with regret; he didn't have the strength to say that he saw through them when all the time he ashamedly wanted them, needed them, like a drug to quell his pain.

'Haven't you made mistakes?' she asked.

What did she want from him, did she want total absolution? Was this what all this was about, him being the lost link to Eve's forgiveness?

There, she had him, right there at the tip of a needle, him thinking about his own mistakes; his own drunken one-night stands; his inability to say no; to drink; to have sex.

'Yes,' he said simply. He'd given her what she'd asked for; a transformation took place before him, her face brightening, her alluring smile returning.

'To my little girl,' toasted Doug, his voice faltering with emotion as he clasped his wife's lifeless hand.

'To Eve,' they all toasted.

The words released from his throat: were they the last ones? he wondered; gone, soon to become part of a passing memory?

'To Eve,' said Sarah solemnly, the last to utter her name in the room to the side of the bar where they'd gone their separate ways on a Christmas Eve unlike any other.

Chapter Seven

The helicopter circling above twirled, lifted and fell like a leaf before dropping its winch, delivering three body bags to the waiting orange-jumpsuited man below. The Good Samaritan, Jim, talking to the officer by the flashing police Land Rover, was shaking his head as he occasionally pointed in the direction of the sea. As if watching a silent film, the stage directions heavy on his shoulders, Kev interpreted the hand signals as the man in the red fleece pointed out the way he'd gone as he relayed (no doubt) the grisly details of a tale he'd told so many times before.

Instinctively he half waved at them, stopping himself from drawing too much attention to himself as he pushed his hair back out of his eyes and made deliberate long strides back up the headland as if he were on an important mission.

'You back again?' He had to say something. It was the photographer he'd crossed paths with most of that morning, her fuzzy hair standing upright on end as she loitered on the chalk trail in front of him.

'Kind of,' she replied and he hated her instantly: the clever reply, her I-couldn't-care-less attitude.

'You're not a birdwatcher then?' he said menacingly, noting her large, yellowing teeth, ginger hair, and orange cheeks which made him stare longer than he would normally.

'No,' she said nonchalantly, as if he were a piece of shit.

'Why do you do it?' Kev asked, his chest tightening as his anger began to rise.

'What?' she asked curtly, grabbing her camera as she unscrewed a lens and put it in her pocket.

'Take pictures of jumpers.' He was shaking now. If she'd been a man he'd probably have hit her.

'It's my job. If I don't get a picture then somebody else will.'

She was the robot type, the kind you might find working as a guard at a labour camp: affirmative, awkward, and arrogantly focused.

'Well, you missed that one there,' he spat, gesturing towards the helicopter.

'Ah, you win some, you lose some,' she stated, shrugging her shoulders and moving swiftly towards the flashing lights in the hope of getting a shot of the bodies being airlifted to the living world.

'Make sure you get a good shot of the dead baby, you bastard,' he shouted after her as the copter, having secured its cargo, lifted it above the waves: a blot in the diminishing visibility of a drizzle which was getting heavier by the second.

'Gotcha!'

Turning at the sudden cry he could see the photographer giving herself the thumbs up as she got the shot she wanted, celebrating with her camera as if scoring a winning goal in extra time.

'Ahh!' Kev shouted back – an inarticulate animal response to an uncivilised act. 'Ahh!' he repeated, throwing his arms up in the air and feeling like an ape as he scanned the ground for a heavy piece of wood or rock that would end a primeval disagreement. Feeling the urge to run and confront her, he instead took a deep breath and reminded himself that he had to remain calm and alert to other eventualities.

Wiping the lenses of his binoculars as best he could, he now tried to focus on the strangers still out walking: a woman and an elderly man; a father and son; two teenage girls; a lone hiker – the possibilities were endless, he thought, each one of them perhaps writing their final chapters here on this unfortunate lump of white chalk.

The sunlight peeping through the slit in the curtain woke him with a start, as did the new odour in the room and the patterned pale lavender wallpaper with brown cubes overlapped by pink oblong boxes. A distant car alarm and a barking dog were more familiar sounds, so much so that his mind temporarily calmed as it tried to nudge him back into the dream he was having. Startled again, he awoke. The scene was still the same, though the sun wasn't peeping any more, instead the changing light brought a silent blue hue to the room, the pink boxes now appearing grey. The house gate opening and closing; engines running; car doors slamming: it wasn't a dream.

Still in the foetal position, spooning the strewn white duvet, he suddenly felt skin on skin as the warmth of another buttock pressed against his own. Holding the corner tight he tried to fire up his thoughts, but hit a steely blank as his head began to throb and his now certain hangover demanded pints of water and greasy food.

'Hi, you awake?' yawned the familiar voice beside him. She had rolled over and moulded her shape into his back, and exhaled a warm sleepy breath on his neck.

The blank was no longer a cavernous hole but a near clear picture of the events of the past twenty-four hours. Like litter swirling in the mild cyclone of a gust of wind, the pieces fell and became hideously and sickeningly real.

It had started with Aunty May and Sarah's sudden declaration of guilt, then drifted, dreamlike, as if sitting on the back of a white swan as he'd floated effortlessly to the next zone. Away from the small room and into the warmth of the saloon bar, that's where the drinking started (5.30 to be precise).

With most of the family dispersed, many leaving with Aunty May, only a few friends of Eve's, a couple of Doug's nieces and of course Sarah were left.

'Leave it to the young ones,' were Aunty May's parting words as they loitered in small clusters. 'To Eve' quickly became the rousing call to arms as the drinks came fast and furious, still available on a generous tab left by Doug and his brothers at the bar.

'Steady, Kev.' It was Sarah who had been flitting between the three groups, the same drink in hand she'd been given upon arriving in the side room.

'Me shoes,' he laughed to himself. 'Me shoes.'

'What?' she asked, obviously bemused as to what he was on about.

'Nothing,' he said, his eyes glazed. 'It's a long story.'

'You going to get smashed? Wouldn't blame you. I might even join you,' she reasoned, shaking her half-empty wine glass between her thumb and finger.

'*To Eve*,' came another chorus.

'Yeah, to Eve,' mouthed Sarah, knocking back the last of her drink.

He couldn't understand where his earlier mistrust of her had gone. Was Sarah just another fuck-up like him? Looking at her now, the vulnerability and guilt, perhaps he'd got her wrong? Of course he knew it was the drink talking, but he let it chat merrily away, knowing that when pissed it was an easier option.

9.30 p.m.: 'Where've they all gone?'

'Who . . .?' She was giggling now as Kev tried to put together another sentence that would make sense.

'The grievers: the mornings.' He was slurring now, standing on the edge of his heels, one hand in pocket, the other cradling a double whiskey to his chest.

'Do you mean mourners?'

'That's the one: mourners.'

'Sit down – come on,' she said, tugging his sleeve.

'Sorry,' he said to no one in particular and plopped down next to her.

'You've had a hard time, Kev,' she said patting his shoulder. 'Couldn't have been easy today, being surrounded by people you didn't know.'

I love her eyes, he thought. He went to say it, but he didn't. 'Did Eve ever draw your eyes?' he asked, the words just pouring out but in a different order and a version of what he was just thinking.

'Yes, she did. When we were kids and into pony club. When we used to get on,' she added, her initial smile leaving her face as quick as it had arrived. 'She was my big sister. I used to look up to her. One day after school she just burst into my room, pad and pencil in hand,

and told me to sit cross-legged with the back of my hand pressed under my chin. She really freaked me out. She was so intense as she drew away. It was like her eyes had pierced through my skin and were chipping away at me inside. She was weird like that – in a good way,' she added. 'If I moved,' she laughed, 'Eve would hit me hard with her ruler.' She appeared sad now, as if reflecting on a past that couldn't be changed.

'Do you know what?' He was going to say it earlier but a lump had formed in his throat and his memory of what he intended to say had deserted him. 'I got you all wrong, you know; you're OK.' There, he'd said it. It was as if Eve's earlier spectral intervention had failed.

'Thanks,' she said, placing her hand on his as Eve somehow frowned. 'I can't erase the past. I wish I could, but I can't,' she added tearfully, solemnly lifting her glass to what was the last toast of the evening.

10.30 p.m.: 'Oh, it's alright, come on!' he hollered, pulling her up from the glass-strewn table, 'dance with me, will ya?'

Was it a devil that raged when he reached a certain number of beverages or was it just wild abandon; the likeable drunk that would make his peace with the world as he played with peoples' reserve until he broke down their self-consciousness? It was probably simpler than that, just a switch, he thought, blinking for a second as more of the same crazy became the norm in his drunken haze.

'Alright then.' She said it as if she was answering a challenge rather than a drunken request which could easily have been for a cigarette or a pound coin.

'It's 15a' he confirmed, pointing towards the jukebox, '*When it Rains*, by Fleetwood Mac. You know, you look a bit like Stevie Nicks,' he added, placing his hand on her waist.

'Do I?' she answered.

It was as if he'd always danced with her: the height, the shape, the moves – a natural dancing queen. The way her leg side-stepped inside his, their steps (in his mind) as one, like his mum and dad, effortless and smooth.

11.30 p.m.: 'Haven't you got homes to go to?' It was the second bell and last orders were well and truly over.

'Come on, let's go.' He was surprised at how strong she was as she lifted him from his seat before helping him to the door and bundling him into a waiting taxi.

Driving through the brightly lit neon streets he felt as if the night somehow stared back at him as he viewed himself from outside the taxi. He was silent; still; dreamy; empty of emotion; engulfed in nothingness; alone and detached from reality and the possibilities that may lie ahead. A drunk crossed the road close to the taxi. He waved and the swaying man waved back. He wanted to look at his shoes, but he couldn't raise his leg. He turned and looked at Sarah, who was putting some money together for the fare; he wanted to say something but his mind drew a blank and he waved out the window at the passing darkness.

12.00: 'Not a bad place.'

'Well, Mum and Dad helped with the down payment, but the mortgage is double.'

'Yeah, it's nice,' he said, his jacket slung casually over his shoulder. He shuddered at the thought, but he always felt like James Dean when he did it.

'You can have my bed, I'll take the couch,' she said, throwing a fresh duvet onto a chair.

Now standing turned towards him, it was as if her eyes said something else: that, just maybe, they should fuck. He knew the look, or had imagined it so many times before; it was a now or never transmission of real intent, almost screaming out to him: *It's for Eve – it's what she would have wanted.* Ludicrous; absurd; macabre; sick, but he'd drunk a lot and the night's toasting of the dead – *for Eve* – had got lost and redefined in a dark recess of his soul. Hearing the words again as clear as he was drunk, it was as if a summons had leapt from some dark distant corner of the bedroom.

12.45 a.m.: 'Jesus Christ! Oh yes; Christ!'

He'd momentarily closed his eyes. *Eve* – it wasn't the name, but the letters of her name etched into his closed pink inner lids. Opening them, suddenly he was sure it was her: her smile, her whole body, which had melted and sunk onto his. Closing his eyes he sadly came.

'Yeah, I'm awake,' he replied watching one of the boxes on the wall change back to its original colour with the new ray of light.

'You OK?' she asked pushing herself in closer.

'Not really,' he said, 'we shouldn't have.'

'Stop right there.' She was almost angry. 'It happened – end of! Things happen.'

'But . . . on the day we buried her?' He didn't want to say her name; wasn't sure he could again; he'd shagged her sister, for God's sake.

'Don't think that way.' She'd swung over onto his side of the bed and was now facing him. 'We were drunk, emotional, and we wanted to do it,' she insisted. Christ, he wanted to do it again – he was surely going to hell?

'Come on; things happen,' she said soothingly holding his face in her hands and kissing him tenderly on the lips as the whole sordid episode repeated itself, mixing passion, regret and self-loathing, and coming up with unforgivable sex.

Chapter Eight

Sometimes you feel so alone; a mere heartbeat within a skin-tight shell. Standing; swaying; alone; eyes aching, squinting to see beyond the drizzle: a man on a cliff; watching; waiting; while others pass by without a glance in his direction; everyone going somewhere; up and down the worn paths; pausing; thinking. Jumping. Wet, cold to the bone, he marvelled at the madness of it all.

Opening his notepad Kev checked the times written in rushed black ink: 9-10 (tick), 12-1 (tick) and 3-4. Checking his watch - 2.30 - he swallowed hard, went to walk one way, then changed his mind and went the other. Deciding on his first position further up the headland where he'd watched the old man with the dog, he now moved with haste, like a man with something hanging heavy on his shoulders, an uncertainty that made his breathing laboured and his chest tight. Reaching the same spot as before Kev turned and faced the now familiar scene replaying: the boy scouts; the young exhausted woman with the toddlers, and the photographer – nothing he could really put together or perceive as relevant; though what he was meant to see was vague; unexplained and unimaginable. Maybe he wasn't looking in the right places?

The cold sweat on his forehead was trickling down into his eyes. Binoculars in hands, he scoured the landscape one more time. More erratic this time, he was hurrying, checking; stopping; swinging his line of vision low and high, desperately trying to solve a riddle which had no real definition.

Suddenly, a scruffy-looking man with flowing dreadlocks walked past, so close that it made him jump and want to curse the intruder who unwittingly blocked his line of vision. Now standing still, the man too had opened up his binoculars case and was scanning the same contours as himself. Birdwatcher? he wondered. No, too far from the rocks and the crannies at the edge for that. Was this it? Was this what he'd been waiting for? It didn't make sense: another watcher.

Checking the time again: 2.55. Kev knew it was close. Still conscious of the intruder, who'd taken a couple of steps backwards, he continued with his now obsessive searching – his eyes sunk deep in their sockets, his mind playing games, becoming unreliable as he found it harder to comprehend the landscape; focusing on the cackling gulls and changing cloud bursts and each time wanting to turn his fists on himself as he anxiously willed the badness to begin.

Battersea Park and the Saturday-morning football was in full flow, the shirts a cluster of all colours of the rainbow. An all-black team sporting Brazilian colours were thrashing an all-white, anaemic-looking team playing in light blue. The calls from the touchline, of excitable dads hollering at the ref and the PE teachers of their sons' schools, were like a frantic morning bird chorus: *Man on! Get forward! Keep going! Go on – tackle 'em.* Judging by the looks of frustration on the faces of the coaches and the confused expressions of the sky blues, the dads weren't helping.

The hangover from hell was pounding the walls of his skull and the yelling wasn't helping as Kev took a deep swig of his triple shot takeaway Americano. If he was honest with himself the drinking was becoming a bit of a problem. Now back at work he was downing three pints of Guinness every lunchtime. Choosing the black stuff, it tended to satisfy his hunger and get him mellow at the same time. Convincing himself of the benefits of the new weekly iron intake, it only helped to pump up his already protruding belly. And then there was the after-work onslaught, drinking till closing time, running up tabs and getting the last drunken tube home back to his cramped one-bedroom flat. Steve was always there for him, though choosing lemonade at lunchtimes and a maximum of a couple of pints after work before leaving for home. It was then that Kev was in the presence of similar lost souls who drank in city pubs after work: middle-aged men avoiding their marriages; functioning alcoholics who were good at their jobs but shit at their private lives. Kev was somewhere between the two. The whole Sarah thing was slowly becoming an on – off arrangement. The more he drank the more he desired her; their relationship becoming more and more casual as they met in between Guy and his new commitment to ruining himself with drink.

Meeting her in Battersea Park by the pagoda was a safe place, it wasn't his place or hers. The cafés and pubs, unless on the other side of the river, were out of bounds. And they couldn't just have sex all the time.

Strolling across the playing fields, cut grass and sunshine flooding his senses, he felt warm inside. Even his headache appeared soothed by the unpredictable weather, which could fool you that you were midway through summer. A distant cheer from the crowd supporting the Brazilian colours and the shriek of *Referee*! from the others. He was soon approaching the Thames. Strangely, she was already there: a dot becoming bigger with every step. Wearing orange and yellow she could easily have been mistaken for one of the Buddhist monks banging drums and ringing bells beyond the pagoda. Pacing up and down with an air of nervousness, she puffed restlessly on a cigarette.

'Kev,' she said, a pained expression on her face.

'Hi,' he replied as she hugged him. 'You OK? You seem strained,' he added now standing back to look at her.

'Well, no,' she began studying his face. 'Guy's moving in. We're combining our finances to save money,' she said, the words obviously Guy's and not hers.

He'd been waiting for a get out of jail card of some description. Through the fog and drink he knew it had to stop – for both their sakes. Sensing the pending brush-off, he clasped it firmly with both hands. 'Well, maybe that's a good thing,' he said carefully.

'It is?' She seemed surprised. 'But our thing – you know?'

Bingo. He had to stop the inner glow threatening to expose him like a hundred-watt lightbulb. 'It's fine; it couldn't last for ever.'

'Well, as long as you're alright with it?'

She certainly had read more into it than he had. How could shagging two guys (one *called* Guy), one of whom was the ex of her dead sister, be sustainable?

'We both know it was circumstances, different emotions coming together – it happens, and now it's over,' he concluded, relieved and astounded at how cold he sounded.

'Thanks for being so understanding,' she said, stamping out her cigarette. 'I was just worried – you know, with all your drinking and everything?'

The *everything* part he knew meant Eve. As for his drinking: what else could he do with the rest of his miserable life?

'But we'll keep in touch?'

Why did she have to go and spoil it? he thought. 'Maybe we shouldn't. Not for a while, anyway. Let things settle down.'

'I suppose.'

She had tears in her eyes now (there, but a long way from flowing). 'Oh, come here you,' she demanded, pulling him in close for what surely would be their last embrace. Kev felt trapped as if in a bird cage, their hug appeared to last for ever, each squeeze adding to the tension in his limbs, which wanted to spring into action and run. It was then that he understood his trepidation as he sensed the tense presence creeping up on them.

'Hey! What are you doing?'

A situation that demands a quick response: always slower than you anticipate. He was glued to her; dumb; paralysed by the shock of it all. Of all the people: the one who'd been so kind and welcoming towards him.

'Dad!' cried Sarah. 'Shit!' she added through hushed clenched teeth.

'You bastard!' Doug was striding towards them. 'How could you?' It was the weakness in the blow which upset him the most: the feeble punch to his neck and the helpless look of disappointment and despair in his dewy pale eyes. 'And as for you!' he screamed turning towards his daughter, 'your sister, for God's sake. Your poor dead sister.'

'It's not what you think,' pleaded Sarah.

Doug was having none of it. 'Please don't, Sarah. Just don't!'

Stepping back, the unfolding family drama made him feel a spectator – and a worthless excuse for a human being – as he watched father and daughter disintegrate into desperate, broken emotional wrecks.

'Dad, it's not what it seems,' she tried again, the guilt in her eyes giving her away.

'Sarah! I know you,' Doug raged, the blood in his face getting dangerously redder.

'Nothing happened.'

She couldn't give up the lie because the truth was so despicable.

'Sarah, stop it,' he said lifting her chin.

'Dad,' she pleaded, knowing that she'd been found out.

'Just grow up,' he said irritably turning towards Kev as if he were the Turner on his living-room wall.

'But . . .' He didn't know what he wanted to say. It wasn't important. He just had to appear to at least attempt something.

'No buts!' shouted Doug. 'Just go,' he pleaded.

'Just go,' echoed Sarah softly avoiding eye contact with him and holding her father by the shoulders. He was now visibly shaking.

Kev went to walk away but turned robotically towards the fallout again, as if being controlled by a TV remote. He wanted to apologize sincerely this time, to tell them both he was really dead inside and that none of it mattered – well not in his world anyway. Holding out her hand she ushered him away. Watching her pale fingertips as he turned, he knew that he'd never be contrite again, nor would he ever attempt to be. He would never be that honest man.

He was wretched, though relieved, and miserable. Had he really fallen so low? he wondered, remembering Doug's words at the dinner table: *you know she's fond of you, don't you?* He only looked back once as he trudged back towards the shouts and cheers of the dads and the thuds of struck footballs in the blinding sunshine. In the distance Sarah and Doug walked away together, their bloodlines thicker than their regrets and disgust. Reaching the gates of the park he knew it was all over: Eve, Sarah – their family. He'd lost and ruined everything; wrecked their lives and his own. Hearing the last cheer of the afternoon as final whistles blew across the park he knew he wanted one thing and one thing only: to drink; to drink and become nothing – a mere rambling fool. He knew as he crossed the road that he was heading on a downward journey which would only end when he crashed and burned, ridding himself of all dignity, relinquishing the will to carry on, curling up on the pavement of a worthless life.

Part Two

Part Two

Chapter Nine

Once upon a time there was a girl. She was sad and in Love. It wasn't the first time she'd fallen for someone, but it was probably going to be the last. A pure, untamed, unfathomable, unattainable love: the stupid kind that greedily eats away at you, feeding like a tapeworm until you're white with death and unable to notice how much you've changed. You see only in black and sludge grey as you shiver and ache, your stomach squelching, moving up and down as it shifts sunken to one side every time he enters the room with that disdainful, uninterested look on his face.

Her name was Anabelle and her disturbing resolve was steely real. If she were to colour in her exact (yet to be discovered) emotion with a waxy crayon, then it would be a cold morning blue moulded like a quivering jelly into a misty mauve within a fuzzy green delicate stem. Though she loathed the word (more the sound it made when unleashed from her pale pink lips) she was a dote: Anabelle the devoted, fluffy, quiet as a mouse, doting dote!

Blinking at the screen of his laptop, Kev shook his head in desperation and then wiped a bead of sweat from above his eyes and forehead feverishly dripping with perspiration, streaming down his cold, pale, drawn face. The round spotlights of the ceiling, atmospherically more suitable for the movies, made him look as though he was a starving clerk from a Russian labour camp.

Was this his best bet, so far? he wondered, scanning the first of three chapters in front of him. She, Isabella Morton, could certainly write. The synopsis was intriguing enough, but he hadn't been fully grabbed by it either. Though he liked the title, *Deadly Mouse,* he thought the writer was perhaps a little too deliberate in trying to keep some aspects of the plot hidden. That aside, he'd decided to give it a second read but was finding it harder to get beyond the first paragraph. Maybe it was the whole *dote* thing? That twisted unrequited love theme perhaps, that stirred a cruel streak in him which would willingly have cradled the love-struck Juliet in his arms before releasing his grip, letting her fall, sniffling, to her knees, broken, loving him unconditionally more as he strutted away like a bastard? Just a crappy passing thought, he mused, clicking his mouse and dragging the arrow down the page. Was Anabelle really feasible though? he wondered, snorting back the phlegm of his impending cold. Her obvious sensuality and gangly beauty didn't quite sit well with her meekness.

'Hi, Kev,' came the booming voice of confidence.

It was Josh. 'Hi,' he acknowledged, barely looking up from his screen.

'Christ, it's hot in here!' he continued undoing his top button and loosening his tie. 'Have you not seen the windows before, they've got little latches on the top you can pull and open?' he added sarcastically.

'If I opened them, I'd be tempted to jump every time you entered the room.'

Kev hated having to share a rather small airless office with someone who was continuously on a happy sarcastic high. More than anything he detested Josh's manic energy and quick mind which tended to bounce off the walls, never allowing for calm to descend and always putting him on edge. Kev didn't mind being touched, but Josh always seemed to be in tactile over-drive. If he wasn't slapping your back, he was hugging your shoulder. Most people just got used to it, saw the Josh hug as part and parcel of who he was. For Kev it was like having a finger continuously poked into a festering wound.

'How's your new list going? Mine's bursting at the seams,' Josh gloated, casually throwing himself down at his desk and whistling 'Rule Britannia'.

'Fine,' answered Kev unconvincingly struggling with a sudden intrusion of Anabelle's pale pink lips, puckered and primed.

The list wasn't as bad as in previous years, but he had to move up the gears. He needed what all agents did – something fresh and intensely absorbing. He still hadn't gone the YA route yet, though he was getting reluctantly closer.

'What's that you've got there?' enquired Josh, gesturing towards the screen. 'Another supposedly tantalising but totally predictable thriller?'

'Unfathomable, unattainable love,' he paraphrased as if taking part in a tedious game of snap. 'A bit like your love life,' he added dryly.

'That's not what Rebecca said last night,' Josh replied instantly, eagerly awaiting Kev's reply, which would compel him to disclose his latest grubby conquest.

'Thought you were seeing that Notting Hill poet's daughter. What's her name?'

'Charlotte.'

'That's the one,' Kev agreed flatly as he briefly scanned the last two paragraphs of Chapter One.

'Let's just say that the new one, Rebecca, is even more insatiable than the old one.'

'Jesus, Josh, you really are a little charmer.'

'You're just envious.'

Kev sighed, not for the first time, before adding: 'I think I'm a little bit classier than that.'

Josh didn't reply but annoyingly began drumming the edge of his desk.

'Do you want me to give you something to play with: some cymbals or maybe a toy trumpet?' smiled Kev, focusing on the flashing words on the page: *she wished she could suck the life out of him.*

'Fuck this, I'm off,' said Josh, restlessly fidgeting with his crotch before springing to his feet. 'Wet supper with a publisher,' he said playfully, punching Kev's arm.

'Sounds good,' answered Kev aware that Josh was itching to parade his feathers some more.

'Don't you want to know who it is?' he asked, smiling broadly.

'Not really.'

'Oh, well, I'll leave you to your admin then,' he concluded spitefully with a smile as he grabbed his coat and left.

Relieved Josh was gone, Kev switched his focus back to the screen and clicked on Isabella's covering letter.

'*Love Iain Banks,*' he laughed, reading the small font of the email. 'She's almost perfect!' he cried a little too loudly as he heard Vicky and Melissa's shrill voices rise and fall in the next office. Contemplating paying them a visit, he hesitated for a second and read on: *Now ready to enter the world of publishing, I'm looking for someone to take my work forward and complete the process. Having read* **with interest** *your profile and a lot about your agency, I would like to offer you a first read. Find attached synopsis and first three chapters for your perusal.*

Pretty standard, he thought. The only annoying thing about it being the blurb at the beginning: *a compelling, psychological must-read,* thrown in at the end of the first paragraph.

Not registering at first the **with interest** part of the letter left ominously in bold, he soon returned to it. It appeared to now reach out to him from the screen. What does that imply? he wondered, squinting at the letters as if they were somehow going to change shape and meaning if he didn't stay with them. His profile was hardly a riveting read, unlike Josh's which oozed egotistical confidence and swagger. Kev's was more clinical and dry. A prosaic account of the worthless facts about an ordinary person who happened to be in the privileged position to maybe make someone else's dreams come true: *Kevin Parker (also known as Kev) joined Hargreaves and Bennett after a successful career in publishing* (though he didn't mention the Book Circulation bit), *he is an Iain Banks fanatic* (that's where she got it from) *who is always on the lookout for authentically weird fiction* (a bit over the top) *which stretches the imagination and keeps you guessing to the last word left on the page* (more blurbs and a bit dramatic). Josh had predictably remarked that he should have included at the end: *Always on the lookout for new talent* and that he could then pass a few wordy babes his way. How Josh ever became a literary agent was anyone's guess.

Where had all the nice people gone? he wondered, taking a sip of water. At Townsend Publishing there had been Mick the hippie proofreader come-sub-editor who brought in his mum's freshly baked fairy cakes each Friday; Brian the harmless fantasist who used to tell people he'd once dated Kate Moss, and then Bridget his boss in Book Circulation: a functioning alcoholic from East Ham who was told by a gypsy woman that one day she would stop drinking and open a French patisserie on the Mile End Road. If Josh was at least just a little bit off the wall he'd be more tolerable, he thought, as he listened to the familiar sounds of packing-up, shuffling and logging-off going on next door.

One more look, he reasoned, checking the time on his screen (6.00 p.m.) before clicking back to the sample document and scrolling down past Chapter Two where he fell upon the familiar words of his original read as he continued to read the thoughts of a stranger.

Anabelle knew what she wanted to do to Karissa if she called him once more. It had first come to her in a dream where she and an old school friend were standing by an open window overlooking an ornate garden and lake. They'd been talking mainly about boys, when suddenly feeling a chill in the air she'd asked Susan to close the window. Still in mid-flow, talking about a boy named Sam who'd kept staring at her at a local fair, she'd not heard Anabelle's request.

'I thought I told you to close the window?' Anabelle had howled uncontrollably, grabbing the strap of Susan's pinafore.

Beyond the calm flowing lawns of summer and the sound of humming bees competing with the warbling birds, a frightened rabbit scampered in and out of the morning shade before stopping abruptly, standing tippy-toe on its hind legs as the cloud moved on. Suzie, as Anabelle called her, was gone; pushed. The last she saw of her were her shiny, buckled, black shoes and knee-length white school socks, reverse side up, as she was comically lifted as if on the wind, gliding majestically to the cold York stone waiting to crunch and smash her below.

'Crunch,' he read aloud, his mind made up in a split second that *Deadly Mouse* was probably no more. Clicking on compose, he began to type:

Dear Isabella. Thanks for this. We're a small agency and therefore very

selective. Your synopsis and opening chapters just didn't quite do it for me.
Erase . . . Too pompous, he thought, holding his finger down until
the words magically disappeared.

Maybe a short, sharp, declining Josh: *This is not for me, but all the
best in your search for representation.* Definitely not. Or maybe a positive
Melissa: *Thank you so much for sending me your work. However, having
considered it, I'm afraid that I don't feel it's right for my list.* Or possibly a
regretful Vicky: *I'm really sorry not to have better news, but I wish you the
very best of luck with other agents.*

'OK,' he said to himself as his fingers suddenly came alive again:
I'm sorry it's taken so long to respond (good start). *I've been rather deluged
and have fallen quite behind with my reading* (a bit whiny). *While there is
much to admire about your writing* (slightly condescending), *I'm afraid,
on balance, I'm not quite enthusiastic enough to ask to see more at this time.*
Erase . . .

*Thank you for sending us your material which I have looked at with inter-
est* (shouldn't I be looking at everything with interest?). Erase . . .

Hearing the scraping of chairs, the quick opening and banging of
doors, he repositioned himself in his seat, keeping one eye on the
clock, and returned with renewed certainty and intent to the bright
screen.

> *Dear Isabella, thank you for sending me samples of Deadly Mouse,
> which I have now read and considered. Sadly, I'm sorry to say that it
> is not something I could feel 100% confident of being able to handle
> successfully. However, there are as many opinions as there are agents
> and publishers, so I wish you all the success in finding suitable repre-
> sentation elsewhere.*
>
> *Best Wishes*
> *Kev Parker*

Satisfied with the rejection he hesitantly clicked send and felt sad
as he always did, that somebody, somewhere wasn't getting what
they'd hoped or, even more distressing, prayed for.

'Kev, you coming for a drink?' It was chirpy, immaculate Melissa, dressed in a French blue flared trouser-suit with a red polka-dot neck scarf with heavily painted ruby lips to match, who'd popped her head around the door: 'Vicky's celebrating another acclaimed book review,' she gushed.

'Why not, I'm celebrating sending out another agonising rejection,' he replied as an instant response flashed up on the screen. 'Be with you in a minute,' he said opening the email only to find Isabella's original enquiry letter, synopsis and first three chapters sent again. Coincidence, he reasoned as the door closed behind him. Perhaps it didn't send or she was just blitzing agents? After all, he had kept her waiting a month.

'Right, let's do this.'

Click – send – beep! – mail. Click – send – beep! – mail. Click – send – beep! – mail. Click – send – beep! – mail.

'Four love,' he said to himself as the rally seemed to eerily intensify as his fingers competed with another set elsewhere and the same email came bouncing back.

Click – send – beep! – mail. Click – send – beep! – mail. Click – send – beep! - mail. Click – send – beep! – mail . . .

'Come on Kev.' It was Vicky now: a tall Nicole Kidman lookalike who smelt of pear drops. 'What are you doing?' she asked looking at the chequered inbox twitching on the screen.

'I don't get it; look, watch,' he said sending off another volley of clicks only to receive instant responses every time.

'Aggressive emailer?'

He didn't reply for some time, trying to decipher the oddness in the room which now seemed to have a gloopy texture all of its own as a sudden lull in the messaging made it appear as if someone had just died, while the airless office began to feel tight; the anxiety and anticipation of another beep adding to the compressed feeling around his now inflamed, clinched tonsils.

'Quick, before they reload,' said Vicky, opening the door wider as her odour of fresh pears swept through the room on a whoosh of cold air.

'Right,' he said unconvincingly, still dazed and more freaked out than he imagined. 'I'll just get my coat,' he concluded, grabbing it with urgency as if racing against the now ominous silence.

Now outside his office he grappled with the sounds circling his head: the loud girlish laughter of Melissa and Vicky further down the corridor, whooping at the prospect of an after-work drink, which essentially spelt freedom; the cleaners switching on their hoovers, and the trundling, wheezy buses outside, their diesel engines spluttering and moaning. Straining his ears above the din, he heard what he expected and strangely wanted: the touché beep from his darkened office, before a succession of what appeared to be angrier blips as he pulled at the front of his sweaty shirt for air before turning and making a dash for the evening.

Chapter Ten

'Overtime?' remarked Steve as they arrived at the same time at the doors of The King's Head.

'No, some mad one kept volleying off the same email to me,' he said with a sniffle.

'Technology, eh?'

'Used to be able to just take the receiver off the hook back in the day.'

'When we were boys, eh?' What's with the added *ehs,* wondered Kev, who'd not noticed his friend's verbal affliction before.

'Who's in there?' asked Steve, blocking the entrance as Kev went to walk ahead of him.

'Melissa and Vicky.'

'Not Melissa, she annoys the fuck out of me.'

'Well, at least Josh isn't there.'

'Probably licking another publisher's boots, eh?'

What would he do without Steve? He was like the earth wire in a plug, keeping him grounded and safe from disappearing up his own arse, away from the trapdoor of self-importance.

'What's with the ehs?' He had to ask.

'Eh?'

Laughing and throwing a few more ehs at one another, they entered the bar.

'What's the joke?' Melissa had to know everything, it was in her DNA. It was why she effortlessly climbed the ladder while Kev had faltered on the first rung.

'It's just an . . . eh thing,' said Steve, prodding his friend in the ribs.

'Oh, cool,' she gushed, because she always gushed at everything.

'Drinks?' enquired Kev trying to contain his amusement.

'We're fine,' chimed the girls, holding up their white Zinfandels.

'Steve?'

'Pint of cider.'

Ordering himself a lager shandy and Steve's cider, Kev acknowledged the solicitor type cradling his gin and tonic at the end of the bar – one of the ghost train brigade of the Monday to Friday club he used to keep hours with. The look in the man's eyes was almost one of betrayal and recognition that Kev wouldn't be joining him later on the drinkathon before the neon go-slow drudgery of a last tube which stopped at the last kebab shop in town.

He wasn't teetotal but he'd cut down a lot, shandy now being his preferred drink. Glancing at the hunched figure sipping his double gin at the bar, he reminded himself of just how far he had come from the abyss. Almost two years since he'd last seen Sarah, and the drunken course that he'd decided upon he'd eventually stopped and got himself fixed. His doctor had prescribed anti-depressants and told him to stop drinking. He realised he needed help when he'd stopped going to work, spending a whole week in the pub. Red-eyed, filthy and lonely, he'd collapsed on the way home and fallen asleep under a hedge. Waking, he discovered he was covered in dog shit, while the loop in his head obsessively played day and night: Christmas Eve; Eve: didn't tell her I loved her; let her walk home alone; dead; shagging her sister; repeat; repeat; repeat; and so on until the sequence drove him near crazy, affecting his work and what he had left of his life. Waking covered in crap and instantly returning to the loop he had arrived in and crashed. The first time he took the anti-depressant he knew the slight sensation shift to the left side of his brain was a good thing as a clear nothingness turned up unannounced and set up camp, making a space as it swept and dusted until there was nothing there but a distant memory of Kev Parker. It was as if the pain had been temporarily numbed, cloaked and folded neatly in bubble-wrap. After a brief spell back at his parents', he'd taken a two-week sun holiday alone in Portugal. Just his pills; a book a day; good food, and swimming – he slowly brought himself back to life. Returning to work relaxed and tanned, he knew he'd somehow escaped the brink and broken free. His new interest in literature guiding him with the help of some old friends – Conrad, Greene and Orwell – he'd retrieved some of his humanity. Writing again: he was trying out different styles and ways of expressing himself, trying to write the way a portrait artist would paint or the way a surrealist would throw colours at a canvas. At work he was putting together a new list, fresh new talent replacing the stale as he revamped and upgraded, convincing himself that one day he really would find that bestseller.

'Jesus, I thought you'd never return,' whispered Steve as Melissa continued with her gushing running commentary of Vicky's book review. Why Vicky allowed her to talk for her only Vicky knew.

'Mad email tennis, huh?' asked Vicky, presumably glad to hear her own voice again.

Suzie: the last she saw of her – her shiny, buckled, black shoes and knee-length white school socks, reverse side up, as she was comically lifted as if on the wind. She could write, he thought as the words flooded his mind. Remembering it word for word, he wondered if perhaps Isabella was really special and that he'd got it all wrong. 'Yeah,' he replied, at last aware that Melissa was critically surveying his face and probably viewing his *yeah* as somehow lacking. She was very similar to Rachel Winkler who'd moved on a year previous setting up her own literary agency. As her replacement, Melissa was a mere replica.

'Steve, have they sorted out that problem with Michael Fontane's expenses yet?' Melissa didn't care about Michael Fontane's expenses, she just wanted to make the distinction that Steve was from Accounts and they were Literary with a capital 'L' Agents.

'Think so,' he replied exaggerating his cockney accent. Kev knew Steve played it dumb sometimes; it was part of his weaponry which read: treat me dumb, I will act dumb psychology – a technique known by all suppressed peoples throughout the world.

'Stella! Good to see you,' gushed Melissa, standing and kissing her on both cheeks. It was almost a ghostly entrance, and everyone turned to notice the beautiful woman who'd suddenly appeared.

Rising to his feet, Kev tenderly gave her a peck on the still moist cheek Melissa had slobbered on and pulled up the vacant stool next to him.

'Finished work early,' she whispered, squeezing his knee as she sat. 'You've got a cold,' she stated as he answered *yes*. 'Steve, how's things?' She smiled, reaching across and patting his arm. 'Vicky,' she acknowledged – 'how did the review go?'

'Brilliant,' Vicky said, beating Melissa to the gallop.

'You deserve it,' Stella added, snuggling into Kev's arm as her crisp brunette bob swished every time she moved her head; all the time her hazel eyes making contact with everyone at the table, radiating warmth and a niceness which was hard to come by these days.

Ten months and five days. He could never have said it, but he thought it nonetheless as the anti-depressant he was taking neatly parked Eve's name in a distant corner of his brain. They'd met one year into Kev's new clean regime at a firm's do. Sitting quietly with Steve in a swanky London hotel, he'd noticed a very attractive young woman staring at him; her hairstyle was the same as it was now, but dyed blonde. She'd seemed familiar, though given his history, most women did. When the music had started with Soft Cell's 'Tainted Love', he'd of course made it onto the dance floor with Vicky and Steve. It was there that Stella had joined them with a friend. Dancing over, they'd arranged to meet at the weekend, a date on which they appeared to want to cram everything in: The National Portrait Gallery; coffee in St Martin's Crypt, followed by lunch in Chinatown; a matinee Woody Allen film and a comedy club by the evening; the closing kiss as they separated at Tottenham Court Road tube cementing a perfect start. He had really come a long way from the groper on the dance floor, now appealing to Stella's love of simply curling up on the sofa and watching old black and white movies. Running her own small marketing company, Stella had a comfy lifestyle. Getting over a bad marriage, she was now searching for romance. Kev, who saw himself as a good reader of people, had seen her as a lost romantic, a searcher who wanted to be protected from the world. She was what he needed, generating calm, uncomplicated security and ultimately sanity.

'Might be an admirer,' Melissa said out of the blue.

'No, definitely a nutter,' interrupted Steve, getting the gist of it before the others.

'What's this?' enquired Stella, increasing her grip on his arm.

'Oh, some woman named Isabella wants me as her agent. Went a bit crazy on the emailing this afternoon.'

'But is she any good?' asked Vicky.

'She can write. Just missing something,' he said as Steve smirked.

'What is she missing?' Stella was now facing him as if awaiting an instant reply.

Christ, I love her smile, he thought as he answered. 'Just . . .' He was lost for words; he really hadn't thought it through. 'Maybe she's just a little bit too flowery,' he managed at last, though not certain that it was actually the reason.

'How would you change it or write it?' enquired Melissa, who'd been uncharacteristically quiet during the exchange.

'Well . . .' It was one of those long, drawn-out replies. The type you might have started when asked a direct question by your lecturer in a seminar room. 'I'd keep it basic; shorter sentences, less of the over-description, and perhaps speed it up a bit.' Everyone was looking at him now and he hated the attention. 'Cut to the chase; paint the picture and move on to the next outline.'

'Let the reader fill in the gaps,' concluded Vicky.

'That's what I always say to my writers; it's simple writing,' agreed Melissa, an expert at taking others' ideas and summing them up as her own.

'It could be that Isabella is writing just as it appears in her head,' added Stella, smiling. She loved talking about literature, something Kev only did when prompted to do so.

'Yeah, as I said earlier: a nutter,' concluded Steve as they all laughed, although Melissa and Vicky's chuckles were through gritted teeth.

'I hear you're off at the weekend?' said Melissa, happy that the laughter at Steve's inane comment had run out of air.

'Paris,' Stella said, the very mention giving her a rosy-cheeked glow – or maybe it was simply a blush at the announcement that they were heading to the Capital of Love.

'Just one more day of first three chapters plus synopsis and copy-cat letters,' added Vicky, smiling Melissa's way.

Maybe it was their in-joke? Perhaps they never trolled through the slush pile like he did, instead going down the recommendations or contacts routes instead? He didn't trust them, they just seemed too polished.

'Is that what Isabella is?' asked Stella, 'part of the numerous "synopsis and first three chapters"?'

'Sadly,' replied Kev answering for them all. 'It's the only way to get your work out there.'

'You'd have to be crazy to start in the first place.' Steve appeared to want to seal the conversation once and for all with a flippant comment which probably annoyed the hell out of Melissa and Vicky.

He was right, who in their right mind would spend the good part of two years writing and editing, then continuously redrafting a piece of work, a piece of themselves, and prostituting it to every agent in *The Writer's Year Book*, only to get near identical refusal letters from individuals like themselves?

'Another drink?' Steve asked.

'Not for me,' said Kev. Steve still hadn't got used to his friend's revised drinking management scheme and looked a little hurt, changing his mind when realising he'd be stuck with Vicky and Melissa who no doubt felt the same. 'Want to get an early night, mate,' he said to his friend as Stella melted into his shoulder once more.

Chapter Eleven

'Kev, you OK? You seem someplace else.'

Their first night in Paris; staring out across the skyline dominated by the Eiffel Tower and awaiting the monument's nightly *lumière* to begin, they held hands – but his slightly sweaty hands and distant stare were a sure sign of the conundrum racing in his mind.

The morning before, he'd returned to work expecting an email explaining a virus or maybe disruption to the network to account for the previous day's game of email ping-pong. Instead he counted the fifty emails sent by Isabella; the last one arriving half an hour after he'd left the building. Randomly checking them to see that they contained more of the same information he'd instinctively landed on the last one (the fiftieth). Instantly he saw it was different and not the expected synopsis and first three chapters.

Chapter Four (She was ignoring him now. She was sending new chapters). Hesitantly he started to read: *Her eyes saw everything. She knew every corner of his house, his life, just as she did each new line on his face. Oh, how he ridiculed her: the cheap put-downs, the insignificance of her very being – if he really, truly saw her at all? Anabelle the dote; the map maker who saw his next move before he did. The transparency of his selfishness easily read, like a* Ladybird *book, had led her to the bottom of his soul, where his darkest secrets festered and played. She didn't have to push him (Suzie could tell you how easy that would be), oh, that was too easy; no, she just had to watch and he'd do the rest.*

He hoped it was his imagination playing tricks, but he couldn't help thinking that in a deranged way she was threatening him. It didn't take a literary mind to see the intent of the piece. Of course it meant nothing to him; but shit – the fact she'd sent it meant something. Choosing not to reply, he stored it in a newly created file entitled *The Mad One*. It was the only way he could put it into words. Like the character Anabelle, it was *unfathomable*. The rest of the chapter had concentrated on Anabelle's infatuation with the mystery man. From a practical point of view it annoyed him. OK, she was keeping his identity hidden for dramatic effect, but he preferred to know people's names. For him it was a precursor to good writing. Reading towards the end there was still a lot of vented anger. The last sentence though was an odd one, a statement of sorts from the mouth of the dote: *Always; always to be concluded; her true love for him a pain; a longing that would **never end**.* The strength of the two words in bold bothered him: simple; definitely not flowery, more biblical; the opposite to the traditional final curtain: The End. Scribbling it down on his pad, he knew it held some significance. On a lighter note, he thought, he'd use it himself one day if he ever got round to writing a novel. It held a resonance for his own pain; that even given all the medication he was now taking his own torment probably *would never end*.

'Fine,' he replied. 'This is beautiful, isn't it?' he added, placing his arm around her shoulder when, as if on cue, the Eiffel Tower erupted in red, white, and blue lights, glittering in a menacing inky sky.

In truth he thought it was an anti-climax. It was big. It was grand, but he felt nothing, only the need to get moving and as far away as possible from a public spectacle and its *oohs!* and *ahhs!*

'Shall we buy one?' she asked playfully picking up a miniature Eiffel Tower from one of the small pop-up stalls selling numerous gaudy knick-knacks. 'It's a pen; it lights up – see?'

Paying for the gifts, they made their way to a small café they'd spotted earlier near their hotel. Painted in a variety of moody Renoir blues, it oozed Parisian style, mixing the odours of fresh coffee, pastries, and Gitanes wafting in from the tables outside, into an evocative multi-sensory orgasm.

'Two coffees with milk,' announced the waitress. It was the first time he'd thought of Eve since they'd been away. The young woman was petite, dark, and had that impish art student, dressed in black with matching Alice-band thing going on. Even the way she spoke, although with a French accent, had the same sing-song quality of Eve's voice.

'She's cute, isn't she?' said Stella, noting Kev's lingering gaze as the waitress swung her hips off to another table. 'Petite,' she added smiling.

'Smells good; something special about French coffee,' said Kev, ignoring the comment and picking up the light blue cup, sniffing it as if it were a fine wine.

'Eve . . . she was petite, wasn't she?'

The mere mention of her name nearly made Kev spill his coffee. 'Yes, smallish,' he managed.

'You don't mind me mentioning her, do you?'

Stella had never really pushed the ex-girlfriends button as Kev had hardly shown any interest in her ex-boyfriends or, more to the point, husband. Having attempted on a number of occasions to extract the odd snippet of information, she'd given up the chase and, seeing how the relationship with Eve had ended, was sensitive to his silence on the matter.

'Not at all.'

It was just the kind of answer Stella was used to: nothing to follow it up; no reminisces. She smiled at him and didn't take it any further.

'My hair is annoying me today,' she said, suddenly pushing it up on top of her head as if facing a mirror. 'I won't be a minute.' She rose and he was sure she was swinging her hips the way the cute waitress had. 'See if I can do something with it,' she added, making her way to the toilets.

He'd given away enough on the Eve front, he reasoned; he didn't want to be continuously bringing her alive. Telling Stella the whole hit and run story a week into their relationship, and then disclosing the utter breakdown of his life that had followed, he felt he'd said all that he could. As for the affair with Sarah, it was something he would never admit to anyone no matter how much he loved them. Why did all new relationships contain this need to go through the whole history of one's life as if it were a prerequisite to starting another one? he wondered as the waitress caught his attention again. She was now speaking on her mobile, her face down-turned and serious as her voice rose and then dropped as if involved in an emotional exchange. Probably a boyfriend, he reasoned as a writer would, his mind flooded with numerous storylines, twists, and turns as the young girl slammed the phone down hard on the counter, picked up her pen and pad, then retrieved her smile and went to take another order. He could watch her all day, not in a sexual way, but as a living, breathing, talking piece of French art.

'That's better.' As if she'd been there all along Stella was back facing him, her hair miraculously changed into a small bun. 'Improvisation – a wonderful French word,' she said playfully.

He was going to say that *communiqué* was also a wonderful French word, but looking at her hair said, 'What's that in–' Stopping as if paralysed with panic, he knew he'd used the same line before. She may as well have said that it was a pencil and that she drew eyes (it was that surreal). 'Your hair,' he finished at last swallowing hard.

'A pen. Watch,' she said, pressing the end of it as the Eiffel Tower briefly lit up. 'Knew it would come in handy,' she laughed, reaching for a pastry. 'You OK?' she asked after taking a small polite bite and wiping a stray crumb from her lip. 'You look like you've seen a ghost.'

Irrationally, he wanted to scream for her to take it out. Wanted it sprung from her scalp.

'Go away,' shouted the waitress, having answered what was probably a call from the previous caller. 'Do what you want,' she concluded in English, catching Kev's glance, blushing and turning away ashamed at having been observed.

'Quite a drama unfolding.'

'Quite,' he said, simply trying to avoid looking at the pen.

The sudden twinge in his groin registered in his brain as a hand moved across his thigh. 'The toilets are nice; meet me there,' Stella said, rising again, her swagger more exaggerated than before.

Could the coffee shop date get any stranger? he wondered, following her a moment later, trying to control the growing erection creeping down his trouser leg.

On his way to the toilet he felt he had an obligation to smile at the waitress as if saying sorry for witnessing her earlier disagreement. The return smile was fake and professional; her eyes revealing an inner pride which said *fuck all of you.*

Pushing open the door she was there, waiting for him, holding up her red knickers, dangling like a dead mouse from her outstretched hand. Instantly turning around and facing the sink and mirror she steadied herself and guided him into her. 'Fuck me,' she mouthed over her shoulder. Facing the pen perched upon her head, he obeyed her orders, his mind racing all the time, pictures from his past whirling around his mind and spinning out of control as the thrusting got faster and faster, as she pushed herself back onto him and let out a satisfied series of yeses as they both collided and came.

'*Très bien,*' she said, pulling back down her skirt and smiling.

'*Très bon,*' he replied, as she flicked open the catch on the door. As he followed her out the pen activated itself and sent a scurry of light to the top of the Eiffel Tower and back down again.

Chapter Twelve

She searched high and low; under the bed, behind the huge oak wardrobe which was turned upsidedown (the result of a search to find the cause of a scratching sound), even the cleaning cupboard where nobody dared go after Edward had sworn he'd seen a ghost there. Scurrying around beneath the stairs, she'd even found the rabbit's paw she'd lost, given to her by some strange distant uncle who kept calling her 'girl' and smelt of turf and sweet tobacco.

'Come on, boy – come on – there's a boy.' She'd heard the smelly uncle use the same words when Ollie (the now deceased budgie) had escaped his cage on one of his last adventures before he misjudged a turn and flew straight into a closed window. Dazed and bewildered, he'd died of fright in the clutches of Mits the cat. 'Come on boy – there's a boy.' She could just make out its little sausage tail wagging under the old range. When it had worked the maid would keep the newly hatched chicks from the farm in a tray underneath it to keep them warm. Now it was Max who'd found a dead field mouse and was toying with the idea, forming in his evolving mind, that he was indeed the fierce, fearless hunter who'd killed it. 'There's my boy. What a big boy you are.' Pulling it out by the scruff of its neck she lifted the hammer high and let it fall with all her tiny might on the pup's head as . . .

Sighing at his screen, Kev couldn't read any more, his eyes stinging as he tried to avoid the onomatopoeia which surged out to him: *Split! Smash! Splint! Crack! Fleck!* The sick soundtrack to the vile scene of a puppy having its head smashed to a pulp by an angry Anabelle.

'Oh, look at this,' cried Josh from the desk behind him as he restarted the YouTube video. Turning around, Kev saw a fat naked man being pushed out of a tree by a monkey who proceeded to pee in the fallen man's direction. 'It's called pissing from the evolution tree', announced Josh, leaning back in his chair as if about to sip a Scotch and blow smoke from a cigar at a gentleman's club.

'About right,' answered Kev returning to his screen.

'So how'd the dirty weekend go?'

Josh was predictable. Kev was surprised he hadn't said it earlier in the day. 'Filthy,' he replied simply.

'Go on: do tell,' Josh said before becoming distracted again. 'Oh, look at this,' he continued, nodding towards the naked man who was now climbing back up the tree.

In truth, after the toilet incident it *had* been a particularly sexually charged break. Stella had been strangely turned on by the whole café episode. He'd certainly returned with the look of a man who'd seen very little of the sights of Paris and more of the four walls of a hotel room.

Sex apart, they'd probably moved closer to the scene in the play where their relationship was becoming serious. There had been an intense chat about being truthful with one another. Stella had opened up a lot about her ex-husband and how he'd kept secrets (not just the women, but the bank accounts she knew nothing of and the child he'd fathered some years ago and had been paying maintenance for – all becoming crystal clear after the divorce when the sheer number of lies broke her completely). As she'd stroked Kev's hair on their last night away, his head resting over her beating heart, he'd said that he would tell her everything and that there would be no secrets between them. Right there, vulnerable and naked in each other's arms in the blue shade of the hotel room, he believed it; kidded himself she knew everything she needed to know about him. As soon as he'd said it there was a thickness in the air, a gap not filled with sound: a pause; a tense space. If Stella had sensed it she'd have known that he was already holding back; keeping his history locked up tight; or was she allowing him more room to unpack his things and lay them all out neatly in front of her?

'You now know more about me than I do,' he'd joked, the words not letting him down, when really they should have choked him.

'He's pushed the . . .' Josh was laughing hysterically, half on half off his swinging chair.

'The monkey out of the tree,' finished Kev not bothering to turn around as another unwanted email flashed on his screen.

Clicking on *The Mad One* he read the next instalment. It was all becoming so familiar. A pattern was forming. No sooner had he read a piece of her work, pondered on it and tried to understand it, than another sequence would arrive to confuse him even more. There was Anabelle the little girl who causes harm to everyone and rages against everything; Anabelle the grown woman: a dote, an easily offended Cinderella type; and then of course the more disturbing Anabelle: vindictive, psychopathic, plotting her revenge against unrequited love. And just as he thought he had the running order worked out there was another Anabelle.

Slapping his forehead he continued with the new entry, more lyrical than the previous ones and unlike her usual style.

Sitting close to him – near enough to imagine his breathing in the next room – she pulled her grazed knees up to her chin and began to speak to the wall. 'If you hear me, my love, please don't be afraid. I will always love you whatever hurt sails my way. I know you can't hear me through this stained old wallpaper. I am but a crushed bird hoping and praying for a stray crumb to fall from your lips. I will continue to live for you, to breathe your stale air until it is fresh and you are once again alive. I will save you as you will me. We will live and we will die.'

As a trickle of blood gently oozed from the cut she'd made in her knee with the blade from a pencil sharpener, she licked at the warm, red iron taste, sucking it until it landed at the back of her throat where she held it, then swallowed hard and wept like a child.

'The Mad One still hounding you?'

'You bet,' sighed Kev nervously biting a fingernail.

'Why don't you say the police have been contacted? That'll keep her away,' said Josh, lazily swinging his keys between his fingers. 'Did the same once with an ex of mine who was threatening to tell my then girlfriend that I'd first slept with her for a bet.'

'Had you?'

'Yeah, but it all turned out right in the end.'

'How?'

'Told my girlfriend everything.'

'So, she forgave you?'

'No, she chucked me. Though I was glad, it had run its course anyway.'

'And the police thing?'

'Oh yeah, scared the shit out of her. You see, she knew my father was a Police Commissioner.'

'Shit! Never knew that.'

'He was all over the papers some years ago for fabricating evidence in relation to the jailing of a well-known London gangster.'

'Right.'

Josh astounded him. There was always something new to find out about him. Only recently, he'd found out that his great-aunt had been a high-class escort who had nearly brought the government down during the sixties.

'Put the frighteners on her, it always works,' he added defiantly, getting up and reaching for his coat. In all the time he'd known Josh their conversations always ended in the same way: Josh getting up and going somewhere in a hurry, keys in hand. Today was no different. 'Tell her you know where she lives; that will frighten her,' he called back as he slid out the door.

Bit strong, thought Kev, opening up a new message. Niceties aside, he knew something had to be done. Running his fingers over the keyboard apprehensively like he was about to sign a death warrant, he began:

Dear Isabella (erase – too nice). *Isabella, this is getting a little strange* (better). *Although I think you're a good writer, I'm afraid I can't represent you* (he was on a run). *I thought at first there may have been a problem with our network when I received so many emails from you. However, as we both know, this is not the case.* He was pleased. It sounded mature and measured. Swallowing hard he continued. *I am asking you nicely* (erase – too weak) *I want you to stop emailing me* (strong and to the point). *I feel that there is an undercurrent of intimidation within what you write and I wish you to cease sending it to me. I have been advised on the matter by my solicitor* (OK, he was lying) *who states that unwelcome emailing to the degree I have received from you is tantamount to harassment. If this continues I will be compelled to contact the police.*

There, he thought, as if drawing a line under the last sentence. It's fair, he decided as his finger hesitated for a second, resting expectantly on the green mouse for the signal from his brain to fire. Something was kicking away at the bottom of his stomach, until: boom! His finger released the trigger. Breathing hard, he waited, his chest tight in anticipation. Scared, vulnerable and, irrationally, nervously excited for the outcome, he fidgeted.

Mail! came the inane *beep, beep.* Shit! he thought, clicking on *The Mad One.*

You'll be sorry you did that.

No exclamation mark, almost too definite, so much so that it didn't have to be stressed. It was the casualness of the threat that bothered him.

As soon as he'd read the last word for the second time, the familiar pattern returned, as he received round after round of the same in succession. The sheer ferocity of it astounded him: forty emails in total, followed by an eerie silence.

Maybe that was the end of it? he thought optimistically, patting the sweat streaming from his armpits as if trying to stem a substantial leak. Her last hurrah, as Josh would say – bluster. Calm and now gone, he thought, wishing that to be true. Relieved at the sudden stillness, he rose and went out into the corridor for some water from the cooler. Waiting, perhaps sadistically willing the beeps to begin again, he stood stolid. Watching Vicky and Melissa in the next room intently staring at their screens within the dim lighting, he felt a warm glow come over him. Why? He didn't know, but he said to himself that he really was going to find that bestseller. Maybe the whole Isabella thing had become his mental block, affecting his judgement and ruining his intuition and sense of smell for the next Iain Banks.

'Shit!' He thought it was a series of beeps, but it was his mobile vibrating manically on his desk.

'Stella,' he said, relieved.

'Kev?' She didn't sound right. Like another person. 'I've just received a couple of weird phone calls.'

'In the office or on your mobile?'

Why was he being so particular? she must be wondering. 'At work,' she replied, sounding lifeless and frightened.

'What did they say?'

'They didn't say anything, just screamed; screeched like an animal. It was pain; anger; hatred. It was just awful. Three times they called.'

'Shit,' he replied unconvincingly. Her breathing was shallow; her voice strange and yet his almost uninterested and cold. 'Probably kids?' he reasoned numbly. 'Maybe a prank call.'

'It wasn't kids.' She sounded exasperated. 'There was no giggling or laughing. Whatever it was it was real,' she concluded coldly.

He understood the silence between them, but still he didn't act; didn't know what to say. Something was holding him back. He knew the answers, but didn't articulate them as he faltered and failed to be valiant. 'I'll come round later,' he bumbled at last, knowing how weak and ineffectual he sounded.

'As you said: it was just a prank. I'm fine, really,' she added as if he'd actually expressed his concern for her. 'Come later, I'll cook,' she said, now sounding herself. 'I'm fine.' She hung up.

Maybe it was the whole Isabella show and then the suddenness of Stella's call which had tripped him up? Convincing himself that it was all a consequence of events, Kev told himself that he'd make things up later, that the pressure had just got to him. Yes, that was it: he was emotionally exhausted.

Looking at his inbox, he wondered what Isabella was doing. It was the first time he'd thought of her in this way: human like him. Doing normal things. Was she staring at a laptop screen in some one-bedroom flat, maybe in another part of the country or even beyond? For some reason he pictured her cross-legged in pink polka-dot pyjamas, sitting on a single bed eating a bowl of cereal while aimlessly flicking through the pages of a gossip magazine; a long folding curl in her hair falling down in front of her eyes as she bobbed her head backwards from time to time to free up her vision.

The sound of Vicky's laughter, then the numerous goodbyes and see you tomorrows resonating from other parts of the building, reminded him again of the impending time and the fact that his list was almost extinct. Deciding to call it a day he clicked on sleep as his screen went grey, and then blank. Sitting for a few seconds more, he marvelled at the emptiness, the slowing of energy and eventual nothingness of a closing office, knowing that the calm was a luxury which was perhaps slowly disappearing the more he noticed it.

Chapter Thirteen

'They'll have the results in half an hour, said they could easily track the address,' added Josh, sliding a written name on a post-it note across to Kev's desk. 'It becomes official once they have total access to your emails.'

It wasn't something that sat comfortably with him and maybe he was foolish to be advised by Josh who'd have sent in the notorious SPC (Special Patrol Group).

'Jan?' read Kev looking blankly at the piece of paper as if it were a wedding invitation.

'Janet,' smiled Josh.

'What, you know her?'

'Once; intimately, of course; old uni friend.'

Josh was slowly becoming his man in Havana. 'Who don't you know?'

'You'd be surprised,' smirked Josh. 'If you want to get on, you have to know.'

The world was full of people like Josh: not talented, but connected enough to be taken seriously. The Arts was rampant with Joshes, Melissas and Vickys: mediocre painters, sculptors, writers, filmmakers, photographers, performers and, of course, literary agents, all linked by a network which sees and perceives what's good on the basis of who knows who. There was a part of him that wished perhaps just a little bit of Josh would rub off on him. Observing Josh's straight nose, confident gait and clean hair swept back like Hugh Grant's, Kev almost admired him. If he was on your side, he wasn't the worst, he reasoned, returning a smile of thanks.

'Stella: what did she say?' asked Josh, briefly turning around and giving Kev a friendly slap on the back.

'What do you mean?'

'The threat; the *You'll be sorry you did that* bit?' he said, squeezing and kneading Kev's shoulders before turning back to face his screen.

He'd said nothing that night. Facing her across a heavenly chickpea and coriander curry he'd decided to keep it in and concentrate on trying to paper over the cracks of inertia and the notion that he should have done more. 'No more calls then?' he'd said, trying to read her mood. She'd changed her hair again. The grown-out bob was now wild and wavy, the odd ringlet flopping down in front of her green eye shadow. The tight black polo neck and torn at the knees jeans made her appear younger, studenty, or perhaps a wannabe member of the Baader-Meinhof gang. Settling on her being a part of the Velvet Underground, his words appeared to falter before her beauty.

'Just one of those days, I guess?' she said, lifting her red wine to her lips and smiling teasingly. 'What about you: anything strange?' she asked, clasping her glass with both hands as she rested both elbows on the table.

'Not really,' he replied sheepishly, and not remembering their discussion back in the Parisian hotel room. He gave up, asking her to pass the mango chutney instead, his eyes resting briefly on her long fingers, giving him enough time to recover. For some reason she didn't mention the prank call again although he was sure it was going to fall onto his plate when the conversation picked up.

'Sorry about earlier. I should have been more supportive.' There, he'd said it. Best to get it out of the way, he thought. It was as if he'd stumbled, lost his footing. He wanted to mention it before she did. Yet again he sounded lame and ineffectual.

She barely looked up as she told him to forget it and that it wasn't important.

'I know,' said Josh, 'you just didn't want to bother her with it. I get that.'

'Are you a mind reader as well as an MI5 agent?' joked Kev.

'From my experience, the less they know, the better,' announced Josh. 'Here,' he said, picking up his buzzing mobile, 'it's Jan.'

'No, it's Kev,' Kev said, noting the confusion at the other end.

Jan was extremely affirmative, establishing a narrative of events once again. She proceeded to succinctly provide the intel she had. 'Various locations have been used, though none of them from a residential address. We have libraries, pubs, cafés; mainly cafés.' She spoke as she read. 'One particular café used for at least eighty per cent of the emails,' she concluded.

'Can you do anything?'

'Not really. Although an official complaint, it's not an investigation. It might be a threat, but nothing significant has really happened.'

'What's the name of the café?' It was all he was going to get for now.

'The Purple Onion Café in Balham.'

'I know it,' he said breathlessly, 'it's . . . just around the corner from where I live.'

'Of course,' replied Jan, who already knew as much.

'Bit weird,' said Josh as Kev handed him back his phone. 'Probably knows where you live as well.'

'Cheers!' said Kev who'd turned pale.

'A storyline a few of your writers could do with,' chuckled Josh, flicking a paper clip in Kev's direction. 'Perfect thriller.'

Although he was hardly going to forget the name of the café Jan had given him, he felt the urge to write it down nonetheless, to see the words. Seeing it in its entirety gave him some hope; a naive notion that somehow he'd solve the equation. 'Yeah, perfect thriller,' he called out over his shoulder as Josh, who'd already fired off another volley of clips, burped loudly.

Chapter Fourteen

'Anything to eat?' enquired Noah, his name glistening in gold on his ID badge which had two stars above it – no doubt a position of responsibility dished out by a McDonald's lieutenant

'No, just the coffee.' Kev was always polite whatever the situation, but language, or rather communication, baffled him at times: you order only a coffee, it's obvious it's only a coffee you want, and they ask you if you want fries with it. Looking around him at the sterile, lifeless surroundings of the fast-food outlet, he wondered why he'd never visited it before. Although busy, it was quiet (probably because it was morning), people coming and going, quickly eating and then leaving trance-like and going about their lives; no one chatting, everyone alone, engrossed in their phones or newspapers. He liked it; liked the calmness of fast food, a process of sorts that he'd never given much thought to; a concept dumbed down by people like himself who wanted to be pampered and made to feel special every time they sipped their Americanos and read their papers. Maybe he'd been looking for Ronald McDonald all his life and all the time he'd been living in the next street? He had to stop himself from saying 'Thanks, Noah'. Was that what the name badge was for? he wondered.

He sat across from a FedEx man, who like most of the people seated at the anaemic white tables, was a Saturday worker: there were shop girls and boys, hunched in solitude before the security gates came up on their places of work; luminous advertising signs switched back on to guide the hordes back to their religion.

Opening his laptop, Kev looked around him. Covert wasn't exactly the right word, but it was close. Clicking onto *The Mad One*, he opened up Isabella's last entry. Reading it again he felt different, less freaked; the words had lost their strength, they were sitting ineffectual, hunched over like the worker bees to his left and right.

You'll be sorry you did that, he read before hesitantly clicking reply and making eye contact with the FedEx man, who briefly observed him before getting up and leaving his tray for someone else to clear away. Right, he thought, here we go.

What do you mean by that? he typed. Holding back the tightness in his chest, he loaded, aimed, and fired.

'Complementary refill?' It was Noah and his coffee jug.

'Just a drop,' he replied. 'Thanks, Noah.' He wasn't concentrating now and blushed at his faux pas as Noah appeared to redden himself and wished Kev a nice day. Right, good: nothing yet, he thought, taking a big gulp of coffee and savouring the effect; the beautiful addictive quality of instant calm, followed by an injected rush. Christ, he loved the stuff; even more than alcohol. One more minute; let's go, he thought, logging off, closing his laptop and placing it neatly in his rucksack.

After a minute's walk towards the posher end of the high street, he was soon at the door of the Purple Onion Café. Naturally painted purple inside and out (though more pastel within) it was a place he'd gone once or twice with Eve when she'd stayed at his, taking in brunch and the Saturday-morning papers in an idyllic middle-class sanctuary, where professionals relaxed in expensive casuals, safe in the knowledge that their busy week had been rewarded with a pastry and a latte which wasn't *to go*.

'Morning.' The arty student in front of him was no Noah: swept-back pink hair, goatee, and an assortment of rings and studs with an aroma of petunia oil, wearing an ethnic headband and a T-shirt which had written on it: *If I was a surrealist, you'd know – wouldn't you?* scrawled across it.

Feeling a little shaky at the last shot of coffee, he ordered another and positioned himself in the corner by the window below a poster print of Paula Rego's human dog poses, the one where a near-naked woman was grooming herself. Opening his laptop, he somehow knew what was waiting. *Oh Kev*, it read; the casualness of it sending a chill up his spine; the familiar use of his name startled him. *I thought you were a literary agent – do I really have to spell it out to you?* More interested in when it was sent – 10.20 – he then glanced at the clock on the wall which read 10.27. Just maybe, he thought, giving a quick sweep of the room as he typed *yes* and pressed send, he might get lucky. His senses heightened, he leaned forward, hunched, primed for a beep in another part of the café.

A loudly confident man to his right boomed into his mobile just at the wrong time, opening up the room to a bellowing chorus of 'You must be joking – really – that's just brilliant.' Further on a woman with a baby in a cradler was intently scanning her phone, while a young couple shared a mobile together and a Kate Winslet lookalike flicked through some party pics; a man at five o'clock, something of a young Piers Morgan in a French rugby shirt, was typing away, intermittently smugly, smiling to himself, no doubt entertained by another witty observation he'd written. He never realised before how engrossed everyone was in their social media, even their conversations involved sharing or holding up a screen to one another.

Beep! Beep! Like buses all coming at once in a techno chorus, though the arrival of each one was knocked off course by the continuous sonar-boom of the man who wasn't even slightly self-conscious at the noise coming from his cavernous gob, negating each new beep like an intercepting missile. Stiffening, Kev looked daggers at the man, wishing him the most heinous of violent ends. Getting the message, the man instinctively turned his large shoulders and lowered his voice, managing a manly smile in Kev's direction. There were no women on their own, thought Kev, trying to locate his tormentor. As for the beeps, their location was lost as soon as they were fired.

A flash and that familiar sound: you've got mail. He'd almost forgotten that he'd just sent a message.

You thought I'd be there didn't you? mocked Isabella. *Do you want me to be there? Nice café, isn't it? Love the grooming dog woman above your head – bit like Anabelle, don't you think? Oh, don't bother looking around –* YOU MISSED ME!

'Fuck,' he muttered. She'd spotted him and moved on; but how? He hadn't been checking outside. That could be the answer. He gazed out of the window at the empty tables and chairs, and the sunny morning which was in full bloom: affluent couples holding hands, weekend papers stuffed under their arms; families out walking with fathers pushing trendy baby combos cruised by like a speeded-up film reel. Two women, one with purple hair and another wearing a green trench-coat and a Greek fisherman's hat, strolled casually past arm in arm, laughing loudly, their heads turned towards him as if viewing the subject of their joke. For some reason he felt like shaking his fist at them and telling them to fuck off. An extremely tall sad-looking man, not unlike himself, perhaps a caricature of his future self, stopped briefly and stared up at the sky, shook his head and briefly laughed to himself, before picking up a piece of litter off the ground and moving on. There was nothing before him that he could read clearly, thought Kev, except perhaps the defeated expression in the man's eyes.

Just then a strained-looking Sarah rushed past. She stopped for a while, looked at her phone, peeped nervously into the café (all the time trying to shield her eyes from the sun) and then returned to her mobile. Surely not, he thought, going to get up and go outside and confront her – 'Sarah? It's Sarah,' Kev said to himself, closing up his laptop and pushing it frantically into his rucksack. As if a shadow, a thick-set, beefy, bearded hunk of a man appeared at her side, his big hands resting protectively around her waist as he moved into her stride. Guy, he presumed, admiring his autumn brown corduroy jacket, with elbow pads, and orange check shirt. Whatever the situation, Sarah wasn't happy. Maybe Guy was late or just messing her around, he thought, trying to read her tortured expression as she swished her hair to one side. They walked away deep in conversation; hardly bothering to look at the cars as they carelessly crossed the road to the other side. *YOU MISSED ME,* he thought, recoiling at the words and at the same time baffled by the whole experience; his whats, whys, whens and ifs confusing him even more as he stood and faced the grooming dog on the wall behind him.

'Sorry about that, mate. My brother's coming home from Australia. Haven't seen him in years,' said the man, now without the big booming voice.

'I'm pleased for ya,' Kev replied plainly, pushing his chair into the table as another chorus of beeps leapt around the café and the sun went in.

Chapter Fifteen

'Are you sure you still want to come?'

'Why wouldn't I?' replied Stella, lying beside him, her hand stroking his belly in rhythmic circles. 'It'll be interesting to see how the publishing world works; plus you'll be there,' she whispered in his ear as her hand slid down and delved into his brown and beige retro underpants.

Why anyone, himself included, would want to attend a laborious book fair at Croydon's Fairfield Halls was anyone's guess. To him they were just exercises in sycophancy where publishers, agents, and the not-yet-discovered mingled with near successful and successful writers, some who had found their lucky contacts at such fairs and those who just turned up exuding the only real public kudos they could muster, reading from average novels which in that moment when they deliberately, slowly, dramatically ushered the words from the page to their mouths gave them a temporary self-importance which would soon be forgotten until the next time they got the opportunity again. He was cynical, but even Josh tended to shun them, preferring his own methods of contact which involved a lot of wet lunches and spot on recommendations from some secret source he kept close to his chest. Melissa and Vicky were naturally going; Melissa more out of a need to control and monitor to her advantage any deals which may be in the offering. Vicky saw such events as a portal to finding a new man – a professional (as she put it) like herself. 'Imagine finding that bestseller and fucking him at the same time!' Melissa would tease her friend when the white wine had flowed.

Getting the train to East Croydon they'd slowly walked down to Fairfield Halls. It was a town he knew well, having worked at Bonaparte Records for a time when he was seventeen, when his main love in life was vinyl and building up his Motown collection and scoring weed off a hippie down at the Surrey Street Arms. He liked Croydon: its modern understated skyscrapers reminded him of a mini-New York, its alleyways, spray-painted walls, The Damned and The Croydon Punks sprayed across them, giving the whole area both an aura of past rebellion and modernity in one daub. Stella held on tightly to his arm as they walked. It probably had something to do with the intense sex they'd had that morning and then Stella's revelation that her ex-husband wanted to take some once-shared items from the flat that she was still living in. She needed him physically and now it seemed more than ever emotionally too; so much so that he felt compelled to tell her that he loved her as they lay in bed that morning. The first time the word passed his lips he felt a deep betrayal, as if Eve had shed a tear and thrown herself in front of a bus. He loved Stella, he kept telling himself as he held her in his arms. As he told her a second time that he loved her, a distant voice whispered that he'd loved Eve more.

Although tempted to open up more that morning about the charade at the café, he decided to keep it to himself for now, reasoning or maybe relieved that Stella had her own problems to contend with. If he was honest, although he'd meant it when he said that he loved her, he did also see it as a softener for his previous inability to show enough empathy when she'd needed him to comfort her over the weird phone calls. Besides, the whole Sarah incident wasn't something he wanted to share at that moment with the woman he'd just told he loved.

'Come on, then,' he beckoned leading her up the steps to the book fair. 'This is where all the shite starts.'

'Kev, Stella!' It was Melissa. Dressed in a grey pencil skirt, white blouse, and navy scarf, she oozed moneyed sophistication. He hated the way she treated every event as if it were her own.

'You look great,' said Stella, kissing her on both cheeks.

'Thanks; you too. Love the dress. Where did you get it?' she gushed. 'H&M!'

'Oh, must take a look there,' she replied unconvincingly. 'Oh, Kev,' she continued now trying to sound sincere, 'you must track down Robin Bloom. He's not bad. Could do something for your list.'

God, he hated her. Robin Bloom, real name Robert Clarke, was a mediocre thriller writer who'd gone down the self-publishing route some years ago. Since then he'd come close, but not quite close enough, to finding himself on Melissa's list on the very rare occasions she failed to fill it. An old university friend of hers, he was a nearly man, strung along but kept in the loop with choruses of encouragement. And now she was trying to dress him up and flog him to a colleague she pretended to care for.

'Mr Clarke,' he said sarcastically. 'Will do – thanks, Melissa.'

'Oh, that's Graham Reacher talking to Vicky,' she stated now waving in her friend's direction. 'Must dash; got to mingle. See you later; great look,' she added again limply, squeezing Stella's hand as she left.

'Fake,' he mumbled.

'Oh, Kev, she's not that bad; she's just a little bit insecure – that's all.'

He'd never thought about it that way before. 'About what?'

'Wanting to be the centre of attention is a starting point; probably wasn't listened to as a child. Maybe had an overpowering sibling or uninterested parents,' Stella reasoned.

'Suppose,' he replied, not totally convinced.

'So, how does all this work?' she asked looking around her.

'What?'

'The book fair, silly,' she said, playfully punching his arm, the touch making Josh temporarily flash before his eyes.

He'd never given it much thought nor, more to the point, any running order. 'Well, there's the independent small publishers over there and then the bigger ones like Penguin, umm, and then there's us,' he pointed to his company's stand, 'and other Literary Agencies and of course the writers – there,' he said gesturing towards the podium where a small, middle-aged man with half-moon glasses was reading rhythmically and slowly from an opened book before him. 'That's Jeremy Sparring – author of *People Always Become Wrecks*. He's a kind of psycho-loon-novelist; writes about a subconscious human matrix from an existentialist point of view.'

'You don't really know how it all works, do you?'

'No.'

They laughed.

At the far side of the hall he could just make out Vicky still deep in conversation with Graham Reacher, her back turned away from Melissa who was talking to well-groomed men with sculpted beards and designer glasses. Vicky must have found her man, he thought, wondering which direction to step in. He didn't have to think for long as the boss was soon within his personal space like an inescapable cloud. 'Martin, you know Stella?'

Martin Hargreaves: tall; tanned; white teeth; fiftyish; pink silk tie and blue pin-striped suit, clutched Stella's shoulder and kissed her cheek. 'Of course,' he said, 'best-looking woman in the room – apart from the wife,' he added playfully as Agatha Hargreaves held out her hand for Kev to shake or kiss (he wasn't quite sure). Remembering how he'd nearly crushed Eve's mum's hand, he decided on a limp handshake - which didn't go unnoticed by Martin, who Kev knew judged a person by their firm grip.

'I'll show you around if you like,' said Agatha, taking Stella's arm and steering her towards the chattering throng of people.

'She's a good one, that one,' said Martin nodding towards his wife. 'Knows the drill,' he added noting Kev's confused expression.

'Right.' The single word acknowledgement didn't help either. Bosses can sense indecision and lack of commitment anywhere.

'So, how's the list going?' asked Martin, getting straight to the point.

Kev got a little paranoid that it appeared to be now everyone's line of enquiry upon meeting him.

'Good,' he lied, having learnt nothing of Martin's irritation at one-word answers.

'Probably should do some mingling then.' It was an order rather than a suggestion as he quickly left Kev's side and headed towards a group of similarly dressed gentlemen who oozed the same prestige and confidence he did. Maybe Melissa had said something to him, Kev thought, remembering her own *mingling* comment.

Seeing them all together, he hated them; loathed the industry and at the same time felt sorry for the talented unpublished writers who had to deal with them. Why couldn't art just simply belong to art? he wondered as Martin began laughing loudly, having no doubt walked in on the end of a boys-only punchline as the circle of upright men slapped each other's backs.

'*Sometimes when you scan a crowd,*' Jeremy Sparring was reading painfully slowly, '*you don't naturally see what is before you.*' As if following Jeremy's words of wisdom around the room Kev surveyed the heads of writers, agents, publishers, and waiting staff, stopping to note the odd pair of shapely legs, as he tried to muster up some professional strategy in which to seek interesting leads and points of reference. Looking at the familiar smiling faces, he knew before he started he'd fail. His mind loose and aimless, he took the stairs where he guessed there would be more seminars and presentations. Nearly colliding with a man who was descending at the same time, he wondered whether the climb was worth the effort. He walked over to an information stall where he focused on a poster which read *How to get an Agent in an ever-changing media-dominated world* – 'which doesn't give a shit,' he said to himself, now leaning nonchalantly against a pillar which strangely vibrated and trembled in a very familiar way.

Looking at one of the numerous stalls, he noted that each one had in one form or another a list or a display of their best-known writers. Remembering how happy he felt when he'd seen Sonia Allen's name on a similar poster, he sighed and felt a faint tinge of pride. Reading the blurb in front of him for award-winning Samantha Green's new novel, he smarted at the relevance of it to himself: *A tantalising must-read from the depths of a ruined soul.* Reaching for his mobile phone he took a picture of it and typed a caption beside it that read: *Am I a story or am I a man?* Smiling to himself and then nodding at a familiar face (though one he couldn't place) who'd acknowledged him earlier, he swiftly moved on.

To the left of one of the seminar rooms was a much smaller one, its double doors sprung open as if in a fit of pique. The silhouette of a woman partly blocked the sunlight pouring through the window in the room; the glare was making her turn her head away and to one side. Distracted or merely bored by whatever was going on in the room, Sarah turned and faced him. As before her face was pained, pinched, preoccupied. Watching her for a while, Kev thought of their lovemaking as he tried to fight off the sensation between his legs and then the anger which was slowly growing. Like the vibration running down the pillar, his anger was an energy; an indecipherable blind ache which screamed for attention. It was an intent he barely understood, one which had no meaning and could only be expressed by a violence he could never partake in.

'Why are you doing this?' He'd taken hold of her wrist and was squeezing it just hard enough for her to realize he meant business. His hushed yet aggressive tone made her step backwards and assess what now loomed before her.

'Why are you holding me like this?' she said pulling her hand free. 'Are you drunk?'

'No, I'm not bloody drunk!' he spat, trying to control himself.

'Maybe you should take a deep breath then?' she reasoned, tears now visible in her eyes. 'Just back off!'

The tears calmed things down considerably, his anger now reduced to trying to get the facts. 'OK, Sarah,' Kev said, now looking surreptitiously around him. 'Why all the weird stuff: the emails and the threats?'

'What?'

'Oh, come on – you emailed me!'

'I don't even have your email.'

'You sent me a message two days ago: *You'll be sorry you did that!* Crap! And what about Anabelle and the mad psychotic chapters you keep sending me – don't deny it!' It was all coming out at once in one mad blurt. He knew it sounded crazy, but he had to get it out, it had lain dormant for long enough.

'I don't know what the hell you are talking about.' She was relaxed now, smiling in disbelief at the ridiculousness of it all.

'And then at the Purple Onion Café where you've been sending the emails from; you were there outside; two days ago!' There was doubt in his mixed-up sentences, becoming more jumbled as Sarah failed to react in the way he expected.

'I was meeting Guy outside! Is that against the law?' She was angry now. It was her turn to raise her voice.

'What about now: why are you here?' He was panicking. Perhaps; just perhaps he'd got it all wrong?

'Look, Kev! Look,' she said pointing, her voice now sarcastic, 'that's why I'm fucking here!' And there he was: Guy, camera in hand, wearing the same outfit he'd admired two days ago. 'We shag and work together – remember? We're doing a crappy shoot for some shitty little literary magazine.' She was mad; the swearing he'd never heard from her before and he wished she'd keep it down a bit as people were now beginning to stare.

'OK,' he said trying to calm her down, 'so you're not "Isabella" then?'

'Jesus, Kev, you really have lost it.'

'Right, so it's not you. Sorry,' he said at last, tapping her forearm which appeared to draw a line under it.

She seemed to now melt before him, her familiarity softening and turning him into play-doh as his heart rate began to slow.

'What's been going on?' She was the Sarah he remembered from the park. Telling her the whole series of events, he was surprised at how thoughtful she now was, as she nodded, raised her eyebrows, while littering her responses with soothing phrases: *I understand; you poor thing*; *that's just crazy*. The more she appeared interested the better he felt, though creeping up not too far behind him was the guilt, the reality that he should be telling the woman he loved.

'Guy, this is Kev – the boyfriend of Eve I told you about.' By the look on Guy's face he only knew what he needed to. He vigorously shook Kev's hand.

A big friendly American, he thought, feeling the strength of the grip penetrating his bones as he saw a picture in his own mind of Guy's tough-looking hands cupping Sarah's breasts.

'So, you're a writer then?' beamed Guy.

'No, everyone thinks that – an agent.'

'Gotcha,' he replied, distracted, gazing back into the other room, 'I think I better get back, nice meeting you, Seth,' he said haphazardly before turning to Sarah and saying: 'Five minutes – final shot.' By the look on her face the strain was back as she merely nodded in agreement.

'Problems?' asked Kev.

'I'd say we're near the end. I know he's been seeing his ex-girlfriend.'

'Sorry to hear that,' he said while thinking pot-kettle-black.

'It never lasts very long with me, I'm afraid,' she said sadly.

Even when upset her expression attracted him. He felt wanted by her sadness and her presence. The fragrance of her perfume and the pinkness of her lips sent his senses whirling as he now longed for her touch and the physical connection they once had.

If Kev had been standing where Sarah was he would have seen a woman slowly climbing the stairs behind him, each step accompanied by an analytical stare which processed and interpreted what she believed she saw before her. Reaching the top steps she began to count.

Step seven: she's pretty.

Step eight: she knows him well.

Step nine: he's sharing something with her.

Pausing at the last step, she took a deep breath and moved forward. 'So, this is where you've been hiding,' she said, smiling at them both.

'Stella,' he said trying not to appear alarmed.

He's pretending, she thought; trying his hardest to be casual. He's different, she decided as she waited for the introduction.

'Stella, this is Sarah – Eve's sister. She's here doing a photo shoot with her boyfriend Guy.'

Clumsy, she thought smiling. He's giving a lot of information because he's off guard.

'Sorry about your sister. I never knew her,' Stella said now linking arms with Kev.

'Time heals,' Sarah managed with good dramatic effect.

'Do you two keep in touch?'

'No.'

'Yes.'

The replies came all at once as they all laughed in an attempt to hide the growing embarrassment.

'So, which is it?' asked Stella smiling.

'Well kind of yes,' replied Sarah.

'We don't regularly keep in touch,' added Kev who hoped Stella hadn't read too much into his *no* answer, which he was going to put down to word confusion or a Freudian slip.

'Mainly through my dad,' said Sarah, awkwardly, the irony lost on Stella, but not on Kev who suddenly developed a nervous cough.

Stella patted his back. 'Well it's important you do,' she said. 'Make sure you do,' she added, nudging Kev in the ribs.

'Better get back; nice meeting you, Stella. Bye, Kev,' Sarah said, tapping his arm as she quickly made for the seminar room.

'Nice girl, pretty; you never mentioned her before.'

There's a lot I haven't mentioned before, he thought trying to resist the impulse to follow Sarah's retreating figure. 'Never thought it was important,' he managed. 'Wanted to leave all that behind.'

'I get it,' she said kissing him on the cheek. 'But you should keep in touch – for Eve's sake.'

'*And remember, people,*' continued Jeremy Sparring deliberately and condescendingly, '*there are pockets of reality that cannot be picked even by the brightest of minds. The End.*'

As a restrained ripple of applause rose and died from the main hall downstairs, Kev held Stella's hand tight and wished she'd been the only woman in the world he'd ever known.

Chapter Sixteen

Sarah's story

'Why, Guy? Christ, your name's so awkward to use! It rhymes with every fucking word I want to say.'

There had already been a mix-up that morning. They were supposed to meet outside the Purple Onion Café. Thinking that he may have meant inside the café, she'd made a quick scan and had really only seen the dog/grooming woman poster gazing nonchalantly out at her as she passed.

'It was the traffic,' he'd explained gruffly, catching her strained expression as they walked briskly across the sun-soaked tarmac to the other side of the road and away from the café.

It was her; he was with her, Sarah kept telling herself as they headed towards Guy's studio, a small rented industrial unit beside a railway arch in nearby Tooting Broadway.

He'd been with the ex; he reeked of her: the perfume, the cigarettes, and the odour of sex that not even the morning's rigorous shower could wash away.

'Christ! You're so cranky all the time,' he stated as if somehow he was the wounded party in what was becoming a hostile atmosphere.

'You were with her; weren't you?' she said at last, slamming her handbag down hard on the work-bench and trembling at her practiced assertiveness – a paragraph learnt from an old book of Eve's entitled: *Be Free And Assert Yourself.* She'd borrowed the book back when they were teenagers; when they'd got on better; when Eve was taking on the role of big sister, passing on her intellectual knowledge and understanding of the self to her little sister. It was an exchange of sorts, with Sarah in return offering her stories of sexual exploration and conquest; racy made-up escapades involving a fictional classmate named Tracy Wildo (will do anything), who did things she shouldn't. It was a childish fantasy, though Sarah had injected some of her own experiences into the tales.

'If I said I wasn't, you'd insist I was,' Guy replied, examining a black and white still of the previous day's shoot which showed a family all dressed in white eating from tins of baked beans in an idyllic picnic setting.

'You were.' She was slowly losing her concentration and will to carry on with the *I wasn't – You were* match of wits. Guy was always going to deny everything. He'd even deny being Guy if it meant keeping his secrets intact. He saw himself as old-school like his dad and his granddad before him; men who had flings and nothing more; men who loved their families and would never walk away from their marriages for sexual risk-taking or the odd fumble with an ex, she knew that. He knew nothing of Sarah and Eve's problem. If he had, then it might have been easier for him to win the morality war. At the moment it was clear he was just waiting for the get-out ship to come sailing along. He knew she was high maintenance and it wasn't what he wanted to commit to.

'So, you weren't with her?' she said with a mixture of defeat and apathy.

Christ, she was needy, he thought. 'I wasn't.'

'Right,' she answered, 'but if you were,' she added, searching for the right words – the assertiveness from the handbook abandoning her somewhere in the muddle between her eyes, 'I'd . . .' She couldn't finish and came to a bumbling end.

'I know,' he said, reassuringly placing his big trunk of an arm around her and kissing her cheek. Weaker than dishwater, he thought trying hard not to smirk.

A potentially bad outcome shelved, they soon fell into the rhythm and necessity of the morning's work, editing parts of the previous day's shoot and organising possible shoots for a book fair in Croydon.

'Do you want coffee?' asked Guy, taking off his jacket and switching the dial on the radio to Jazz FM.

'Sure.' She felt demure, calm almost. Maybe the coffee wasn't such a good idea, she thought.

'It's French,' he added, opening up a new packet.

Sarah didn't answer, but smiled instead; she already knew what she wanted to talk about that morning and it wasn't Guy's ex and the messing around she knew he was doing; no, it was darker than that; much darker. She couldn't talk to Kev any more (that was over), though she probably wouldn't have told him anyway – it just didn't sit right. It had to be Guy. It didn't matter that he probably wouldn't be around much longer; in fact she preferred it that way. He was merely preparation, a talking post; someone who wasn't going to be there in the future to remind or judge her. It was dark and she knew it; the worst thing she'd ever done.

'I need to tell you something.' *No,* she corrected herself remembering the chapter on *direct speech patterns and their relationship to being assertive.* 'I must share something with you, Guy,' she concluded, glad that her inclusion of *Guy* at the end hadn't rhymed with any of her previous words.

'Shoot,' he said.

It didn't matter, she thought, closing her eyes to the fact that his empathy began with such a cheap and casual word. But she just needed to tell.

First it had just seemed like an odd feeling inside; then it felt as if something in her body had changed. She felt like she'd been occupied, as if a stranger had casually stopped by and taken shelter, taken off its clothes, laid down and waited. Yes, that was it: everything in and around her had just stopped and waited; that's what happened. Then it was her breasts: constantly sore and achy, not like before a period, but more intense – and of course the blood stopped coming, the monthly stream had dried, her belly feeling as if the sun had warmly bleached it and that the stranger lying on the floor had decided to stay and get a tan.

120

They'd only done it five times. The fact that she'd felt so horny should have been an indication; a warning of what her body clock was ticking towards and screaming out for. Three months pregnant by her sister's boyfriend, Stuart. The sex had been great, though not worth the hurt it would eventually cause, but like everything else in her reckless life it was exciting. Oh, and she'd got her own back; that was the reason she'd started flirting with him: beautiful, vindictive revenge.

'Sarah, why don't you show Stuart your dolly collection?' Eve had been drinking. She'd just gained promotion and although she wouldn't admit it, was feeling superior to Sarah who was still work-ing as a part-time telesales person for a double-glazing company. To Eve they'd been harmless quips (the first one in particular), though she knew only too well how Sarah was struggling to find anything worthwhile or interesting to do with her life. 'Sarah might sell you some double glazing if you're good,' giggled Eve. There, she'd said it – couldn't help herself – and as Stuart laughed the wicked glint in her sister's eye made Sarah think of Tracy Wildo and what Sarah now might *well do.*

He was putty in her hands. She passed him a piece of paper with her number on it and a message saying that she found him attractive and did he want to meet up? He called the next day and invited her round to his flat. The rest was history; her sister walking in on them on her birthday; planned to the last detail: despicable; unethical; destructive and intentionally cruel. She'd thought it through and yet she hadn't; their relationship ruined for ever. But the stranger grow-ing inside her: that was her cross; her punishment and hell; the thing she'd keep to herself. Her abortion, the paid-for death of her baby (the child she could never have); a sin, a stain on her memory for ever: the doomed ex-convent girl, silent in her crime, in her murder of the unborn. Eve, oblivious to the end. The *Unwanted Pregnancy Unit;* the forms, the questions, the sympathetic, compassionate, yet seemingly accusing eyes of the nurses; then the sudden emptiness inside; the other pregnant women you'd pass in the street who you'd begun to see everywhere suddenly had meaning, their bumps crying out accusingly at you every time they passed. The physical pain and emotional pain you feel when you leave another life behind; the invisible scar which reminds you that another being has been sucked from you, that you've been violated, as what was a stranger in your belly becomes more of a living being rather than just words: *terminated*; exterminated by a sad bitch that wanted to get her own back.

'Fuck! You did that to your sister?'

'Yes, I did that.' As she replied she knew it sounded affirmative, unemotional, blasé; but that's what it was now: a cold, steely reality. She'd done *all that* and now it had been said. Whether he judged her or not, she really didn't care, but she'd told it; she'd temporarily let go of her filth.

For a while he'd looked sad. 'It's all in the past,' he lied, squeezing her hand as an image of a little baby popped into Sarah's head and let out a silent cry.

122

Chapter Seventeen

A bench and a takeaway coffee was all he needed. Back on Clapham Common for the first time since Eve's death, Kev smelt the sweet cut grass and the whiff of tarmac drifting down on a freak bluster of wind which was spent as quick as it blew in; an empty KFC snackbox lifting and then dropping within a whirl of dead leaves and dust. Above his head a flock of geese forming a V-shape flew, their wild flapping breaking the silence which at its best was the slow, humming drone of cars in the distance.

After a difficult morning in which he'd contacted a writer in relation to representation (in his opinion a near dead-cert), he was pretty sure that Jean Myer, author of *The Only Nice Thing Left*, would jump at the opportunity. Acting on a rumour that Jean was worth a read, he'd been coerced into action. It was the kick up the backside he needed – only for it to be the first time he was to be turned down. Jean merely told him stolidly that she had an agent and that she was surprised to hear from him considering she'd emailed samples of her work a little over six months ago (all of which he'd missed completely or hadn't read with an open mind). Sickened and dejected, he'd left the office without a word and made for the Common.

Christ, he needed to empty his head. Watching a dad and his son kick a ball around, he wondered how long it had been since he'd done the simplest of things. OK, he'd danced, he always danced, but what about the rest, when had he ever really said or done anything important – saved a life, even given to charity? He was a selfish bastard whose eye easily wandered and strayed; a sewer of a mind, filled with garbage and a gaze which followed a woman whatever her shape or size.

'Hey, you! Yes, you!' called the old man in the blue and white bobble hat and oversized duffle coat done up to the top. In truth, he thought he was alone, lost in his own self-loathing and misery; he'd overlooked the old man who'd been feeding the pigeons and crows upon his arrival. 'Mind if I join you?' the man asked from the bench to his left.

Given his feelings of selfishness he could hardly have said no. 'Sure,' Kev said, pushing himself towards a charitable act but at the same time wishing the man would just leave him alone.

The old man was over in a shake, plopping down a tightly packed laundry bag by Kev's side. He got a distinct smell of urine from the man, who ran his fingers through his yellowing white beard and scratched the crotch of his stained trousers.

'I'm Chelsea,' said the man, 'what are you – Arsenal, I bet?'

'Manchester United.'

'Where's your accent gone? You ain't got one,' stated the man, his blue eyes sparkling, set deep within his heavily lined leathery face.

'Never really had one. Me mum and dad do, but I was brought up here.'

'No London accent? Are you posh?'

He'd never thought about it before; he was pretty much neutral in that department, only dipping intentionally into a Manc accent when it suited him or he was showing off, a bit like Steve and his cockney.

'So, what do you do?'

After a slimline summary of his life's work, Kev felt depressed at having used the same account so many times before. His words sounded futile; he didn't really know what he did or what he was.

'Sounds pretty boring,' replied Sam. He'd already slipped in his name a couple of times, speaking about himself in the third person: 'Sam, everything is shit; go and join the merchant navy.' Sam referring to his job as boring was the most refreshing thing Kev had heard in his life.

Finding out more about Sam in his preferred third person, Kev learnt that he lived in a derelict basement off Battersea Rise and that the council had tried to evict him on many occasions. Sam wasn't married, though he had a son somewhere in Singapore, the result of a prolonged shore leave for which he'd been docked a month's pay. Lastly, Sam loved birds, particularly crows and jackdaws, loved the anarchy in their nature as they scrapped away for the best pickings and had no regard for pleasantries, swooping down on each other and landing on each other's heads, arguing all the time until nest-time.

Kev quickly came to the conclusion that Sam, unlike himself, wasn't boring at all.

'You should come down to Stamford Bridge some time. Sam here is a non-paying fan, courtesy of his dear old dad who was a Chelsea Pensioner.'

'So the children of Chelsea Pensioners automatically get free attendance at Chelsea?'

'No; crikey, no! Sam's dad dies; Sam takes his badge and uniform; they don't do the maths; Sam gets into every home match. The other old boys know, but they keep schtum!'

Kev wished he had a lively adventure to tell, but all he had presently was chaos, though he did tell Sam he liked dancing. 'At last,' Sam had said, 'you blinking are alive after all. Sam thought you were dead when he spotted ya with that mopey boat-race for all to trip arse over tit – just bloody dance, boy!'

He must have sat there for hours listening to Sam, who left his perch only once to urinate behind a tree, making Kev chief look-out.

'Look 'ere,' said Sam suddenly after a lull in conversation in which they'd both been happy to watch a fancy-coloured kite dip, weave, and glide on the breeze, as two dots (the father and son who'd been playing football earlier) cheered the kite's ascension. 'Sam can see you got problems, son,' he continued, gathering his bag together on his lap. 'Sam thinks you need to learn to fly again. You see, we all could fly once, you know; when we was children,' he began. 'Sam would fly over Wandsworth Bridge, past Battersea Park, down to the river, up to the Power Station, back up Queenstown Road and back 'ere to the Common; regular, even during the Blitz; more exciting then,' he said, his eyes wide with joy and wonderment. 'Now you might think old Sam 'ere is loco. Well,' he paused, pulling his beard, 'he might be, but,' he said, looking Kev deep in the eyes, 'all children fly; all of them. We just can't remember, that's all.'

Wishing Kev well and firmly shaking his hand, Sam was slowly on his way, shuffling back over the flats of the Common, where he briefly waved at the father and son who didn't wave back. Knowing Kev was still watching him, Sam turned and did a little jig and shouted 'Wahey!' before continuing his journey.

As a light drizzle started, Kev jumped to his feet; pulling up the collar of his overcoat he smiled at the blob on the horizon who'd reached the far side of the Common where a rainbow now arched overhead like a stage drape. Deciding to go the same way as Sam, he didn't walk or fly, but ran, ran like the wind now at his back as the tails of his long coat flapped like a sail behind him, followed now by a swirling murder of crows and jackdaws who'd decided to see him off, high above his head like black ashes from a bonfire, squawking and diving on the wind like an aviary rebellion. *Faster! Faster!* A voice in his mind demanded. *Run – run – dance – run you fool.* 'Fly! Fly!' he roared, feeling the blood pumping in his veins as he laughed out loud: 'Flyyyyyyyyyyy!' His arms now flapping, he rose a metre off the grass. 'Fly! Higher! Higher!' Then a swoosh! And the wind had taken him high up above the tearoom and bandstand below, further still, towards the concreted-over air-raid shelters rising beautiful, bluey-grey like a ripe black grape.

Out of breath he'd caught up with Sam who'd picked up a leaf and was intently studying it. 'Sam: here,' he said handing him a piece of paper. 'My number; call me if you're ever in trouble.'

'Thanks, son,' he replied, a glazed look on his face, 'but Sam's dad always looks after him; he's Admiral Nelson's right-hand man, you know – see ya,' he said, continuing with his shuffle and an expression which suggested they'd never ever met.

Chapter Eighteen

Getting off a stop before Balham, Kev enjoyed a leisurely walk back to his flat. It was still raining, the air was muggy and the heat from the slow-moving traffic was rising, creating an eerie pastel effect around the varied coloured cars, the grey-blue of the road and the green grass verges washed into one. Marvelling at the ordinary scene, it reminded him of a Renoir, the colours straight from a palette, smudged in parts – a dripping, atmospheric watercolour.

The talk and walk in the park had done him the world of good, his perception of his surroundings clearer than they had been in weeks, as if his thoughts had been pumped and cleansed with menthol cleaners.

At his front door the calmness stopped.

'Shit!'

The door was open; he'd been broken into. Not for the first time; it was still a run-down area, but one which was slowly on the up. Still, it was better than being mugged at knife-point, he'd considered when it had first happened. Gingerly passing from room to room, he noted the obvious: laptop, TV, sound system – nothing taken. Maybe they'd been startled, perhaps spotted or disturbed by a passer-by?

In the bedroom the wardrobe door was left open and one of his suits was laid out on the bed (his brown pin-striped). The weirdness of what looked like a body prepped for cremation was one thing, but there was something else in the flat: a smell, not a bad odour, but perfume, as if deliberately sprayed throughout the flat, the smell left as if a message or a puzzle to be solved, a residue he'd have to live with for a couple of days. Naturally, he thought of Isabella and imagined her laughing manically as she sprayed her scent and lay beside his suit on the bed. There was no evidence, no clues, and strangely, no message when he checked his laptop and email. It was strange, but for some unknown reason Kev felt he wanted to keep it straightforward as he dialled 999 and logged the break-in. Maybe he'd had his fill of the mad and bad, he thought, staring down impassively at his laid-out suit, the creased right sleeve reminding him of Eve as she would constantly hang on and drag on his arm, much to his annoyance.

'So nothing taken then?' asked the desk sergeant as Kev tried to refocus on why he was making the call as a little bit of Eve flew like a Tinker Bell around his mind.

'No, just forced entry,' he said, picturing himself in his suit lying with an imagined Anabelle (or was it Eve?) on his bed.

'Do you want us to send someone round?'

By the tone of the sergeant's voice, he knew what he was expected to say. 'No, it's fine, officer; just a broken lock,' he said, seeing Isabella tap-dancing with his suit on.

Taking his mobile number and address, the officer told him that they'd be in touch if they came up with anything, though the reality was that they wouldn't as nothing was stolen to sell on. Kev now felt vaguely disappointed that there hadn't been an email explaining the intrusion. He briefly considered a psychic attack, as he had read somewhere about how paranormal disturbances are often accompanied by strange smells . . .

The humming mobile startled him. It was Stella. She was supposed to be staying over.

'Hi, Stella.'

'Kev, you sound odd,' she said instantly.

'Broken into again; nothing taken, just a strange smell of perfume in the place,' he managed, realising how monotone he sounded.

'Oh my God, that's so weird. Are you OK?'

'Of course. It's nothing new, well, apart from the smell, oh, and the laid-out suit.'

'What – your suit?'

'I know it's weird.'

'Christ! Crazy stuff.' The pause which followed suggested that she was worried and perhaps a little freaked out.

'I'll be fine,' he said, as a brief exchange of *are you sure*?s and *will you be alright*?s took place.

Telling her the whole story, detail for detail, he was relieved that he for once had told the whole tale, instead of closing up shop.

Asking him again if he was alright seemed to be the last words on the matter. 'Look,' she began – he knew there was something up – 'I know it's bad timing, but I can't come tonight; there's a conference in Cardiff which Amanda was supposed to cover. Well, she phoned in sick this morning, so I have to get the train up there tonight. I'm really sorry,' she added.

'It's fine,' he said, making an effort to sound upbeat. 'I might call round to Steve – his girlfriend's left him.'

'I'll make it up. I promise.'

'Really, don't worry.' This seemed to do the job as he could sense by the static pause that the conversation was coming to an end.

'I'll speak to you when I get back, but call me if anything odd happens again.'

She was busy; he knew that, though he wished she could have come over. 'Bye.' A simple word, but it felt like a lingering hernia.

'Bye,' she said, blowing a kiss down the phone.

I'll bolt the door from the inside, he thought, deciding that it was the best he could do until the locksmith arrived. Making a cup of tea, he sat quietly reading the Arts page in the *Guardian*. His mind distracted, he flitted from article to story, gathering the odd piece of information and not really settling on anything for long. A loud rap at the door made him spring upright from his hunched reading posture.

A large black-haired man with a thick moustache and a stern expression stood before him, his huge frame blocking out the glare of daylight behind him.

'Kevin Parker?' came the officious enquiry.

'Yes.'

'Detective Inspector McGuire.'

'That was quick; you caught them already?

There was a pause. 'Sorry?' McGuire said impatiently as he briefly turned and glanced at a speeding motorcycle which had just zoomed past.

'The break-in.'

'No, it's not a break-in. Can you come down to the station for a chat?' McGuire replied, shifting restlessly from foot to foot and then standing legs apart.

'A chat?' He was lost. 'About what?'

'Probably best we do it there,' said McGuire, and an awkward pause followed. 'Just ask for me at the desk. Unless you want me to give you a lift?' he added, raising an eyebrow.

No way was he going to get into a police car and have the neighbours speculating. 'I'll walk – it's not far,' Kev replied, nervously coughing and clearing his throat.

'Take your time – I'm going to grab a sandwich on the way back. Even the police take breaks,' said McGuire, managing a false smile.

'Right.'

'See you at the station then.'

'Of course,' Kev said, slowly closing the door.

The sudden visit had left him cold, as if Eve had died all over again and the police were contacting him and not Doug with the news.

After making small talk with a rather too chirpy odd-job man he reluctantly made his way to the station, the pit of his stomach feeling empty and jumpy, an electric, uncertain energy gushing down his limbs and attacking his nerves.

The street was empty, as if he'd just stepped into a western, a stray dog barking at him on the corner by the post office as he passed the church whose bells started to toll. Maybe Clint Eastwood was going to stride into view, he thought, waiting for a tumbleweed to come spinning by.

'Kevin Parker to see Detective Inspector McGuire,' he said, detecting that the desk sergeant perhaps knew the reason for his visit, the look of indifference on his face temporarily interrupted by a deadly glare as he said his name.

'Take a seat, sir,' said the sergeant, motioning towards the cold blue plastic seats.

Like a prison cell, the waiting room was bare and overly clean, the bareness of it only broken by the assortment of drink–driving, solvent, sexual abuse, domestic violence, and *say no to drugs* posters splattered across the walls like accusing fingers pointing down on whoever happened to be waiting.

'Kevin?' said McGuire, opening the door and ushering him towards a heavily scarred table where two chairs ominously waited. 'Over there,' he nodded as he wiped a trickle of mayonnaise from the corner of his mouth with a serviette.

'Look,' he began after Kev had followed him and was firmly seated in what appeared to be a sparse interview room. 'This won't take long.'

Long? Kev thought, glancing at the bars of the window and recoiling at the sterile brightness of the small menacing room.

'Right,' he replied nervously, not knowing what to do with his clammy hands.

'A complaint has been made against you.' The words sounded longer than they should have as his mind slowed, searching for clues, alert to the seriousness. 'Of a sexual nature,' McGuire concluded. Like a cold steel bolt pummelled into a cast rivet, the hammer head dropped, his mere being smashed and dragged to his spinning, scared mind as the words Sexual! Sexual! spun out of control through his brain then tore into every sinew in his twitching body.

'What?'

Sensing his trepidation, McGuire sat down opposite him. 'Maybe it would be better that you just listen. You're not being charged with anything. Yet.'

Yet, thought Kev, crossing his arms defensively.

Reading from the notes in front of him he began: 'A complaint has been made against you from an anonymous source that you performed an unwelcome sexual act upon a woman on a disco boat on

131

the Thames at the Embankment. That drunk, you proceeded to force your hand down the front of a woman's undergarments and didn't stop when told to, instead ignoring the request and trying to kiss the woman, who eventually was able to pull herself free and make for the safety of her friends. The complainant is apparently a friend of the woman who didn't want to come forward at the time of the assault.'

Assault: his mind a tornado of images; lost faces, lipstick, limbs, dancing, tongues, the groper on the dance floor; Eve – fuck! What did he do? Couldn't see it through the fog of that night. Had he really done that? Possibly, he thought, but only – he was sure – if it was OK, he reasoned naively. But if told to stop, surely he would have? Wouldn't he? The girl on his lap; she'd sat on him, hadn't she? Or had he pulled, no, forced her onto his lap? Fuck! He couldn't remember. Would his mind have instantly locked down if he'd done something as bad as that? No, it would have plagued him to kingdom come. Now half-listening to McGuire's summing-up and his insistence that it would only be followed up if the woman herself came forward, Kev started to doubt his humanity, his sanity and ethical being. Perhaps he *was* that monster. The 'groper on the dance floor' sounded a lot more serious now than the humorous observation concocted by Eve; now it was a probable tabloid headline to his debauched episode aboard the *Nell Gwynne*.

'Do you remember there being a woman?' asked McGuire, his voice breaking through Kev's paranoid haze of possibilities.

'There were women,' he replied, instantly thinking that it sounded a bit sleazy and that he should have phrased it differently.

'So, there were *women* – plural?' said McGuire, with a hint of sarcasm.

Kev wondered whether he needed a solicitor present, but gauging that it was a fair enough question, he answered that there were many women and men and that he'd been with colleagues all night.

McGuire stared intently at him for several seconds as Kev coughed again.

'Maybe you should get a tonic for that?'

'Just a dry throat,' replied Kev unconvincingly.

'Be in touch if anything more comes to light,' McGuire said abruptly, closing the file firmly and standing.

The comment made it all seem so casual, like he'd just undergone a job interview and they'd be getting back to him if he was successful. That's it: no counselling, no therapy? Kev thought, remembering the odd celebrity who'd been wrongly accused and driven to the brink. 'So I can go?' he asked.

'Yes, you can go.'

'But what if nothing happens?' It sounded absurd; it was absurd, but was that really it?

'Then nothing happens.'

'So it's unfounded – it means I'm innocent?'

'If you're innocent you've got nothing to worry about, have you?' McGuire replied curtly. 'We'll be in touch,' he added firmly as he roughly pushed his chair under the table.

He knew that the more questions he asked the worse it could get. He'd met police officers before and knew they would never leave themselves open to *well, you said this.* They were programmed to be direct, but also politely vague.

As soon as he left the station and the sunlight smacked his face, the loop began and played in his head with unforgiving ferocity. Faces from that night launched themselves at him followed by hands, legs, thighs, skirts, tongues, breasts, and drinks. They danced with abandon, kicking him in the head and guts every time he attempted to rationalise and place events into any kind of decipherable order.

The groper on the dance floor? No, the out-of-control sexual predator.

Chapter Nineteen

'Bloody hell,' said Steve, his eyes dark and heavily ringed by lack of sleep and an unhealthy new appetite for late-night drinking alone. 'They said that?'

Kev had arrived dishevelled, wet, and in a vulnerable place, having decided that a walk in the rain was better than returning home where he knew the accusers would play havoc. Instead, walking the three miles to Steve's flat in Tooting, he appeared at his friend's door like somebody who'd been walking for days, lost and mad, across a desolate moor. Stupidly, he'd taken a short cut through what was locally known as the pick-up point, where he was propositioned by prostitutes and stared down by frightening pimps who sat in parked cars. 'Not your liking?' a man had called to him as, scared, Kev quickened his pace. Passing the girls, one of them giggled and another stuck her tongue out at him and called him a wanker.

'Yeah, have me down as a sexual predator. I mean, fuck Steve, did I do that?' he pleaded to his friend having divulged the whole episode to him.

'Christ, no,' said Steve.

'How can you be sure? I mean, there were a lot of women that night. I did, you know, have a few . . .'

'Liaisons.'

'Yeah, liaisons.' He'd dropped his head in shame now, sure that Steve had seen all and was just being a friend.

'You did what you did and you were pissed,' said Steve, lighting a cigarette. 'You want one?' he asked as an afterthought.

'Yeah, why not?' Kev replied, his hand slightly shaking as he fumbled to get one out of the box offered to him.

'You better light it,' said Steve, passing the lighter, 'bit shaky myself.'

'Sorry about your girlfriend,' Kev remembered, trying to light his cigarette.

'Ah, we were always fighting; better that it's ended.'

'Sure.'

'Look, fuck my problems; nothing compared to yours.' As if searching the room for something to help him, he continued, 'Would offer you a drink, but I know you don't.' He smiled for the first time.

'So,' Kev began – he had to try and get some validation from some-where – 'did you see me . . . you know?'

'Mate, you did nothing,' said Steve. 'I had your back all night; OK, I'd been to the toilet a few times and the bar when you were on the dance floor and I'd had an argument with Jane, but apart from that.'

'What about the girl on my lap, did she seem like she wanted to be there?'

Steve was laughing now. 'She seemed happy enough.'

'And I didn't have my hands down her pants?' He hated saying it, but that was what it was all about.

'If you had, she didn't mind,' was Steve's answer, though Kev would have preferred it if he had said that he definitely didn't have his hands down her pants. Although hardly perfect, Steve's declara-tions had made him feel slightly better. And what about Eve? She'd seen him, and if he had and she'd seen something then surely she wouldn't have gone out with him. And what about Stella? He'd have to tell her – wouldn't he?

'Do you think I should tell Stella?' He valued Steve and wasn't sure of his own reasoning just yet.

'Oh, Jesus, Kev,' Steve began rubbing his stubbly chin and push-ing his glasses back further up his nose, 'that's not easy.'

'I know; but what would you do?'

'I'd probably have told her.'

'Right, so what do you think – tell her?'

'You probably should – if she loves you, she'll stick by you,' added Steve after some reflection, 'after all, you've done nothing wrong.'

He'd tell her, he thought. Hadn't he hidden enough from her already?

'No worries, brother; no worries,' he said, sadly retreating back into his melancholy.

Hearing the beep of his mobile, Kev knew by the sound he had mail. Isabella, brilliant timing, he thought looking helplessly at his friend.

'Go ahead, open it. I'll go and make some coffee,' he said reading his hesitation. 'Go on, it's fine.'

Dear Kev, just another page to add to the last chapter I sent you; an afterthought perhaps? It was as if they were friends. It was all he needed: more weirdness, he thought, reading on. *Anabelle had seen that look before: distant, lost, unpredictable, like a wounded hound, mad with fear. If he only understood the hurt he inflicted upon her, the way he mauled her and then spat her out as if she were just a dirty taste in his mouth.* It was more of the same, he thought. *Surely an intelligent man like him realized that his actions had consequences.*

'Jesus,' he said to himself, scrolling down to the message at the bottom. *What do you think?* it read. *It fits – doesn't it? That he should know what a bastard he is?*

It all now sounded so familiar; the fiction, now the reality that was his life, all being moulded together without his consent, the layers of words confusing and pushing him to the edge of insanity. Whatever Isabella was striving at, he was now sure that he was somehow the protagonist and she was the pen pushing him further into the dark depths of his soul.

'The Mad One again?' asked Steve returning with the coffees.

'Yep, The Mad One.'

'There's no let up there,' he started with a defeated sigh which could easily have been Kev's.

'That you can rely on,' he said closing his eyes. 'You know what?' he continued, 'I think I will have that drink.'

Chapter Twenty

Broken, fallen, splintered rigging; hell-fire; muskets and cannon-balls; rich, cracked, navy blue brush strokes, the texture of each uniform: lighter blues, smudged, blurred, tucked within a violent white spray, scratched into the canvas. The men with silver wigs, some coiffed, the ones wearing shoes – their faces stern – bark instructions to those without, bare-chested and grim, their fearless faces turned to battle. In the centre, the focal point – the stillness and serenity of a noble death. Nelson lying in the arms of Hardy. Elevated, floating, he almost leaves the picture. You have to stay focused or the artist's brush will play tricks on your mind as the great man exits for heaven. The look: ghostly, noble, or lost?

Today, though, Nelson was gone. Ripped from the wall; not even an outline where it used to hang. The whole interior of the café repainted, the walls daubed with photo-prints of Hollywood stars from the thirties, forties and fifties, a portrait of Bob Hope, smiling through perfect, gritted teeth, playing to the camera – the exact spot vacated by Sir Horatio.

No longer the Trafalgar Café, but the Bluebird Café, it sat, changed, but still remembered affectionately in its previous state. Opposite Clapham Junction station and a short walk from the Granada cinema, it had survived the Blitz and was still feeding the changing communities of that part of South-West London.

'Josh, it's Kev,' he said gazing up at the photographs and thinking it strange that the stone-faced John Wayne to his left had an uncanny resemblance to his dad. 'That's right, you guessed it: off sick today;

will you pass on the message? Good; no, it's not a hangover, just a stomach bug. OK, cheers!' Job done, he thought, placing his mobile next to his steaming coffee cup. Though he had to be careful, pulling sickies was contagious and a slippery slope; a few more and the spotlight would be on him.

Please! he pleaded with his mind to leave him alone as the mystery woman on his lap episode began to play again in his head. It was relentless, the images even more fuzzy than before, his reasoning changeable and unreliable as he questioned every memory from the boat, his morality in doubt, unsympathetic and spiteful, taunting him all the while as he sat on the brink of believing himself to be a despicable monster.

Coffee: the fix; triple shot Americano; the second one arriving at his table. The instant hit nudged him back into the present. The waitress, a bubbly young woman with an impressive back-combed beehive and heavy mascara, smiled at him sympathetically as she unwittingly came to his rescue, breaking the cycle of torment.

'Let me know if you want a top-up?' she repeated, having said the same upon delivering the previous one.

Smiling at her instead of saying anything, he waited, her singsong cockney accent still ringing in his ears, soothing his troubled mind. Letting the caffeine attach itself to his senses, he felt happily anaesthetised, averting his eyes as she swaggered back to the service area. Closing them, he remained still, the inside of his eyelids red, and the more he squeezed them shut the darker his inner self seemed.

'Kev, I really missed you,' came the words as if on a breeze.

She seemed lighter, as if she'd floated into the café, the trip to Cardiff perhaps the detox for her troubled relationship with her ex, who by all accounts was still being unreasonable. Her skin appeared clearer, freckles he'd never really noticed before scattered across the bridge of her nose, fading as they spread across her cheekbones. Her warm, tender, somewhat wet kiss made him want to weep and rest his head on her breast for ever as he welcomed her scent; her distinct smell making him feel suddenly warm and safe.

'Ditto,' he replied, hugging her a little tighter than usual.

'It's good to be back.' Stella began placing her travel bag on the seat next to her. 'Cardiff was great, but the travelling was a nightmare, the train seemed to stop at every station in the country on the way there. Coming back was fine though,' she added breathlessly, 'got the express.'

'Do you want to see the menu?' asked the Beehive.

'No, just a coffee please.'

'Want a top-up?' she asked Kev again, who out of habit said *yes*.

'So you phoned in sick today?' Stella began, looking at him intently as he answered, noticing the dark rings under his eyes. 'Have you not been sleeping?'

It was his intro, the opening he didn't think would have come as soon as it did. 'Not really,' he began, 'there's a few things I need to tell you.' He lowered his head on the last word, focusing on her clasped hands. Slowly he relayed the events of the night on the boat (a watered-down version, of course). Placing emphasis on the fact he was drunk and could remember very little, Kev was surprised at how effortlessly he was able to tell his sordid tale. As he did he wondered whether he would stop at Eve or even mention her at all; deciding the whole truth and nothing but the truth, he ended on Eve. Only the sexual accusation presented a stumbling block, Stella visibly wincing at the mention of it though he didn't go into graphics. Worried, his hands a little clammy, he now looked up as if awaiting a verdict; the guilty and totally wretched before her.

It was everything he wanted. Holding his hands between hers, she told him she understood and that everyone had baggage and that the accusation would work itself out. As the words poured from her precious lips it was as if everything was alright, as if it had never happened; that his mother was comforting him, saying that it was all a bad dream and that none of it was true. It seemed she didn't doubt his innocence; loved him unconditionally: sex predator or not.

'Come on,' she said. 'I know and you know it's all nonsense.'

He nodded in agreement as he wished he could be as certain, muttering a strained 'Yes, I know.'

Was that it? he wondered. Odd given the fact that there hadn't even been any questioning on Stella's part; she'd taken what he'd said at face value. She'd merely listened and told him what he wanted to hear, he was completely absolved.

The subject was soon dropped, though he wondered if he should have gone further and mentioned the emails? For the moment he was just pleased to have her back and happy that the conversation was merrily mundane and casual, much of it concentrating on the conference in Cardiff. That was until there was a sudden lull and the silence led him to a revelation he hadn't expected nor appreciated.

'You don't seem worried about me,' she began, noting the confused expression on his face. The weird delivery of the statement throwing him somewhat off balance. 'My past,' she elaborated, 'sexual history – that kind of thing.' She stopped abruptly, waiting for a reaction.

It was out of character, thought Kev. It was Stella being direct and perhaps recklessly so, he thought, weighing up his options. Suddenly he felt annoyed at the question, particularly because he'd been down this road so many times before with previous girlfriends (though not in the same, sudden way), the *let's tell each other everything we've done; and who with; let's completely fuck with each other's heads and we'll be the better for it and we'll love each other more for it*. She'd said it and there was nothing he could say or do to put her off, particularly after what he had divulged – though he was willing to give it a go. 'Well, I don't think it's that important.'

'It's not?' She seemed put out. 'But it is important,' she continued, 'if the other person is carrying something around with them that is stopping them from fully enjoying a relationship. Don't you think?'

'Well, yes,' he replied, wanting to say that he thought it was just transference, shifting the problem on to someone else – was that love?

'Look, I'm just going to say it,' she said.

He saw himself leaping across the table and smothering her mouth roughly with his hand. 'OK,' he said because he had to.

'The night before our first date, I had a one-night stand.' Fuck, he thought as his mind quickly logged on to that time in history;

when he'd phoned her full of expectation and made arrangements for the next evening because she couldn't make the previous one, she was going on a girls' night out. And now it seems that very same evening she'd had a one-night stand. 'I'm sorry,' she said, holding his now limp hand. 'Bad timing, I know, but we weren't officially going out. I feel bad; I wish it hadn't happened, but it did. His name was Mark. It was just sex.'

That she didn't have to say. The *Mark* and the *sex* went straight to his urgent information feed and he wanted to throw up as a cold shiver encased him. Why did she have to say it; couldn't she have done as he had with Sarah and not mentioned it? But that was before they'd met. *It doesn't count*, he told himself. And then the next night, on their first date when they'd kissed goodbye at the tube station . . . the night before, she'd willingly fucked a stranger. He didn't know what to say, his feelings for her had suddenly changed and he knew it was shallow, but it was what it was. Her altruism of earlier had thrown him and now he wasn't sure of how to react – wanted to say it was fine, but he wasn't fine with it. He knew it was wrong, loathed himself for thinking it, but it was there nonetheless and he hadn't the courage to fight it.

Just as one loop in his head had subsided a new one had been born: the woman he loved writhing naked above a man named Mark, who was pleased to be getting an uncomplicated shag before returning to his other life, having got his rocks off and not needing to worry about the consequences.

'It's going to take a while to digest,' he managed, at last noting a tinge of disappointment in her eyes.

'Thanks,' she said before adding: 'You know I really love you – don't you? But I had to tell you; you have to have me whole,' she said, tears in her eyes. 'I couldn't carry it any longer. Surely you understand that?'

He was wavering; what else could he do? Challenge her? Tell her it's over? Christ no, he loved her. He could just get it – couldn't he? He could run with it; what she'd said made complete sense and he could take it or leave it. Fuck, he hated it, wanted to put an end to it as quickly as she'd told him, but how could he when he was stuck in accusation-land with his innocence still in limbo? It was only his pride which urged him to battle on, to be a man and do the irrational thing and dump her. But he wasn't that man; he was on the ropes and he knew it.

'We'll get over it,' he said, the words squeezed through a set of tonsils which wanted to clamp shut and suffocate him.

For some reason he felt almost aroused, suddenly attracted to her more than ever, ashamedly turned on by her sadness and regret and, if he was honest, her disclosure, though he'd never ever admit it.

'Thanks,' she whispered lowering her eyes as if in prayer. 'If I could . . .'

Instantly looking up and expecting to see Nelson staring sternly back at him, the rest of Stella's words merely floated past him, circling the discarded rigging and broken sails way above the fallen hero and expectant men.

'. . . turn back the clock I would,' she finished, the words lost someplace beyond gunshot, smoke, angels and an artist's brush stroke as they sat facing each other hoping that they too had moved on beyond the battle.

Chapter Twenty-one

'Turn around.'

'Hold on.' She wanted to make them wait.

'Hello; you still there?'

'Sorry. Just getting into position; how's that?'

'Yeah, that's it. Start slowly.'

'Is that good?' Not that I give a damn about your special, sad, oh so shitty needs.

'Ahh, yeah, that's good; a bit faster; grind a bit. That's it.'

'Oh yeah.' I say this to every twat that's dumb enough to want it.

'You bastard!'

'What?'

'Say: you bastard.'

'Oh, right – you bastard.'

'Louder!'

'You bastard!'

'Now take your bra off.'

'I can't; it's only nine thirty.'

'Oh. Sod the bra, then; just touch yourself a little; that's it: in circles. Faster! Faster!'

'You bastard!'

'Yes. Oh yes!'

'Yes!'

'Aaaaaah!' Silence followed by frantic rustling, wiping, zipping, then he'd hung up.

With the abrupt ending still ringing in her ears, she quickly shifted herself into the sitting position and readjusted her bra and knickers. Anna (not her real name) continued to smile into the camera, waving the mobile phone in her right hand while signalling with the other (thumb to ear and little finger to lips) for an imaginary person to call her.

With another perv in the bag, Stella Mayfield rubbed her worn elbows and reached for the bottle of still water, which had remained out of the frame during her last act, and drank steadily. Above the techno and annoying ambient music being softly pumped into the room, she could just make out the *oooohs* and *ahhhs* cooing from behind the screens of the other girls' sets, where five women were gyrating on a conveyor belt of simulated TV phone sex, the vile requests of the punters lost to the viewer who witnessed what was in essence a silent sex movie. Now and then the light would catch a shadow and the sounds would have more meaning, an identity given to the shapes that could easily have been attending a rigorous yoga class, stretched and sprawled, awaiting further vile instructions. Stella looked at the red digital clock above the camera: 9.45. Great, just fifteen minutes to go, she thought, attempting another seductive pose and a pout.

'Shit!' The dreaded ringtone began again. It was the same every night, always just as she was finishing. Ten o'clock was bras off time. Technically, Stella's shift only went to then and if she finished the punter off quick enough she'd still be able to hang on to a small part of her dignity.

It was a foot fetishist. With a foot enthusiast you really wanted them at the beginning and the middle of your slot, but not the end. Their fantasies were long and drawn-out affairs. Firstly, the shoes or boots had to be on and either fastened or loose. These were then slowly prised off; the toes stroked, pumped, and rubbed. If the punter came at all, it could be an arduously slow, sleazy ride. As customers went they were a quiet, shy bunch, who were rarely aggressive or abusive after their requirements had been met. This one she was sure she'd spoken to before as he kept calling her Sally,

144

a name she used to use, rather than Anna. Luckily, he must have been watching her session with the bastard as he appeared quite worked up and a little breathless already. He went straight for the toes, not bothering to tell her to put her heels back on. A toe-puller, she thought. Stella knew exactly what to do as she held her bare toes up to the camera, licked the tip of her thumb and forefinger, and slowly tugged at her big toe, with teasing pauses littered in between each pull. With the sixth yank and stroke he was done for. A little whimper and a faint *thank you, Sally* and he was gone.

10.05: not bad; mobile phone passed expertly like an experienced relay runner to the next girl who had sidled onto the make-shift bed beside her, topless, wired, and ready to go. Many of the girls approached it in this way, pumped up and eager to get it over with, like a wife who knows all her husband's predictable moves. Get through the night and try to hang on to as much sanity as you had when you arrived. Of course, when the adrenalin had run out and you'd heard enough sick talk and become bored of that too, you soon succumbed to speed and the temptation to at least try and enjoy the process. You always knew them, the ones talking at a hundred miles an hour while grinding their teeth and twerking their behinds like baboons at the zoo. Then there were women like Helen, Tracey, and Kourtney – young mums, who took their work seriously, who knew the moves, the storylines and, although perhaps not completely enjoying their vocations, treated it in the same way they would if they were toiling in a biscuit factory, packing the correct number of Custard Creams. And when all is said and done it *was* glamorous; though somewhere at the rough end of the catwalk. These girls didn't need drugs, they just played the game. There were some ex-prostitutes and escort girls, but the majority (apart from appearing on Babe TV) just lived ordinary lives; had boyfriends, even husbands, and children. Naturally there were impressionable girls who foolishly believed they were models and would soon become super ones. Caught up in their looks and bodies, they desperately needed to be wanted, Stella knew, even if it was by a fat middle-aged man with his dick in his hand.

Stella looked at Erika (real name Mandy) who'd just taken her place, and wondered how far this new rookie would fall. She had already invested in her boobs; the scars revealed under her breasts every time she excitedly bounced up and down, giving the impression she was at the best party she'd ever been invited to. She seemed wired. Stella was sure it wasn't the adrenalin of the novice but the amphetamines of desperation as her pupils dilated like huge saucers. And where was she: Stella Mayfield? Desperation island for sure. Though she tried not to bring it to work with her, drugs had gradually seeped slowly into her world. She smoked pot daily and took coke now and again. This she saw as her home thing: shower, cup of tea, slice of heavily buttered toast and marmalade followed ritually by a joint before zonking out in front of the TV, mind fully deadened, dredged of the madness that made up her life. Stella knew she was tipping the scales, but for now she kidded herself that it was under control – domestic drugs partaken alone and always in the presence of her cat Nibbles.

As Erika, bubbly, received her first call of the night, Stella wondered why she was still hanging about and not reaching for her coat? She didn't realise it, but she felt safe. It all actually made sense; it did something. She hung on a bit longer, as if hoping to catch the last minutes of a film she'd seen a hundred times before. Erika, already on all fours, had reached for the baby lotion and was dripping its contents copiously onto her thonged buttocks. Pretty enthusiastic for a beginner, thought Stella, pulling on her navy woolly polo neck and zipping up her jeans. Overcoat on, she was out the door and into the chill of the night and heading for home.

Her lie had become her reality; the marketing job pure fantasy, as was the ex-husband who was supposedly harassing her. After her first date with Kev, it was just easier to reinvent herself or rather mislead him. On a positive note, if you believed what you read in celebrity magazines then it seemed that reinvention was the new must-have self-evaluation package. She had to be seen as a professional, or as close to what she thought a girlfriend of his would be. She was surprised that Kev showed little interest in her made-up working life, never enquired or delved into the office politics she would lay before him. Much of the material she'd used from a previous part-time job she had as an administrator: a position she easily tired of, preferring to have the days to herself. Her work at the sex factory certainly had its drawbacks, juggling dates and drinks after work with Kev. Most of the time, he was happy to be meeting her after ten o'clock. If not meeting at the pub, she'd either make her way to his or he to hers (though she preferred her own place, where she'd cleanse herself until she found who she really was again and of course become who she wanted to be). 'Tonight, Matthew, I'm going to be Stella: confident, driven, successful Stella Mayfield, girlfriend to Kevin Parker.' Do you remember *The Wave of Time*? And there was always the chance, wasn't there, that Kev would get his break or maybe start his own agency and that they'd move in together, she'd wave goodbye to 0898 Sex Lines and forget (along with the list of lies) it had ever happened.

Given her present job description she had to be careful, especially in pubs and bars, which she tended to shy away from as much as she could. Luckily, with Kev cutting down on his drinking to near zero, they now tended to mainly do restaurants and cafés. She was sure no one recognised her with her clothes on. To be on the safe side she was always changing her appearance, particularly her hairstyle. When she could, she'd wear a wig or glasses if she was doing a school teacher or librarian.

She'd only been recognised once when out with Kev. At the Fairfield Hall Book Fair, when she'd been lead away by Martin Hargreaves' wife Agatha. As Kev had taken the stairs, a man who she had spotted staring at her earlier, brushed by him. Kev had apologised and carried on climbing the stairs. Instinctively, she knew the man was coming her way. Quickly, making her excuses to Agatha, she'd headed straight for the ladies, where she waited nervously for a few minutes before resurfacing. It hadn't been long enough; she almost collided with him as she opened the door. He must have been waiting for her, she thought, trying to read him.

'Anna, isn't it?' he gloated, either perversely pleased to see her in the flesh or delighted in embarrassing and belittling her. 'You're on TV, aren't you? I think we've spoken a few times,' he said, his voice getting louder with excitement.

Jesus, what did he want: an autograph? 'You've got the wrong person,' she said in her best aggressive Scottish accent.

'No, I was sure . . .'

Her stern, murderous glare had done the job, as had her hard, no-nonsense, hard-nosed Glaswegian accent. 'You wanna be careful who you talk to,' she fired at him as she turned on her heels and re-joined Agatha.

She was no different to a lot of the girls she'd met who'd kept their working lives a secret. If you had the right mindset you could do it. It helped if you had a thick skin and knew the ground rules of a covert life. It had been by no accident that she'd seen through Kev's attempts at covering-up his relationship with Sarah. She knew at a glance the lie of the land. When you lied as much as she had you could spot another's hidden story a mile off. To date the secret life had worked for her, even when having to change her plans, like when her boss had pleaded with her to do the boobs-out shift because of a tummy bug doing the rounds with the 10 to 1 a.m. girls. The storyline of the Cardiff trip was effortless; word perfect. Even the break-in at Kev's, which could have provided a wobble, was dealt with steely ease, down to the last details of train times and then the meeting with Kev at the Bluebird Café with a pre-packed over-night bag, seamless to the point that she actually believed it herself; she genuinely felt knackered after the fictional trip, even if it had actually been the combination of two exhausting shifts of thrusting and twerking.

There was always the possibility that Kev or anyone else for that matter would watch late-night soft porn. It had been the first thing she'd taken care of when Kev had first asked her back to his on their second date – the ownership of a Sky Box. He had none; never even bothered watching TV apart from the odd Man United match and the highlights from *Match of the Day* – he was perfect.

The more she'd fallen for him, the more lengths she'd gone to disguise herself on her slot: heavy mascara, thick pink eye shadow, and a blue-rinse bob being her now preferred persona. She'd even recorded the programme repeatedly, playing it through, searching for any changes to her concealment. She never for one moment recognised herself; it was a floor show she didn't know: her pouting lips, the longing stares, the poses of erotica and seduction, alien to her as she watched a young woman who could have easily been Erika, Kourtney, or Kelly – anyone but her.

Chapter Twenty-two

'You're back then?' said Josh stating the obvious. 'Crabs cleared up then?'

'Yeah, got some great ointment,' Kev replied, taking his first sip of coffee of the day from a paper takeaway cup which made his hand and lips burn.

'Early bird and all that,' continued Josh, 'you must be on to something,' he casually threw his jacket across the back of his chair, 'a bestseller,' he quipped, realising that Kev had chosen to ignore his first comment.

'Haven't even checked my emails yet,' Kev answered blankly, and then noticing the brown bruise on Josh's neck, 'Jesus, is that what I think it is?' He laughed.

'Yep.'

'You're a bit old for love bites?'

'I know – bit common, I suppose,' he answered unashamedly, but nonetheless choosing to tighten his tie and do up the top button on his shirt. 'In fact, a friend of yours.'

'Oh, really.' Shit, he'd really had enough of intrigue.

'Jan: the police surveillance woman,' Josh said lazily.

'Oh, yeah,' Kev answered, for some reason thinking that he'd been about to say Sarah.

'Bit of a biter,' Josh laughed, flopping down in his seat and switching on his computer. 'Anyway, it was good to see her again.'

'A casual thing.'

'I think that's what they call it?' answered Josh, now uninterested and lost in his emails. 'Aren't you going to check in on The Mad One?' he said as an afterthought, now fiddling with his ear and then examining its contents.

It was why he was still sitting there; he really couldn't face his emails. After Stella's revelation they'd managed to work through a few things, and although it was still a little strange had enjoyed a restful night in at her place. She'd said that her boss had allowed her to take a few days off after the trip to Cardiff. With more time on her hands they both felt unusually serene in each other's company, cuddling up for much of the night and working their way through a Laurel and Hardy boxset.

Sitting there at his desk, the loops of himself as a sexual predator and Mark shagging his girlfriend slowed to a manageable visual, he just wanted to sit and hold back from taking that first step into a day that so far was problem-free. He often thought of living his life in a more controlled way, reasoning that if you sat and did nothing, then surely through your inaction nothing bad would happen; literally nothing would happen – well, that was the theory anyway.

'Playing the waiting game?' Josh said, briefly turning in his chair and hugging Kev's shoulder.

He was sure Josh had a sixth sense as well as a penchant for hugging everyone and everything. At the moment the man seemed to have the rub of his trepidation; his predictability perhaps.

'No, just relaxing,' he lied, shifting nervously in his seat as his fingers made for the mouse. Two messages from Isabella: one sent at midnight, and the other ten minutes before he logged on. Going for the running order he clicked the first and took a deep breath.

New Chapter for your consideration she'd written as if a good working relationship had been cemented.

She knew it before he did, that hackneyed expression: the endgame was so close; the masterstroke, when the only true player in the game pulls the final strings and the curtains come down on what was – no, is – an honest contest of wits. But he was witless; a donkey to the last hurdle, unaware of the danger that lay ahead. She'd already demonstrated to him what she was capable of, the things she could make happen. And still, after all that had happened, he saw before him only Anabelle: the dote.

To be continued, Iz.

Iz, he thought, wanting to smash his fist through the wall. How more casual and surreal could it get?

'The Mad One?' asked Josh right on cue.

'Yeah, *Iz.*'

'How cute.'

Was that what he was doing, *galloping blindly towards the endgame?* Was he really that *donkey,* blind to what was before him?

He'd contemplated not reading them at all, but how could he when the closing finale had his name firmly stamped upon it.

'Jan, hi,' said Josh, his ringtone hardly sounding. 'Yeah, knackered; oh, you want the good-looking one?' He was winking at Kev now, making a biting motion with his teeth into his mobile. 'I'll pass you over; it's Jan.'

Naturally he thought the worst. 'Kevin,' she said as he smiled at the correct use of his name. She was obviously back to being a police officer again. 'I've been speaking with DI McGuire,' the mere mention of the inspector made him shiver, 'don't worry, no one's come forward.' Spending time with Josh must have also made her telepathic. 'In fact, the person who made the accusation has withdrawn it.'

'Really?' He was pleased, but not totally happy – how could he be?

'She said she'd been mistaken.'

'Mistaken?'

'Yeah.'

'That's it?'

'Yes.'

'Did they trace the call?'

'A payphone: pub called The Shakespeare, by Victoria Station – mean anything?'

'No, nothing,' he answered, feeling lonelier by the second and finding it harder to show any emotion.

'Well, that's it; you're no longer suspected of any wrongdoing.'

'Right.' He felt nothing; a little confused and numb, a deep ache forming in his gut which told him that it didn't yet warrant a celebration.

'Call me if there's anything else strange.' With that she'd hung up.

'Good auld Jan, eh; got you off the hook?'

She must have told Josh everything. Hardly police protocol, but he was bound to find out anyway. Josh seemed to be in the know on most things.

'Yeah, good old Jan,' he replied despondently, before noting the hurt look on Josh's face who no doubt expected a bit more from him. 'Thanks, Josh,' he said at last managing a weak smile, 'really appreciate it.'

'Couldn't have you going to prison: who would I have to flick things at?' he laughed, flicking a paper clip up in the air.

He didn't reply, instead clicking on the very last email.

Did you really think I'd be so cruel as to let you doubt yourself for ever? Anabelle, perhaps – but that's for another day. And you still can't see me, can you? Your hands and tongue that thought they knew me so well. Did you think that you were that capable of anything? You were so drunk. And now you try; you search every part of your mind for an image; for the face before you – don't you? The torture; your confused doubt is enough for me, but not for Anabelle. This is it for now (you'll be relieved to hear). The next time you'll hear from me will be towards the end of April – Anabelle's birthday. Yours, Iz.

'Tough one, eh?' Josh had been eyeing him suspiciously, noticing his shallow breathing. 'Do you want me to ring Jan back? I think you need help, mate.'

Josh had never called him mate before and he felt he wanted to cry. Maybe he would later. Cracking open an aluminium sheet in his pocket, he quickly popped a pill into his mouth and closed his eyes and tried to find his way back to the brief peace he'd enjoyed before he'd re-entered the world.

Chapter Twenty-three

'What happened to Mandy?'

'Who?'

'Erika: the newbie,' said Stella, making sure her wig was in place and that her thong was straight.

'She's dead; died last night, overdose; they found her in her flat,' said Kourtney. 'A punter who was due to visit her got worried at the loud music and the fact that she wouldn't answer the door – called the police.'

It all made tragic sense: the wired over-zealous bouncing up and down, and now the fact that she was on the game; a short life-span for a species that only comes out at night. 'Poor thing,' she said, remembering how Mandy had lent her a tampon the last time they'd met.

'Well, it happens,' replied Kourtney coolly, 'with those that take drugs.'

'Yeah,' replied Stella, thinking of the little nip of coke awaiting her at home.

'If you don't want her spot . . .'

'You can have it,' interrupted Stella.

'You don't like getting them out, do you?' she said, smiling, cupping her false forty-fours.

'Not really.'

'Well, see ya then.' Kourtney was gone, into the next booth.

At least it will be a quiet night, thought Stella, knowing that Kourtney made very little noise when filming, preferring silent pouting and crazed expressions to yells of encouragement and cosmic gasps of pleasure.

Mandy: Jesus! she thought, remembering the soft touch of her white fingertips as she'd passed her a tampon and told her that her sister worked in a petrol station and that she got free toiletries and that she only had to ask as she had *loads of them*.

Alone under the lights, Stella instinctively began spinning her mobile in her hand and mouthing *ring me* to the camera, the red light above it reminding her that she was live and being watched. She hadn't bothered with an outfit – it was too hot for rubber nurse's uniforms and she wasn't in the mood for undressing, instead going for silver knickers and bra and a matching wig. Kourtney had already got her first call of the evening, her soft words just audible above the pumping techno: *'OK, baby; yeah, I'm feeling really hot; do you want me to . . .'* Stella always thought how the dialogues (her own included) sounded dumb. If someone really talked like that, would you be turned on? Remembering that it was men on the other end of the call she quickly dismissed the notion.

Turning away from the partition and Kourtney's silhouette, which was simulating a sex act, Stella crossed her legs and leaned back on the red plastic chair, a prop she'd used many times. Unable to hide her boredom, she stared vacantly into the lens and reached for her water bottle. Sadly, even indifference was a turn-on. In fact there wasn't an emotion, an expression, a pose that wasn't. At least not recognising herself in the reflection of the camera, she was pleased that her new heavy mascara and grey eye shadow had eradicated any trace of her, making her eyes appear as pieces of coal waiting to be mined in some deep crevice of her soul.

Her mind was racing as she tried to visualise herself as a little girl and failed. It was something she often tried to do, only for her childhood to abandon her, as if her own sordid, near-nakedness had somehow rejected the essence of the memory. What would Kev think? she often thought as she stared deep into the depth of the black camera – would he run? He'd hardly buy her roses.

The first call was always the hardest of the evening; having to get into character at the flick of a button on the wave of a ringtone; to be ready to rub, pout, or do whatever the dirty bastards desired. Allowing it to ring for a few seconds longer, she prayed for her preferred foot-fetishist.

'Anna?' came the expectant enquiry.

'Hey.' With the first greeting she was almost there as her hand habitually stroked her right boob. 'What's your name?' she purred, smiling dumbly at the red light.

'Malcolm, call me Malcolm.'

Bristol area, she thought, now a dab hand at accents. 'Malcolm, what can I do for you?'

'Touch yourself down below,' he rushed, his breath heavy and laboured.

Good, she thought, letting her hand drop to her crotch, he's going straight for the wank. 'How's that?' she asked.

'Good,' he gasped.

'Do you want me to go fast or slow . . . Malcolm?' The last word dragged out as long as she could say it without laughing. She knew she had him, the delivery of her words seductive and measured.

'Slow,' he managed, as a thumping sound could be heard on the line telling her that he wasn't that far off. 'Stick your tongue out a bit.' The thumping sound was now faster and accompanied by the odd grunt. Christ, men were animals. Their depravity never failed to surprise her, they were totally visual and easily suggestible: like monkeys masturbating up the evolutionary tree, they unashamedly fulfilled their needs.

'Do you want me to lick you, Malcolm?' She had to stop herself from laughing as Malcolm let out a not-so-manly *Yes!* The slow breathing which followed, then the abrupt silence, perhaps a sign of embarrassment though probably not, which became a strange and weird atmosphere, informed her that mission was complete.

'Bye, Malcolm.' Malcolm had hung up. No need for niceties now, she thought, adjusting her pants as she began the whole phone-waving between fingers and the ring-me mime all over again.

It was always like a surreal dream. The strangeness of it all: taking your clothes off; posing in a small box; touching yourself; talking dirty to people you couldn't see, who live in another town or country – all doing the same things to themselves. When having sex with Kev she had to concentrate and convince herself that she wasn't being watched. It had affected their sexual relationship; she never really knew when to be experimental and daring and when not to be. Sometimes (like in the toilet in Paris) it had its advantages as role play became second nature.

'Hi,' she answered without even thinking: a robotic answering machine, directing a myriad of wanks.

'Sally?'

Again, it wasn't the foot fetishist she'd been hoping for. This was another sad bastard who remembered one of her old aliases. 'I can be if you want me to be?' she teased, popping her finger in her mouth and sucking it.

'You don't remember me then?' came the broad Scouse accent.

She could never work out how these men really believed she would remember them, as if they were important to her or she had total recall.

'Oh, yeah,' she lied unfolding and opening her legs as she leaned forward into the camera.

'Danny.'

He was a chatterer. Would talk you into the grave; bore the hell out of you with stupid inane questions and small talk for twenty minutes or so and then tell you to get on all fours and keep you there on your elbows for another gruelling five minutes, finishing abruptly and then wanting to talk some more.

'You got a boyfriend?'

'No.'

'Kids?'

'What, with a body like this?' She wanted him moved on as quickly as possible.

'Do you work out?'

Christ, he was hard going. 'Only in the bedroom,' she replied, rubbing her thighs. It was now a battle she had to win.

'I work out.'

'I bet you do,' she purred.

'I have a funny feeling you support Spurs?'

Who the hell was this guy? she thought, licking the contours of her mouth in a couple of circular motions. 'Well, I may have been with a few of them.'

'I support Liverpool.'

Really, she thought, not bothering to engage further with the conversation on football. 'Danny?' she said at last, 'just do me.'

'Stella, a word.' It was the so-called floor-manager-come-producer: a small, sweaty, pudgy, bald-headed man with red-rimmed glasses.

'Tom, what's up?' she asked, sliding into her trench coat, wrapping it around her like a comfy blanket as she checked the clock on the wall.

'You didn't follow the rule tonight,' he said sniffing and wiping his nose with the back of his hand.

'Oh, the Danny guy – I know, he just went on a bit–'

'But,' he began, cutting her short, 'they're paying for the right to talk, you have to listen.'

She knew he was right, but felt angry nonetheless.

'Well, maybe you should try spending three hours a night on all fours with your arse in the air, speaking to perverts with their cocks in their hands and maybe, just maybe, you might not always *follow the rule*.'

'Now, Stella,' his eyes were wide with anger and his tone confrontational, 'you know where the door is if you're getting ideas above yourself,' he spat, his sweaty face now purple with rage.

The last part; the very last thing the little prick had said: *getting ideas above yourself*, she could not move beyond. *Well, guess what Tom, you'll never get above yourself; look at the size of you and what you do for a living, and you have the audacity to think you're better than me, than any of these girls here – you fucking little prick.*

This she wanted to say and more. Instead, she just pulled a face, grabbed her bag, and made for the door knowing she'd be back the following evening and the next. Reaching the pavement, two girls on the neon shift passed her: younger, perhaps sexier, laughing to themselves as they went, no doubt convinced they were on the verge of a modelling career or at least the top-shelf magazines.

'Night,' said the tallest one, Kelly, with pretty, large brown eyes and the cutest of smiles.

'Night,' she answered as a group of young men wolf-whistled from a dark corner and a stray dog barked.

Listening to their stupid laughter and drunken high spirits she wanted to rip them limb from limb. At that moment it was as if the men she'd listened to all night were all around her; in her head and outside of her body as well.

'Slags!' was the last word she heard from them as she crossed the road and headed home as the girls shouted 'Tossers!' back at them.

Arriving at Kev's newly fixed front door she stood for a moment, as she pulled a small tin in the shape of a butterfly from her handbag. Opening it she expertly did a quick snort of the waiting cocaine, before quickly returning it to her bag. The sound of her rat-tap-tap on the door had a comforting sound to it. She'd followed the same ritual many times when staying at his: the snort, the warm tap of wood, followed by the needed embrace in his arms and the sudden feeling that her time at the 'factory' had been nothing more than a bad dream.

'You're shaking,' he said as she lay in his arms, her head numb with the cocaine swirling around it.

'Just cold,' she said softly, nestling into his warm side and enjoying the weird sensation of an itchy nose.

Stella knew he never really knew what to expect when she stayed at his. Sometimes she just jumped on him and they had sex right there and then, wherever they found themselves. Unbeknown to Kev, it was a reaction to the factory, a release of frustration, of sexual repression, of the very things she was acting out in her booth. And then there were other times when she craved pure warmth and comfort, when she just wanted to curl up with him, feeling totally sexed-out and in need of a cup of sweet tea and a slice of buttered toast and marmalade. Tonight was that night.

'Do you ever just want to sit alone in silence and kind of wait for something to happen or not happen?' she said, her voice deeper than before.

'Funny you should say that,' he replied, stroking her forehead. 'Yes, just today.'

'Really?' she said lazily, trying not to appear too wired.

'In fact, sometimes, when I wake up in the mornings, I wonder what would happen if I never budged – ever,' he said laughing.

'Do you feel sad?'

'Sometimes, and you?'

'Sometimes.'

All that remained was the tick of the clock and a stillness which they both understood. Their conversation collapsed and they felt good, searching out each other's smiles in the near darkness of Kev's sleepy bed. The things they needed to say lay unsaid, wrapped, secure and safe for another day – unpacked, but lurking ready to explode.

The sensation of her warm closing-down body and the heaviness of her eyelids, the closeness of Kev's deeply breathing chest lying beside her, made sleep the most heavenly thing she had desired that evening.

Chapter Twenty-four

'What do you think; will it do?' Stella asked, her expression strained and lost.

'It's only my dad's eightieth, not the Queen's,' Kev said, looking self-consciously around him at the numerous women who were holding hangered garments to their chests with one hand while grabbing another top with the other. Amazed at their dextrous manoeuvres, it was like watching a horde of shopping zombies. He'd seen the glazed look before: that focused expression of mixed anxiety and euphoria, picking through racks for that elusive piece of treasure. Making eye contact with the only other man in the shop, there was that instant solidarity; that dejected, helpless lost face that said it all – *please get me out of here*. Did shopping, successful shopping, go hand in hand with stress? he wondered, noting the pinched mouths of some of the women. And why did they leave clothes on the floor? Men never did that (well, not in a shop). Deciding that consumerism was an experience he really had overlooked for a number of years, he quickly came to the conclusion that if he just complied and said yes to everything, they'd be out and safely installed in a coffee shop before midday.

'Really suits you.'

'Ah, you're just saying that.' It wasn't going to be easy; plain talking and compliments weren't going to lead to a quick exit. 'I think the blue and white one,' she continued. He said nothing and let the silence decide. 'Yeah, I think this one; what do you think?'

What was the answer? he wondered, noticing that the nearby

shop assistant was also eagerly awaiting a response. 'I think you're right.' He'd thought it through; the syntax was just right and he'd simply returned it for game, set and match.

'I'll take it,' she said.

He really wanted to clench his fists in balls of celebration and shout a victorious *yes*, as the shop girl smiled at him sympathetically and the till opened and closed.

'Costa?' he said expectantly. Although not a great fan of their coffee, which he found was often bitter and stewed, it was better than chancing a risky walk past the remainder of the brand names in the mall to his preferred O'Brien's.

'Fine.'

Something was up. She seemed at times unusually irritable and preoccupied; her mind elsewhere. Her early exit that morning may have had something to do with it. Still drowsy with sleep, he'd seen her quietly opening the bedroom door so as not to wake him. At first he'd thought it a dream until the closing of the front door jolted him fully awake. An hour later she'd texted him saying they were going shopping and to meet her outside Marks and Spencer. And then there was her appearance, which seemed different, almost reflecting her mood. She'd tied her hair up into a tight ponytail on the back of her head, giving the impression that her skin had been stretched over her cheekbones. Still wearing the heavy mascara of the previous night, she looked ghoulish, her face hard, worn and tired.

Looking deep into her bag as if searching for something important, she inhaled deeply and then sniffed.

The nip of coke she'd had upon returning home hadn't energized her nor was it enough to revive her troubled mood as she later made her way to the mall. All she knew was that she wanted something nice to wear for Kev's dad's eightieth (it was what she was trying hard to stay focused on), when all the time she was still fuming over the spat with Tom, wishing she hadn't got so upset and consumed by it. She knew she probably had the look of someone who was visibly

162

weighing up her options as she tried to hide it with a smile which battled every twitch and raised eyebrow, the skin to her internal dialogue and the debate raging within.

'Penny?' he said as the coffees arrived.

'Penny?'

Why had he said it: the very same line Eve had used on the boat? 'For your thoughts.' Word for word; he trembled at the memory.

'Ah, it's nothing,' she said, placing her hand on his.

'Come on, I know you better than that,' he said soothingly.

'Well, it's David.' He wondered for a second who David was. 'My ex,' she said curtly, realising he hadn't registered the name. 'He wants to sell the flat.'

'That's terrible,' he said, anticipating that she'd probably want to move in with him. Nervously, he continued: 'But you have rights. He can't just kick you out,' he said a little too eagerly.

'I know,' she replied, a hint of irritation in her voice. 'I'm not going to move out; well, not yet, anyway.'

His antenna was up. He didn't like the last part. Frowning at this, he really did think that Isabella (whoever she was) had him sewn up: he was a selfish bastard to the core, more concerned that the woman he loved was going to ask to move in with him rather than the fact she may find herself suddenly homeless. He didn't really have to analyse it that much, he'd always shied away from total commitment, somehow scared that if he went all the way he'd just lose his identity. It never once crossed his mind that he was pretty crap in and out of a relationship; that his identity was not necessarily what he thought it to be. What was he waiting for? he wondered, avoiding her hurt eyes. Why couldn't he just do it? It wasn't as if he'd lived with anyone before and had had a bad experience. It was just a block of nothing that he nevertheless wasn't prepared to smash to pieces.

Taking a sip from her cup she eyed him suspiciously.

Sometimes, I could just slap him, she thought, noting his dropped gaze and hunched shoulders. His expression says it all, a voice reminded her as she sipped her coffee and then slowly and deliberately returned it to its saucer. 'Don't worry, I wasn't asking to move in.' For a moment she hated him: a mixture of hurt, surprise and sadness that he was so transparent to her. Could he really not detect her disappointment?

'No, of course you can,' he bumbled, managing a misplaced smile.

'Really, Kev? I don't think that's what you want.' It was an intentionally cold reply.

'Yes, it is.' He felt totally pathetic, like a child who'd easily been found out.

'Just drop it,' she snapped, folding her arms. Maybe it was just bad timing, but he could see she naturally expected more from him; he'd said he loved her and yet it seemed he only wanted to do it from a distance.

'I'm sorry.' He didn't realise he was getting himself in deeper and deeper, his brain no longer connecting with what was really at play.

'Just stop it! Stop it!' she cried. 'I don't need anyone's charity.' She was getting up and pushing in her chair.

'Stella,' he pleaded, putting out a hand to try and stop her.

She didn't reply, instead roughly grabbing her shopping bag, brushing past him and making for the entrance.

'You idiot,' Kev said to himself as he watched Stella's cross face pass him on the other side of the shop front. Thinking of running after her, he hurriedly tried to finish his coffee. It was something he thought he should do, though really the smell of Java was just an excuse to let her go. What was stopping him? Did he just not care? Was his soul now so bare, had he become a worthless amoeba overnight? Had so much happened that he'd simply crashed, his empathy crushed beneath Anabelle's swinging hammer and relentless ravings? And then there was death: had he actually, truly grieved? Had Eve somehow still got a hold on him, unwilling to let him go; ejecting him from the arms of Stella?

Now holding his head in his hands he contemplated drinking Stella's unfinished Americano, as his thoughts began to stray, as he wondered if it was ethical to do so considering they'd had their first fight? Fingering the lipstick stain on the rim of the cup, he turned it around and drank. It was stronger than his – he hadn't known she was a three- or four-shot girl.

It was probably the lipstick which began the loop he'd been resisting since they'd first started shopping: Stella shagging Mark, or was it the other way round? he thought as the drama began again in his mind. It was then that he realised why he'd really let her go; why he recoiled at the idea of having her move in with him. It was the one-night stand and he was punishing her for it. He was the guy he used to despise, the one who sought to get his revenge. And why was Sarah there, loitering in his darkness? Of course he would, he reasoned. If she were to walk into the café right now he'd book them a hotel room and afterwards, lying there totally satisfied, he'd feel better; he'd be that irrational, pathetic man.

Chapter Twenty-five

The heavenly song of the nightingale was soon drowned out by the raucous crows who'd been excited all morning at the arrival of the dustcart and the stray rubbish which the dustmen had let fall from the over-flowing bins to the littered pavement. Their poor orchestral attempts at song had descended into a frantic, hysterical screeching as they fought each other for the tiniest of pickings. 'Damn and stone the crows,' Kev said to himself as he fought for the right to remain dreaming within the predictability and safety of bed.

His mobile in the next room wouldn't stop vibrating and ringing. He had intended to get the horrid ringtone changed from bird-call to something less of this world. The taste and smell of doner kebab appeared to be all around him, his whole slug-like body was a large doner with extra chilli. His tonsils still moist with whiskey, he had a headache to support the fact he'd definitely finished the bottle which now stared accusingly at him from his bedside table.

The dancing fool had made a brief comeback. After walking aimlessly around the shopping centre, buying himself a pair of skinny jeans he'd never get into nor wear and, why he didn't know, a set of binoculars and a red scarf strewn carelessly across the floor, he'd arrived back with his sudden zest for consumerism in a carrier bag and a bottle of whiskey stuffed deep and safe within it. Only intending to have one drink to steady himself, once The Temptations and The Stylistics were grooving, he was dancing around the room; the bottle over the course of an evening sprung a considerable leak, quickly evaporating into his bloodstream. Realising that no matter

166

how many times he called Stella's mobile that she wasn't going to answer, he'd decided to drink himself stupid. As for the kebab, it was a mystery, the shredded cabbage, slice of lemon, and wrapper by the empty vessel meant that the time-line wasn't what he'd thought, the visit to the takeaway, a trip lost in drunken time.

Christ, he was dying: his limbs heavy like felled trees, sunk and left in a thick muddy bog; his brain removed from his skull, resting someplace in another part of the room as his senses merely experienced and then chose to ignore the ringtone which at times he thought was the crows outside his window. He simply registered the sound and then forgot about it as he fantasized about Sarah and tried to remember the lyrics to a tune that was still sounding in his ears from the night before.

When the ringing ceased he felt real peace; the return of the nightingale's song providing the illusion that it may be a sunny day; the smell of freshly cut grass finding its way into his otherwise musty lair. He must have fallen asleep. Outside he could hear a heavy rain, the birds no longer singing and squawking, no doubt now more concerned that their newly made nests would be washed away in the freak spring showers. Opening his eyes to the changing light he soon closed them as the bottle by his head reminded him of how crap he was. He vaguely had some recognition that the ringing had started again, but he really couldn't care less. With his hangover declining and coming to a lost end, he was happy to drift in and out of sleep, returning to Sarah and their sordid little secret.

'Kev!' came the shout as he turned over onto his side to face the intrusion from the draughty letter box. 'Are you there?' He clearly hadn't heard the knocking or the buzzer.

'Yeah!' he managed, rolling out of bed and pulling on his trousers, 'just a minute,' he called out as his heart rate quickened and a feeling that he had let someone down engulfed him.

He knew the voice, although the face didn't emerge until he opened the door. 'Sarah!' He felt like telling her he was just dreaming about her.

'Christ! Don't you answer your mobile any more?' She was

breathless and annoyed, her blue eyes wider, more piercing than usual. 'I didn't want to call round, but I had no choice; I wasn't sure whether Stella was here or not – you know? It could be awkward?' She was rambling now, so much so that her sudden appearance on his doorstep had jarred him into reluctant reality.

'She's not here,' he managed, rubbing his eyes.

'Good,' she said walking in. 'I don't want to get you into trouble.'

Whatever was wrong she was quickly busying herself. Like Eve and her dusting she seemed to share the same gene, as she began picking things up off the floor, before telling him to have a wash (which he ignored) while she made some coffee.

She was holding on to something, wanted to drag it out for as long as possible; it was her thing and she'd divulge it when she was ready.

'What have you been doing? It stinks in here,' she said, placing two coffees on the table and opening a window. He didn't have to tell her he'd been drinking; she'd have had to be senseless not to have detected the fumes seeping through the pores of his skin. 'Sit down,' she told him firmly, taking out a piece of paper from her handbag. 'I've written it down; I didn't want to leave anything out.' She seemed to be enjoying how important she may have seemed, her self-esteem unusually high and a far cry from the woman torn apart by her sister's cutting tongue and cunning. 'OK,' she began, composing herself and spreading the piece of paper out on the table. 'The police have been in touch with Dad.'

God bless her, he thought, she's written it down word for word. 'Is he in trouble?'

'No, no,' she said impatiently, 'let me finish. The police have been in touch with Dad,' she read again trying to make herself sound as natural as possible. 'There's new evidence on the hit and run.'

'Eve,' he stated, his heart leaping from his chest.

'Please, Kev, let me finish.'

'Sorry.'

'Well, at around the same time as Eve was killed, two hours before, another hit and run had taken place in Putney; same car as the one which killed Eve.'

'How do they know?' he asked as images from the last time he'd seen Eve on the Common flashed before him.

'The victim, who survived, saw and knew the driver.'

'Shit!'

'Please, Kev,' she said again, excited and exasperated at not being able to tell her story in her own time. 'She knew the woman; they were in care together as teenagers. She'd nearly killed her then, pushing her out of a window, leaving her with a limp and a constant battle with pain in her spine and hips.'

'Christ!' he gasped, 'and she tried to kill her again – and then Eve?'

'Yes, she just jumped out of the way in time, but recognised her instantly, remembered the car; it all fits with the Ford Focus which killed Eve.'

'And then two hours later does exactly the same with Eve?'

'Yes,' she said, tears in her eyes now.

'Fuck,' he said, clasping her trembling hands.

'That's why I was ringing you,' she said as a tear rolled down her cheek.

'Why didn't she report it then?' he asked as an afterthought as Sarah checked her notes.

'Oh, yeah, I have it here,' she said fingering the words on the page. 'At the time of the hit and run she was wanted by the police for soliciting. In fact,' she continued, reading from another part of the notes, 'she was soliciting at the time she was hit; that's why she didn't call the police.'

'But why now? Why has she come forward?'

'She saw her – says she's back in the area. She's scared shitless,' added Sarah gripping her wrist tightly.

'And the police, have they been able to find the driver?'

'So far there's no trace of her.'

'But they got her name?'

'Oh, yeah,' she said, recovering and glancing at the piece of crumpled paper. 'Her name's Anabelle. Anabelle Waters.'

Chapter Twenty-six

Suzie, as Anabelle called her, was gone; pushed. The last she saw of her were her shiny buckled black shoes and knee-length white school socks. Scrolling down further and checking the words of a maniac, he didn't need to read any more of *Deadly Mouse* to realise Anabelle's intentions; after Eve, who was the only other person he was attached to? Stella. She had to be Anabelle's next victim. Whoever got in the way of what she wanted, she'd soon dispose of them. It was written there in black and white.

Frantically pressing the buttons on his mobile, Stella's phone went to voicemail again. He'd tried texting her, even emailing, but nothing. She was either still annoyed with him or Anabelle had got to her already. 'Think,' he said to himself before picking up his mobile again.

'Jan, it's Kevin Parker, Josh's friend. There's been a development.'

Telling the whole story again, Jan seemed to be in the know, informing him that the Suzie character as named in the story was probably a Karissa Jennings and that she and Anabelle Waters had been in care together. So far they knew very little of Anabelle, only that her deceased mother had a serious drug problem and that her father had been violent towards them both, resulting in a restraining order and Anabelle being placed into care. After the Karissa incident (in which she couldn't be legally charged due to lack of evidence), Anabelle was moved to another home where she stayed until she was eighteen. When she'd left the centre that was the last they heard of her.

'So what happens now?' he asked, feeling as if he'd just watched and not enjoyed a twisted thriller.

'A DCI Mike Reynolds will be in contact shortly; will probably call round,' she added. 'He's already spoken to Douglas Blake and is interviewing Sarah Blake this morning.' She never mentioned it, he thought, peering over at the empty Jameson bottle still goading and tempting him. 'Probably best you don't let on you know all this info,' she said hesitantly. 'DCI Reynolds likes to run his own show – he's a bit old school.'

'No, of course not,' he replied, thanking her and hanging up.

That was why Sarah was in such a hurry to get back, he thought, undressing and getting ready to step into the shower.

'Shit!' he cried as the not too warm water hit his sensitive skin. Letting it cascade down his body he thought back to the last moment before Sarah had left: the natural embrace they'd fallen into and the brief kiss of desperation they'd had before she'd pulled away, shaking her head as if to say they were always going to be making the same mistake. Sure that she'd be there now with him beneath the spray if she hadn't had to meet DCI Reynolds, he felt ashamed and yet guiltily turned on.

Concentrating on a spider that had somehow avoided the spray, he watched it as it lurched forward, stopped, then quickly scurried across the wall tiles, its long legs getting jumbled up as it went. Kev blew in its direction, and it dropped to the floor of the shower basin and disappeared down the hole. Staring at the grate of the drain he willed the spider to reappear, but it didn't. He must have misjudged the time because the water was going cold as the electric pump on the wall began to hum and make a loud chugging noise.

The buzzer was now sounding in the hallway. 'Stella,' he said to himself, grabbing a towel and pulling on his dressing gown; though another voice longingly whispered Sarah's name.

Noting the large dark shadow through the frosted glass, he hesitated for a second, taking longer than usual to turn the latch.

'Kevin Parker?'

'Yes.'

'DCI Mike Reynolds,' he said holding up his badge. 'Sorry to disturb you,' he added, looking down at Kev's open dressing gown.

'Sorry,' he apologised tightening the cord, 'come in.'

Reynolds was a large man, similar in build to himself, mid-fifties with a greying beard and a mop of black curly hair, with large mournful, hazel eyes which appeared to peer up from their saggy sockets every time he spoke.

'Sarah Blake mentioned you'd probably still be in,' he said, surveying the mess.

'Sorry about the state of the place; a bit of a heavy night.'

'Right,' Reynolds replied, smiling, his eyes knowing as much.

'Please sit down,' Kev said, picking up his laptop off the chair and placing it on the table.

'I don't live too far from here, so it was easy to find,' Reynolds said, still looking around the room as if putting together a profile of who Kevin Parker really was.

'Yeah, it's a good area,' Kev said, not thinking of his recent break-in.

'Has its problems, but we're working on that,' Reynolds joked. 'So look, down to business,' he said, clapping and then rubbing his hands as if warming them in front of a camp fire. 'Sarah, I believe, has already filled you in on a lot of the finer details surrounding Anabelle Waters and the suspected murder of Eve Blake.' He stopped abruptly, waiting for acknowledgement. It was a pattern Kev would soon get used to.

'Yes,' he replied, now understanding the procedure.

'I first interviewed Anabelle back in the 1980s when she was fifteen.'

'When she pushed Karissa . . .'

'Yes,' he interrupted, raising his hand. Jan was right: he certainly liked to run his own show. 'Out of the window,' he finished grumpily, now folding his arms. 'Back then,' he continued, 'well, that was that really: routine police work, counsellors, psychiatrists were all called in and the incident logged away. By the time she could legally leave the home, she'd vanished off our radar, well, in fact,' he corrected himself, 'she was no longer on our radar. Her social workers were happy with her new state of mind and in honesty saw great things for her. She'd managed straight As in all her A levels and there was talk of her going to university; so no concern really.' Was he going to continue? wondered Kev, not daring to interrupt again as the DCI sat for a while as if searching for some lost words. 'And then there's now,' he said at last.

'Right,' he managed, not wanting to break Mike's sacred flow.

'No record of her; no tax contributions – nothing. In our book she no longer exists, well, not as Anabelle Waters of course.' There was another prolonged pause. It was as if someone just turned the light off in him now and again and he was just waiting for it to be flicked back on. 'Why do you think anyone would want to murder Eve Blake?' The words were alien to him; a question he'd never anticipated. 'Anyone you know?' he asked as an afterthought, looking deep into his eyes.

'No; no one.'

'What about you?'

'Me?' he answered, astonished at the enquiry.

'Have you upset anyone; someone she may have been connected to?'

Relieved that he hadn't understood the *what about you?* question, Kev answered that he didn't.

'And Sarah?' His stare was hard and slightly menacing now.

'Sarah?'

'You and her; Sarah said you had a thing.'

'After Eve,' he said clumsily, swallowing hard.

'Not before?'

'No,' he said guiltily.

'You can see why I had to ask?' Reynolds said cagily, managing a smile. Could he? Did he mean Sarah had a motive? 'And Isabella Morton,' he started again after another long gap, 'you've never heard of her?'

'No.'

'I had the emails passed on to me. Pretty crazy stuff,' stated Reynolds.

'It's definitely connected then?' said Kev, wanting to get the facts right.

'You mean Isabella Morton's Anabelle?'

'Yes.'

'Could be; although it could be a coincidence; she hasn't used the name Waters, has she?'

'No.'

'But the last emails: the *endgame is close* rant does seem to suggest something, don't you think?' He really had done his homework.

'You mean me; she's going to–'

'Not necessarily,' Reynolds interrupted, 'but maybe, or maybe someone connected to you.'

'Right.'

'And what about that allegation against you? Who do you think wanted to hurt you? Isabella Morton seems to know a lot about it, that suggests that she was there – or maybe there was someone else on the boat that night who wanted to get to you?'

He was a good detective, but not one who put you at ease. 'I've been through that night and I can't put anything together,' Kev said, exasperated.

'Because you were drunk,' Reynolds added, with a hint of mistrust as his eyes darted around the room, again taking note of the mess and the residue of whiskey and kebab still in the air.

'Yes,' he faltered, feeling a little annoyed at the direct questioning now taking place in his own front room.

'I'm not trying to get to you,' Reynolds said, noticing the look he'd seen so many times before. 'I'm just trying to get the facts right.'

'When's Anabelle's birthday?' Kev said, remembering the details of the last email.

'Oh,' Reynolds said, looking in his notepad, 'the twenty-third of April.'

'That's–'

'I know,' he interjected again, 'when she'll be in touch next.'

'You've got it all pretty well sewn-up?' He was feeling brave now, or thought he was speaking to a normal member of the public.

'Yes. DC Janet Goodman's been very helpful.'

This guy knows everything, Kev thought, his lips now dry and his throat still parched from the drink. 'She's very helpful.'

'Keep sending her your emails; I want to know everything,' Reynolds stated, getting to his feet. 'Maybe the next time you communicate with Isabella Morton, address her as Waters; see if you get a reaction? Until then, here's my number; keep in contact and if you remember anything that may be relevant, call me straight away.'

'Of course,' Kev answered, now standing.

'Might be a good idea to keep an eye on your girlfriend; make sure she's OK. I've already warned Sarah Blake to be vigilant; they need to watch where they go, think about their own security.'

Stella, he thought, maybe he should mention that she hasn't been answering her calls? 'I haven't been able to contact my girlfriend Stella for two days,' he blurted.

'Did you have an argument?' Reynolds asked as if he knew they had.

'Kind of,' he answered, sure that DCI Reynolds had made another check on the squalor in the room.

'Well. It's probably nothing; just keep calling her,' the DCI said, 'these things happen – people stop communicating,' he added, smiling for the first time. 'Just remember: call me – any time.'

Kev felt he should have shaken hands or maybe said more, but Mike Reynolds' hands remained firmly in his pockets and his demeanour signalled that the show – the DCI's show – was over for now.

Chapter Twenty-seven

'Are you going to say anything today?' asked Josh, who a second earlier had fired a rolled-up ball of elastic bands at the colour printer, making it reel off a blank page.

'Thought I'd save it for the playground,' Kev said, staring at his empty screen and rubbing his unshaven chin.

'Are you sleeping under the same bush tonight?' asked Josh, watching a forty-year-old man on YouTube put a live hamster between two slices of bread and pretend to eat it.

'May as well,' he sighed, looking down at his pot belly and to where two buttons had popped and gone missing from his shirt.

The bush comment wasn't that far from the truth. After the visit from DCI Reynolds, Kev had raced round to Stella's flat where Nibbles the cat had welcomed him, obviously ravenous and mad with hunger as it meowed and circled his legs in anticipation of a good meal. Judging by the junk mail still sticking out of the letter box it seemed Stella hadn't been there for some time. Peering through the window he could just make out the kitchen sink, where a pile of unwashed cups and dishes waited. Ringing the buzzer and then knocking on the door wasn't going to do any good, but he did it all the same. The more he became physical with the door and the rapping of the letter box, the more his mind turned darker as he saw her in the arms of her one-night-stand boy Mark or in bed with her ex-husband. Irrational fears circled his mind like vultures. Cursing himself for the selfish running order in his mind, he eventually arrived at the dreaded fear that something bad had happened to her.

Wondering if he should contact DCI Reynolds, he thought he'd try calling her again later. She was probably staying with a friend and still punishing him until he came to his senses and behaved like a proper boyfriend.

As he'd walked in the sun that afternoon along Tooting Broadway, contemplating another morose night alone in his flat, something in him just gave up; he'd fallen into submission: strolling into the nearest pub, he'd stayed there till closing time, nursing numerous pints of Guinness and whiskey chasers, while feeding the jukebox and grazing on as much soul and Motown as he could find. By nine o'clock that evening he was dancing with the local drunks – 'I Heard it Through the Grapevine' a particular favourite, continuously pumping out of the speakers, as was 'What Becomes of the Broken Hearted', much to the amusement of the watchful manager who was pleased to have a little light entertainment, rather than the usual dull vibe of old men and desperados watching Sky News updates on the flat screen above the bar.

Asked to leave after a lock-in until 12 a.m., he'd staggered the rest of the two miles home. Falling after trying to pick up a discarded paperback with its pages ripped and flapping in the breeze, he'd landed with a thud near a bush at the front of someone's garden. Moving over onto his side, he'd stared in disbelief at the front cover of the damaged book facing him: *The Wave of Time* by Sonia Allen. Howling with laughter, he'd rolled around on the filthy concrete, holding his bursting belly as the pages appeared to wave at him, taunting him, as they joined in the mockery of the fool on the ground whose shirt buttons had just popped.

'The things people do,' remarked Josh as the same man from the previous video placed his dog's paw between a hotdog bun and proceeded to do the same as before.

'Fancy a pint?' asked Kev, casually turning off his screen.

'Why not; it's lunchtime,' said Josh, a little surprised at the invitation.

The weather was glorious, blue skies, not a cloud in sight, though the forecast was bad for the rest of the week. The small pub across the street was already littered with office workers sitting outside enjoying the soon to be gone sunshine. The men's shirts: white, light blue, and some pink, made a pastel background to the vibrant colours of women's dresses, as their reds, oranges, yellows, royal blues, and purples splashed across the subtle canvas. The sounds of an early London summer: lumbering buses, laughter, and the beauty of glistening wine and pint glasses, tinkling and dinking, the odd cool breeze and the smell of melting tarmac, the light of the sun catching and bouncing off Ray-Bans as even the badly dressed office workers appeared elegant within the fantasy that was a premature summer.

'Enough for us both,' said Josh, putting his arm around Kev's shoulder as they crossed the road, instinctively smiling in the direction of four women. 'They're a beautiful species, aren't they? They're just perfect.'

Normally Kev would make a witty comment, but really, he couldn't be bothered, he just wanted a drink. 'I'll get these,' he said as Josh went to get his wallet out.

'Bottle of Bud; I'll be over there,' Josh said, nodding towards the women, 'I think I may know one of them.'

He didn't protest; normally he would have. Ordering himself a pint and whiskey shot, he downed the Jameson straight away, all the time making sure nobody was watching. Picking up the bottle of Bud he made his way over.

'Kev, this is Becky, Jane, Hazel, and Harriet who I met at a publishing convention.'

Why didn't he ever get invited to publishing conventions? he wondered, as the woman named Hazel asked him if he'd gone to Goldsmith's College as he reminded her of someone she'd met on her semiotics course. Luckily, he hadn't gone to Goldsmith's, so that was the end of that conversation. Josh gave him a look which said: *You idiot, you should have lied – you were in there.*

Like a goldfish in a bowl he was just happy to be swimming around in circles, watching Josh give his masterclass in seduction and smarm, as he complimented, gushed, and spoke of himself in glowing terms, only including Kev now and then as either the butt of a joke or to add spice and realism to a funny story.

Becky, Jane, and Hazel were soon joined by work colleagues Ray and Paul, allowing Josh to corner, monopolise, and re-establish his links to Harriet, who was showing signs that she may be interested in his advances, now leaning in close to listen more intently to his catalogue of stories. Finding himself out of the loop, Kev moved back inside, where he now pumped the fruit machine with coins, losing more money than he was drinking.

'Kev?' It was Melissa. 'What are you doing in here; it's lovely outside,' she stated, swishing her immaculate hair to one side. 'Come on, Vicky's out there with Josh and some other people.'

'I'll be there in a moment,' he lied as another noisy, flashing nudge failed to go his way.

'Oh, and Vicky's got a new man: Graham—'

'Reacher,' he finished for her, as the machine at last paid out five pounds to the chorus of inane sounds and lights. 'The guy at the book fair,' he added with a faint smile.

'Oh, yeah,' she said trying to hide her disdain for him and the fact that he'd finished off her news bulletin. 'You were there, weren't you,' she said.

'Kind of,' he replied flippantly.

'Well, we're outside anyway,' she said abruptly, getting the last word in as she headed for the light and, no doubt in her own head, the fun people in the sun.

After another pint and chaser at the bar he was ready to head back to work. Using the side door of the saloon bar, he'd soon circled the group outside and was back at the office.

There was something comforting about an empty, dimly lit, air-conditioned room, when the sun was burning up everything in its wake outside. Unwrapping a Mars Bar (his lunch) and taking a bite, he turned on his machine as two messages sprang up at once. 'A Publishing Conference in Edinburgh,' he said to himself, laughing and nearly choking on the chocolate. The next one tagged *Are you*

179

alone? was from *Iz*. Instantly, checking the date again, he was sure it wasn't Anabelle's birthday yet; no, it was another week, he reasoned, now clicking onto the next instalment of madness.

Needing to pee and with trepidation he proceeded to read what was entitled the **Final Chapter**.

The next day, the 16th of April (a week from Anabelle's birthday, to be precise), the weather changed and the clouds moved in foreboding formation, sweeping across the already dreary cliffs towards the mainland. And there he was: frightened, lost, unable to control the events which would haunt him for ever. He didn't know what to look out for – well, not at first anyway; you see, the selfish don't see things at first; you have to guide them. Unaware, stranded, paralyzed with fear, he stood. Anabelle was watching him all the time, waiting for him to act, to witness what he had created: the ultimate consequence of his actions. 'Between the times of 9.00–10.00 or maybe 12.00–1.00, or could it be 3.00–4.00,' she'd written neatly on the little pink birthday invitation card with his name lovingly written in her best handwriting above. 'An innocent will be sacrificed in your name, you who never saw, but failed to recognise the woman before you. All you saw was Anabelle the dote; not the lover; the only one who understood you. The price has to be paid in full, as you see them smashed on the rocks below, knowing all the time that it was your hand that did the deed; your ego that spilled the blood of innocence.'

Anabelle: she saw it; felt every changing expression on his face as he stood helpless as another life was taken, swept out to sea, broken. Everything he'd said and done in his life tainted by his resistance to doing the right thing.

Beachy Head – where love never dies.

The End.

'Christ, are you alright?' said Josh, casually bursting through the door and catching the tortured, horrified expression of a man who'd reached the bottom of the pit he'd been slowly falling into.

'Fine,' Kev replied, tears in his eyes, 'just a bit pissed,' he added, logging out of his emails and scribbling something in a small note pad and sliding it into his pocket. 'I'm going home,' he stammered picking up his bag and jacket.

'Is it because it didn't work out with Hazel?' Josh called after him in an attempt to defuse the weirdness in the room. Kev opened the door.

'No, just got to go,' he said turning his face away and gripping the sweaty handle of his laptop case tight as the air-conditioning poured out of the room after him.

Chapter Twenty-eight

Kev, Just to let you know that I'm fine and staying at a friend's (her name's Jane: a mate from college). I'm sorry how things worked out between us the other day. I didn't mean to storm off the way I did. I just got so frustrated. There are things that I need to work out on my own now. I will be back soon and we will talk (I promise). Please don't contact me for now, because I really just want some space. You know I love you. Speak soon.

Stella x.

There are so many ways you can interpret a text. First he'd convinced himself that it was over and that she was just alleviating his fears about her whereabouts, and then that she'd soon be back and that she really did need to have *some space*. Finally he came to the conclusion that things were now so fucked up in his life that what would be would be and that fate and all the bullshit in his life was out of his hands – that it really didn't matter which way he interpreted the text because all the crap was heading down the same pipe anyway.

Relieved that Stella was safe, it was at least one thing off his mind as he struggled to keep himself together that afternoon. Returning home, he couldn't face the isolation. After the text from Stella he knew he had to escape before the real drama was to unfold. His shaky hands told him as much as he quickly packed an overnight bag and threw in some essentials. Looking around his barren flat he knew that he'd probably be a different person when he eventually returned. Picking up his new red scarf off the chair he tied it around his neck and checked his reflection in the mirror. It seemed like months since he'd seen himself. So much so that he hardly recognised the man with the puffy, dark rings under his eyes and a pallor which was somewhere between unhealthy grey and deathly white. He quickly abandoned his reflection and made hastily for the door.

It was the most natural place in the world to go. He now understood how refugees felt when they were frightened and so far away from home. Where else could he be; not judged or tormented, but with his mum and dad? Looking around the kitchen at the familiar setting, he sadly thought of how objects, cups, plates, pictures and photographs all stay the same, unsullied, uncorrupted by time, unlike the human condition which changed and ultimately died. Was it why he'd struggled to make eye contact with his parents when he'd first arrived – was that it? Was he just childishly thinking about their eventual deaths?

'Everything alright, son? You don't seem yourself?'

I really love you, thought Kev, knowing he could never really say it.

His dad still wore a light brown work coat (the kind a metalwork teacher might wear), his hands stained by paint and oil – the remnants of whatever he was presently working on in his shed. His new venture was mending anything electrical which most people nowadays would just throw away, fixing the new neighbours' electric carving knife and charred clapped-out toaster. Margaret had remarked that the Taylors next door were quite poor and that the house had been let to them by the departing O'Malleys, who had temporarily moved back to Ireland for a year. 'Your dad just wants them to feel welcome; you know what he's like.' That was William Parker: always putting others before himself; not something that had rubbed off on his son, thought Kev, noticing that his father's eyes appeared grey rather than blue now, like jellied eels in a glass jar.

'Just work, Dad; I'm fine,' he answered, aware that his dad's deep breathing was something he'd never heard before.

'He's got an appointment on the twentieth of April: X-ray department; they think it's a chest infection,' said Margaret, intercepting her son's concerned look.

'It's nothing,' claimed Bill, waving away the comment with his hand.

'But you've had it for some time, Bill.' She always used his name when she was being serious.

'Ahh!' he said dismissing her with a glint in his eye as he winked at his son. 'They all think we're the same as the soft cockneys down here.'

'There he goes again,' laughed Margaret, her serious tone now lost. 'Still thinks he's a rufty-tufty Northerner.'

'Cold, hard steel,' Bill stated, smiling broadly and lighting up the whole room.

God, he wished he could have been more like them, particularly his dad. Now he knew where the John Wayne apparition in the café had come from. He was of that generation of good, solid men who suffered and toiled for their families, never complained and found enjoyment in the simplest of things in life like gardening and pottering around. This was a man (a dying breed) who still wore bicycle clips, polished the brass on the door-knocker, and oiled the front gate when it squeaked. Whatever he did it was done with generosity and a smile, his only vices being the football pools and the odd bet on the Grand National. He never drank. Where did I get the *I must have alcohol* gene? Kev wondered, his body still awash with the whiskey he'd feasted upon after his hasty exit from the office, his mind still susceptible to the destructive ache in his soul for more.

'How's Stella?' Margaret had asked earlier, throwing a worried glance in her husband's direction.

'Fine.' What else could he say, that he'd screwed up again?

'Is she still coming to your dad's eightieth?' she whispered, holding her hand up to the side of her face and then fiddling with an earring.

'Of course,' he lied. Judging by his mother's expression she probably knew as much anyway.

'So you are still going strong then?'

He really was being pushed to the limits on the concealment front. 'Yeah,' he said aware of how insincere it sounded.

'Good,' she had replied, thinking of how badly her son had been affected by Eve and still a little guilty that she had misjudged her good intentions in trying to protect her son after her sudden death by saying that *he hadn't been seeing her that long.* 'She's such a nice girl,' she concluded as if by saying so that her previous error would be erased from memory.

His mum was right, she was and he didn't deserve her. Looking at the real man in the room, he knew that his dad would have run after Stella and insisted that she move in with him. In fact it wouldn't have got that far; they would have been married by now.

Why are you here again? he asked himself. He felt like crying as the familiar scenes from his childhood whirled around the kitchen, where his mother poured the tea and the cuckoo clock chimed at noon and his father automatically reached for the volume dial on the wireless as the midday news began. He wished he could tell them everything: Sarah; Anabelle; the drinking; the allegation – the whole worthless mess. How could he? Look at them, he thought, watching his mum pat his dad's workman's hands as he wheezed and then stopped himself from coughing, preferring the discomfort to his dry lungs than the upset or concern he may cause others. *Help me!* he pleaded with them; *please be younger; don't die*, he wanted to say it all. *Let me be your child again* – all of them dancing in Streatham; having that treat in the Trafalgar Café; 'eye-eye, hey dad,' and unwrapping that Action Man at Christmas and watching the *Morecambe and Wise Special; Mum, wrap me in your arms and tell me it's all going to be alright. Mum! Dad!*

'Do you think it will take long, the X-ray?' Margaret asked innocently as Bill pulled another face and shook his head, smiling all the time.

'Your mum: she's a worrier, that one,' he managed to say to Kev, trying to control his breathing so as not to alarm anyone.

Why did he find it so hard? He'd said it as a little boy. Gripping the armrests of the armchair he went to get up but slumped back down instead as if an electric field had stopped him from doing so.

'I really love you,' he blubbered, 'I really do.'

'We know, son,' said his dad, glancing worriedly at Margaret.

'We know,' agreed his mum, reaching across and squeezing his hand. 'We love you too.'

'You silly sod,' said his dad, laughing as he stood and ruffled Kev's hair. The distinct odour of oil and paint embraced him and wiped his tears.

'Silly Billy,' said his mum, a little teary as well.

'Watching the match?' asked his dad, in an attempt to re-establish normality.

'United?'

'Of course bloody United,' he laughed.

'No, I have to be somewhere,' he replied sadly.

'Don't worry, son, I'll record it for you.'

He held on to it; cherished it; he knew he may perhaps never hear his father say it again. *Son; son; son* – he kept it as he rose and took it with him as he left.

Chapter Twenty-nine

Beneath

Searching the rock pools below for the odd washed-up household object, a man on the rocks dragged his small wiry frame like a sea snake over the slimy, seaweed surface. Not once did he look up or wanted to as he pulled two plastic coal bags behind him, the contents of which varied, depending on the day. For this particular stretch it was mainly plastics; milk containers, beer ring holders, microwave dinner packs, black bin liners, and a myriad of packaging which you couldn't confidently put a name to. In all his time on the rocks he'd never found anything alive. Mainly it was the parts of those who lived or had lost something of themselves. Fishermen's toes and fingertips being the most common; it was the reason he always kept a cool box with him. Like leftover chipolatas they would often poke out of the sand like sea anemones searching out light and food as they expectantly pointed upwards from the ocean. Never once did he follow their projection.

When he'd first started recycling he was aware of (well, he'd been warned about) the people above who'd just stand and peep down, *who loitered with intent* as someone had put it. He had only looked skywards once and it was the last time as he'd caught the tortured glance of a young woman. Luckily she never jumped (although she had contemplated it), but it was the sheer utter nothingness he'd witnessed in her eyes, that of an abandoned child which stung his eyes and haunted him every time he got close to the cliff face. Busying himself in his work, he only saw what was in front of him, his quick, darting eyes sorting, sifting, and excavating the sand and pebbles like a whale filtering silt through its gallbladder. Thank God for ears, he thought often to himself. The noise of the helicopters were his eyes; their location to be avoided. It was their job to clear up the human mess (as he saw it), not his. It was why he'd managed to avoid the young couple with the baby who had jumped that day. He'd been busy collecting rubber and an uncharacteristically large amount of discarded flip-flop soles on the shingle to the left of the jagged rocks where their bodies had been broken. Was he guilty that he'd hidden when he'd heard the helicopter? A bit; but genuinely, no. It wasn't his business. His was saving the planet from human waste, not human frailty which rained down as unwanted flesh from the world above. Settling himself down between two huge boulders he had a smoke and thought about his mum who was getting remarried later that year and how he really didn't want to go to the wedding; not that he didn't like her new man Tony, only that he really couldn't afford to buy a suit. Feeling the full force of the helicopter blades flattening everything before them, he'd sadly acknowledged the bodies as they were slowly hoisted high above his head. The simplicity of his sigh had said it all as he eagerly set to work again, choosing to try and forget what he'd just seen.

Sometimes he'd bring his girlfriend along. She would do the metals, mainly cans, and he'd do the plastics and rubber. They'd share the glass, though bottles, despite the cliché of them being washed up on desert islands with messages in them, tended to sink out at sea (unless the top was still secure).

Sinead was an artist and used plastics in her work, making huge sculptures of plastic art; large heads with fishtail-shaped ears and milk container noses in the guise of phallic symbols – *fertility plastics* as she called them, or *the infertility of man and the destruction of the environment*. Sinead, who wore a yellow builder's helmet after being hit by too many falling rocks in the past, never looked up. It was probably why she'd been hit so many times before, as she tended to stray too close to the chalk face at times; perhaps too absorbed in her skill at finding just the right shapes to fit the art whirling in her mind.

Today he was alone, lost in his reverie and sad that a small but significant slick of oil had left a tidemark along the bottom of the cliff, like the scum line on a bath. Later he'd make his way round to the lighthouse, he thought, picking up a plastic Waidi bottle filled with what looked like shipping oil. There was definitely a leaky tanker or trawler out there somewhere, he pondered, looking out to sea. He'd move up onto the cliff later when the tide changed, remembering that his spy glasses were safely hidden under the passenger seat of his dilapidated 1960s camper van.

His stomach rumbling, he thought he'd grab a sandwich in the pub. Though the thought of encountering the sarcastic barman quickly erased the idea. As for the locals, he sensed that although he was one of their own, that he was perceived as a bit of an oddball, his long dreads, nose rings, and fifteen-hole army boots portraying him as living on the periphery of their community. 'Nigel's alright,' they'd say in a tone which suggested that he was only just *alright*. Other descriptions of him as being *weird, strange*, and *not really like us*, were freely bandied around. In a small community like theirs everyone had a nickname: his was the *toe collector* or *the finger-toe-man*, depending on who you spoke to. His home-made advertisement in the local shop described his service as an *environmental emergency service* in which he was available at any time to clear human debris wherever it may land. Fishermen in the area always made a note of the number at the bottom of the advert knowing that if anyone had recovered a lost tip of a pinkie or toe it would be Nigel.

Being an outsider, Sinead never really got a mention in the same way as Nigel. Known simply as *the Irish one* or *the artist,* she was merely the girlfriend of *the toe collector.* There had been a rumour going around at one time that she had been a potential jumper and that Nigel had talked her down. *'They'd met over a cliff,'* was the joke which was told.

'Nooooo!' he roared, crouching down by two oil-drenched gulls, still warm but dead, having struggled throughout the night against the pounding waves and the grease which prohibited them from escaping. Shaking his clenched fist at the grey sea, he searched the waves for the culprit but his gaze was only met by a blank, dirty horizon. Placing the dead gulls in a gap between a rock, he covered them in smaller stones until they were invisible. 'Bastards!' he shouted at the sea, whose slow menacing claps reminded him that the tide would be changing at midday. He had until two o'clock, maybe three at the latest, he thought, wiping his oily hands on his combat trousers and trying to quell the anger he now felt inside. He'd have most of the plastics sorted by then and maybe some rubber as well, he reasoned, taking out an already made roll-up from behind his ear, placing it in his mouth and lighting it. Inhaling deeply and then letting the nicotine bellow from his lips he began to sing:

> There you are
> Sweethearts to the end
> Somewhere beneath this sea
> There's something from which I shouldn't hide
> And there you are
> A real life photograph
> And I know it's somewhere in the dark
> I've seen it in my dreams.

As if the song had demanded more than a metaphysical picture to accompany it, he stared down at the shiny wet pebbles. 'A photograph,' he said, picking it from the tangled blue fishing tackle and seaweed. He was never surprised at what littered the ocean's floor: a music stand, toilet seats, a second world war tin helmet, a sword, a McDonald's sign, teapots and toy Action Men were just a few of his odd finds. Though the shop dummies strewn across the rocks was one of the most haunting scenes he'd ever seen as he'd stopped in his tracks, believing that a mass exodus from above had taken place. He'd wondered whether the scattered, broken plastic limbs were somehow a message; a warning sent by God that man wasn't only just destroying himself physically but also the environment as well – the bodies, the plastic, the oil: they were all connected, seamless in their misery and contradictions. The day after discovering the mannequins Sinead had put them back together and painted them pink and erected them up on the cliff. A news cutting of the spectacle had been printed, framed and hung on the wall of the local library entitled *Dummies on the look out for Dummies*. Straightening the coloured Polaroid and wiping off the gull shit, a wedding shot peered back at him of a beautiful Spanish bride and groom, surrounded by family, friends, and blue skies. Instinctively flipping the photo as if anticipating an explanation he read the inscription on the back:

Maria and Tony
Wedding day, Barcelona 1999.
Happiest day of my life.

He'd hand it in at the police station, he thought sadly, placing it in his coat pocket and patting it gently just to make sure it was still there.

Far out at sea the clouds began to roll in: a sign of bad weather he knew only too well. Finding cover in a small cave he'd used so many times before, he sat watching the steady, silver trailmarks on the walls as fresh water trickled down from the earth above. Thinking now as he always did that it was strange that the earth and rock above his head and below his feet was all the same and the cavernous middle that he sat in was fragile and transient, that it could be flooded or collapse at any time. Picking up a flint he began to write, engraving the words *middle earth (I think)* into the rock accompanied by his initials *NG*.

Making a pillow with his jacket he laid down in the foetal position and closed his eyes and listened to the rain hitting the water like shrapnel being sprayed from a diving fighter plane.

'*Nigel Grimes, you will go to prison for one year, three months.*'

Waking from his dream he stared out at the sky which was now brightening, the gulls now leaving their nesting holes in the rocks around him and heading out to sea to fish. Checking his watch he cursed himself for having fallen asleep for so long.

He'd served only six months in total and had been released early from the open prison in Southampton on his twenty-seventh birthday. It had all happened before he'd met Sinead, before he'd become an environmental beachcomber. *An error of judgement; a breach of his civility* was how his solicitor described it in the court room. He wasn't the only one on the proposed Winchester bypass who'd been arrested that day. Others had done worse, i.e. actual bodily harm to police officers, as they had done to the protestors. He was just one of six who'd rocked a patrol car back and forth like a cradle until it turned on its side and the screaming policewoman inside fought to set herself free from the baying mob. He wouldn't have harmed her; have harmed anybody, he kept telling himself as he was led down to the cells at the courthouse. 'He was just caught up in the moment,' as Sinead had said later after they'd met and he'd shed his guilt at having been involved. It was a blot; a stain he could never remove from his past. Carrying it around with him like a rugged cross arched upon his back, he never lived a day without remembering how his judgement had let him down. Soon after his release he'd decided that he had to give something back if he was to move forward again and that his days of just being a road warrior with a chip on his shoulder were over. After attending a talk at the local town hall on environmental issues, he then decided that a small gesture, a sacrifice of sorts in which he'd clear the shores of human waste, would at least help to pay his dues to society and cleanse his soul of a wrongdoing which should never have happened.

Sinead had said something about Yin and Yang and that everybody underwent an internal struggle in their lives and that if they didn't that they probably lacked humanity and had no inner light. One night as they sat around a campfire on the beach, she had told him that she'd once been a drug mule (only once), making the trip from Bangkok with a belly full of dubious packaged heroin, to help pay for her Art degree. She said that it was a bad thing she had done, as the stuff had probably found its way into the veins of the experimental young and vulnerable, but that said, it was done and she wasn't a bad person – well, not any more, anyway. When he sang at the sea (which he did every day) he knew she'd been sent to him, to be at his side. *'Hadn't everyone done things they weren't proud of?'* she'd say to him. It may as well have been in Irish, as the way she said it with her smiling eyes, it could have been in any language and it would have made sense to him. It was why he didn't mind being alone on the rocks – the sea, sky, Sinead, the beach, they were all one.

He didn't have to look up to know when someone was peering down at him. He just could feel it. Like the gulls, who constantly glided above his head he could just contemplate their presence without looking at them. At this part of the beach he was more exposed and easily seen from above. There was more of an assortment of human waste to sift through: shoes, tyres, plastic toys and for some strange reason baby dolls; ten, he counted in all, not bothering to pick them up until the preying eyes had disappeared, knowing that he looked weird enough already without being seen hugging a bundle of freaky triplets.

He didn't know why, nor did he care, but the weekly appearance of a patrolling Royal Navy destroyer barely stirred his emotions. He was alerted by the strange ripple in the waves and the sound of the excited rhythmic slaps against the rocks to the presence of a grey looming monster. The cries and shrieks of wonder from above stated the obvious as he refused to look out to sea, now busying himself with the dolls, safe in the knowledge that he wouldn't be spied.

One more haul (he already had three bags of plastic), he thought, wiping the sweat and the salt of the sea from his brow. He'd be able to drag four bags to the lighthouse and the winding gap which he'd climb back up to the headland. It was the part of the day he dreaded most, when he'd suddenly appear out of nowhere, dragging his bounty as sightseers, walkers, and observers would naturally stand and stare as if he were a returning hero from the ocean: a lost but now found Portuguese sardine fisherman perhaps, who'd returned after being missing for years. Lowering his head, he'd drop his rounded, sloping shoulders, his eyes making contact with the scuffed metal toe-caps of his boots. Letting his dreads flop down over his eyes he saw nothing but distorted light as if sprung from between thick prison bars swinging like jellyfish tentacles before him, as he whistled nervously a tune that meant nothing.

'Bob Marley', was the only thing people tended to hurl at him as he slumped up the beaten path to the trodden green grass. Though to be fair it wasn't very often as the Head tended to be frequented by the serious-minded or those with a deranged focus, rather than the mindless utterances of yobs.

Deciding to call it a day he soon found himself at the gap in the cliff and the windy trail. Throwing the bags over his shoulder he began to climb. Surprised at the lack of interest from those milling around at the edge of the cliff he soon made it ominously to the top. Dragging his plastic swag to the side of the road, he paused for a moment as he looked up for the first time. Was this what a child's recollection was like? he wondered as if seeing those around him for the first time: their shapes temporarily blurred, their figures and frames fuzzy. Until, lastly, their now in-focus faces mooned at him like huge dinner plates, making him dizzy and flustered as their expressions appeared to jump out of their faces and taunt him. A group of schoolchildren who'd just scrambled out of a minibus, their shrieks to his ears more abominable than the gulls', made him want to cover his head and run in the opposite direction. 'Work to be done,' he told himself, looking out beyond their cries to the sea and the numerous trawlers and tankers he could just see on the horizon. He needed names and numbers, he reminded himself as he hoisted two of the heavier bags up onto his shoulder and gathered the others in his left hand and made for the car park. If he was quick enough he'd have his bags in the boot and his binoculars out from under the seat and he'd be able to log the possible polluters before it started to rain and visibility made it impossible to see.

Thank God it started first time, he thought, remembering how Sinead had been stranded a week ago having driven solo to Wales, only for the van to conk out on the outskirts of Bristol. Still, he'd got to see a bit of a city which had eluded him, unlike the slaves who hadn't been so lucky when put up for sale a little under three hundred years ago. What a cool accent, he thought when eventually picked up by a man and woman from the area who took him all the way to Sinead. As they told him about Bristol, their lives, their hopes for the future and love of motorbikes, he just listened as if being told auld yarns by two aging pirates named Vic and Helen.

Pulling in at the side of the road, he did a quick take of those around him, collected his binoculars and made for the cliff. Positioning himself twenty metres from the edge he sought to avoid those around him. Aware of a man to his right who was looking his way he took a few steps backwards to a less obvious position. No longer in a straight line with the man who was now staring out to sea he comfortably scanned the horizon. 'Ah, there's one,' he said to himself reading the name on its side. 'The Santa Maria,' he said making a mental note. Big enough, he thought, noting its size and number, 'and,' he continued, swinging north, 'if I'm not mistaken, The Morning Star.' One more, he thought, moving forty-five degrees, 'and the . . .' He'd stopped abruptly, stamping his foot in anger, 'the bastard Princess Catriona!' he said cursing the sea. 'Fuck you!' he said under his breath. Three times he'd logged it and passed on his findings to the shipping authorities and here it was again leaking its shit all over again. Just then his vision was suddenly spiked and sucked into the surreal. His mind blank, he dropped his glasses and ran as fast as he could towards the cliff's edge and the sea.

Chapter Thirty

Above

Rubbing the scar above his left eye, Kev Parker pressed his binoculars deep into the sockets of his eyes. Scanning left then right he nervously re-checked the perimeter of the cliff's edge. Hearing a car arrive further up the road behind him he tried to ignore it but he couldn't, instead, turning ninety degrees to his right, he did a quick take. It was a taxi from which a man and a woman emerged, paying the driver and walking hand in hand down the coastal path. Stopping briefly and kissing they seemed to have a change of heart, the man appearing to make a joke as the young woman, dressed in a parka with a target on the back, laughed as they turned in the other direction and began strolling down to the car park and the pub. Noting the smart young man's desert boots, straight Levis and black Fred Perry jacket, he recognised the familiar uniform. 'Mods,' he said to himself, smiling, then switching his attention back towards the sea.

Further out beyond the surf and threatening waves a trawler bobbed up and down as gulls glided and swooped, their white chalk wings hanging on the grey sky like harsh scratches on a rough palate knife background, scattered and at times completely still as if captured by a camera from a surveillance shot. Below the bow line of the rusting red ship, the grey had smudged into a darker cold, inky black; a light spray rising from the gloom of the deep every time the vessel moved up and down as if a street artist with aerosol in hand had added extra definition to their graffiti.

3.15, he acknowledged, checking his watch. Nothing in front or behind him; he deliberated whether he was in the right spot as he now took in the coastal path, the lighthouse and the road behind. Surely, she'd find him, he thought, deciding to stay put.

Leaving home the previous evening and getting the inter-city train to the coast, he'd chanced finding accommodation in nearby East-bourne. Arriving late he found a 1970s-style guesthouse on the edge of the resort. Although sparse and lacking in the charm of many of the buildings on the promenade, it was at least clean, warm, and friendly. Feeling overwhelmed by the reason for his trip he'd made straight for his room where he decided he would stay until the next morning. He thought about calling Stella again, but thought better of it, remembering how she'd pleaded with him to give her the space she needed. Lying on the brown eiderdown on the single bed, he knew that he was hedging his bets and that he shouldn't really be there. DCI Reynolds had received the email of Anabelle's final instalment from Jan and had rung him stating in no uncertain terms that he should not make his way to Beachy Head and that they were pretty close to finding Anabelle, having received information that she may be living in the South London area and had been working under a false name nearby. He was being vague and Kev detected that he perhaps wasn't as forthcoming as he was before and was definitely hiding something as he went to say something and then uncharacteristically stopped abruptly and coughed nervously; it just wasn't the polished Mike Reynolds show he was used to. Something in him had changed. It might have been DCI Reynolds' case, but it was his story and he had a leading role. Fuck Reynolds, he'd thought, telling him that he had no intention of travelling to West Sussex. He had to go with his own intuition and follow Anabelle's plot through to the end.

A troubled, sleepless night followed in which he craved coffee and drink. He must have fallen asleep briefly as he remembered shouting out in a dream where his father and mother were drowning in a capsized boat on the murky River Thames and a demented Josh kept flicking his ear. The tense airless night had painfully, slowly led to a wet downcast morning and his frenetic appearance on the Head.

★

From his vantage point he peered at a flock of screeching gulls which had landed close to the edge of the cliff. Their din startled him back to his senses as his ears rang with chaotic shrieking. The birds appeared to attack another one of their kind, who seemed to be the victim and the cause of their consternation. It was now being pecked by a vastly superior, bigger gull, perhaps spitefully encouraging the others to join in the playground beating. Knowing what Anabelle had done (fiction or not) and was capable of, he felt helpless and guilty watching the smaller gull being abused by the others. Theatrically, he waved his arms frantically in the air and shooed them away, only for the gulls to re-group further on and continue their bird retribution with even more gusto and vindictiveness.

'Afternoon.' He'd failed to see the elderly lady who'd now passed him by and having found the spot she wanted was setting up camp, opening up a tiny canvas camping stool, sitting and making herself comfy under her huge umbrella as she took out a drawing pad and began sketching.

'Hello,' he answered on the wind as she lifted her frail hand like the Queen and turned away towards the sea. How had he missed her? he wondered. Annoyed with himself he walked down to the edge for the first time. A metre or so from the drop he turned and checked the view behind him as the old man from earlier was out for another spin with his dog. Like London buses, everyone was coming into view all at once, he thought as the red-fleeced Samaritan drove slowly up the headland waving as he went. Raising his hand in recognition Kev felt a kinship with the man, his comings and goings akin to his own, both watching, waiting and searching for bad things to happen on a landscape littered with human frailty and the oddity of mankind.

The last time he'd peeped down, he'd been a child and the cliff's edge had a barrier and a sign saying: *Beware of falling rocks*. As if on a fairground ride, his stomach had shifted and his testicles tightened. Now it was no different, except for the impulse to jump. He tried to place the possible words of the couple who'd jumped with their baby in his head: *You say goodbye, you kiss, you savour that moment before the fatal step and you tell yourself that what you're about to do makes sense,* he thought as he took a timid step forward and peered down.

Below: a mystery to those above, an unseen world walked only by the dead and the gulls. A carpet of seaweed, washed-up plastics, tyres, dead fish, dead birds, dogs and oil cans. A rusty motorbike and the side panelling of what was once a red Ford Escort marked the sacred site, now the playground for the lost and tormented souls who'd jumped.

As the wind intermittantly whipped itself up and died, it was as if he could hear cries of encouragement from the fallen below calling out for him to join them and jump; to not be afraid of the jagged rocks which peered skywards. *We will stop your pain*, they cried out, *Join us . . .*

'And set yourself free,' he said to himself, completing the cycle. Would it really matter? he asked himself, pulling up the collar to his now flapping overcoat as he tasted sea salt and felt spray in his face. Eve, wasn't she out there? Her soul . . . her soul free on the wind, waiting for him to join her and tell her that he loved her. 'Eve,' he whispered, closing his eyes, 'are you there?' She didn't answer, though had he seen the sudden break in the cloud and the sunlight which poured out from behind it as a sign, a conversion, then perhaps he may have jumped. The ray of light which cut through the grey lifeless sky brought with it a chattering of birdsong and what appeared to be an excited chorus behind him. Expectant whoops and cries at the welcome break in the weather warmed his back, pulling his lifeless stare back from the now silent underworld.

Turning, he saw two parties of schoolchildren beyond on the headland quickly merge into one as their teachers began handing out work packs and pens. They barked instructions, trying to curtail the over-hyperactive amongst their group. A line of blue, each child with an orange rucksack on their backs, like dotted waxy crayon marks appearing as if bright flowers on small blue stems, now waved at the old lady, who did the same back, briefly stooping from beneath her pink umbrella, exposing her wild, white, scattered hair illuminated by the changed bright sky, the deep crinkled lines on her wrinkly face like winding rivers in her now flushed cheeks warmed by the unexpected sun. If he had the time, had a camera, the woman: the subject of his composition would have moved left of centre, the schoolchildren in the background like tiny blue socks with orange dots on a washing line, merging as if on a tiny escalator to the sky.

3.45: out of breath, he quickly scrambled back to his previous spot; the grass still worn by his toing and froing as if a restless circle of anxiety had been left there awaiting his return. Binoculars in hand, he felt like a commander in the field, surveying his military options. The children, now formed into four groups, were scattered around him, heads down, filling in their workbooks as they followed the instructions in their packs – *draw a lighthouse; a horizon. How many metres out to sea do you think the lighthouse is?*

The group in front worried him the most: more boisterous than the others, their male teacher more interested in the young petite special needs assistant than the two lads who were repeatedly falling back onto their rucksacks. If one of them were to roll in the wrong direction, he thought, as a knowing tightness enveloped him – they'd be gone. Swinging to his left, then his right, his line of vision was annoyingly obstructed. He struggled with his glasses as if trying to find a target in a heavily populated civilian area, noting the casualties which may occur if he were to make the wrong judgement or face the wrong way.

3.55: the impending time; the sweat pouring down his back as his legs turned to jelly told him that the moment had arrived and that the next five minutes would possibly change his life for ever – his memory splintered and infected by a virulent disease, locking him into the darkness till his dying day.

'Jason! Mark! Stop that,' cried the young teacher as they failed to get back up having fallen so many times that it had become endemic as the students in the other groups copied them. 'This isn't an idiot convention!' he shouted sarcastically, as the assistant cringed at the remark as she helped her severely handicapped pupil settle back into her wheelchair.

'Sir!' came a cry to his left as he nervously swung around to the shout.

'Yes, Smith?' came the baritone.

'Jeremy's had a nose bleed.'

Merely feet above their heads the gulls had gathered, their searching eyes awaiting the odd discarded sandwich crust or crisp as they glided nonchalantly, squawking every now and then just to let the world know they were still there.

'Keep away from the edge – twenty metres!' shouted the baritone whom it was now obvious was the teacher they all took notice of. 'I need to return with the same number I started out with,' he quipped in that show-off, I'm a teacher kind of way.

It was hard not to follow the school drama without drifting into the past. Thinking of his own school days, Kev thought it was a miracle he'd got this far. The only teacher to have inspired him was Mr Green, who'd started out as a shouty geography teacher before having a nervous breakdown and returning the following year as a mad, peaceful hippie who'd ditched trying to teach and brought in an acoustic guitar instead and played Bob Dylan songs. *'Always be prepared to change, man,'* being the only advice he'd shared with the class. Listening to the dreary instructions of the teachers he wanted to shout for them to stop and get them to sing a Beyoncé song.

'Don't come running to me if you fall off that cliff, Butler,' one of the teachers shouted as he too (like Butler) temporarily froze at the real implication. Suddenly, there was a gasp of wonder as everyone turned and faced the sea. Maybe it was the warship again? thought Kev straining his eyes to see what all the excitement was about.

'Look!' they all shouted, their expectant faces lifted towards the sky, their small bodies standing to attention as they mechanically pointed at the blimp. It could easily have been a cloud or soap suds as it casually floated into view; silent, like a deadly assassin bubble. The kind of menace that made you want to run and hide.

'Anabelle and Kev Forever!' one of the children shouted as the rest followed suit and the baritone teacher told them to watch their steps as a few of them lost their balance. And there it was, in red celebratory letters: *Anabelle and Kev Forever*, flapping wildly on the tail of the blimp. The young eyes that had spotted it before him were now instructed by their teachers to draw the advertising balloon (as it was now referred to) which appeared to move closer towards land and hover magnificently above their heads. If there was now a shadow on the ground before them, then he must have imagined it as it seemed bigger and more foreboding than it actually was.

Coincidence? Yes, it did cross his mind; but no – it wasn't, he told himself. It was a looming stunt of absurd madness he could never make up, let alone put down in words. And there it was above – mocking him, showing a preview of the craziness she had in store for him. As it lingered in the grey-white sky he sensed that somehow it wasn't going to go away; that it would remain there: a witness to a torment which, to use Anabelle's prophetic words, would *Never End*.

The whole thing could easily have been in slow motion (a cliché of course) with the sound turned down when he saw her first: the long green army trench-coat and short, layered, dyed blonde hair. Her figure turned away from him. He knew it (the shape) every inch. The hair had thrown and fooled him for a mere second as she moved swiftly towards the children. Changing direction as she made her way towards the edge of the group, now striding casually, hands thrust deep into her coat pockets, he caught her side profile as it slapped him hard across the face: Stella, as he'd seen her so many times before: focused, calm, her friendly demeanour there for all to admire as her kind expression remained locked within a warm smile as if she'd just remembered a pleasant memory.

'Stella!' he called out, still holding up his binoculars and examining every move she made, as he scanned all around her for a crazed knife-wielding Anabelle, who couldn't be far off.

'Stella!' There was no change as she slowed and looked out past the students towards the sea.

'Stella!' he tried again now taking a few steps forward. Why was she here? Had she followed him – or maybe DCI Reynolds had been in contact with her and let slip that he may be heading to Beachy Head, or maybe it was Anabelle who'd led her here with some cunning plan? She just seemed motionless; poised and quietly content as she stood there as if contemplating life itself.

It was then that he came to a halt, the full screen now appearing in his head as the image became static and played: Stella, her face now changed, hate and pure loathing turning for a split second to face him. It was then that he sadly realised that he'd perhaps seen her before; before she became the Stella he knew. It was the sharp haircut, the peroxide seductiveness and the edginess of her now familiar face, mixed up somewhere within the dark corner of a sticky, boozy, disco boat dance floor, his tongue deep in the throat of a stranger and the hands, lipstick, thighs and buttocks floating in a montage of a drunken haze, which was now unfolding and clearing before him as the woman he'd groped and fumbled with in the shadows stared back at him – Stella; his Stella, was the one he couldn't remember – lost, distorted in drunk time and now found.

It was a charge; a planned calculated surge towards the children. Her prey: a small plump girl with glasses who'd temporarily strayed from the group, like a young innocent antelope who'd slipped away from the herd, left behind, happily nibbling on a blade of grass as the lioness pounced. Grabbing hold of the girl in full flight she soon held her tightly by the shoulders as she ran with her towards the edge of the waiting cliff.

'Sir! Sir!' cried the boys and girls, unsure of what to say or do.

'Jennifer!' shouted the baritone, now running down from the back as the girl screamed uncontrollably and fought to free herself from Stella's grip.

'Stella!' Kev called out helplessly as another man surged into view – the very man he'd seen earlier with the dreadlocks, now sprinting towards them as Jennifer struggled desperately to flee the clutches of a certain death. The man with dreadlocks now dived at the girl's legs, pulling her down in a rugby tackle as the two of them spun free from Stella's clutches, landing four metres from the edge and what would have been a certain death.

'Stella! Stop!' he cried as she walked with purpose towards the edge. He still couldn't differentiate between the Stella he loved and the one he saw now. Throwing his glasses to the ground he at last gave chase, his lungs heavy and laboured, each step like lead, his belly bouncing uncomfortably up and down as he went; past the huddled school party and oblivious old lady and heading heavy-footed towards the sea, his steps slower and slower until he couldn't move any more.

The vast expanse: inky sea torn by white foam as if a blue velvet curtain was opening before him. There she stood, silent, her back to the sea, facing him: both of them locked into one another, transfixed in time as an unfathomable stillness engulfed them and the sky above them appeared to wobble and tremble before reverting to its previous state.

'Anabelle,' he said at last, catching his breath, 'you're Anabelle.' He felt stupid. The words sounded ridiculous, not what were really required for such an important opening line.

The voice was not hers, the pitch higher, the speed of her delivery quick and affirmative, her lips almost puckered as she spoke. 'So you worked it out then,' she said with lightning speed as he tried to keep up with this new way of speaking. 'No, don't come any closer,' she warned. 'The penny dropped then?' she taunted, pulling her collar tight up around her neck.

'You killed Eve,' he stated mechanically.

'I had no choice,' she laughed, 'you used me, thought we'd just have a quick, sordid, squeezy fumble and that would be it.' She spat the words out with venom at machine-gun speed. 'And then I saw you outside with her: all coy and lovey-dovey; her with her pencil in the hair and you posing like a film star, both of you gazing out at the oh so romantic river – you must have thought it was perfect?'

'It was perfect,' he replied coldly.

'Oh,' she said theatrically surprised, 'I'd thought you'd be a little more sympathetic; I mean, you probably know of my *disturbed background* by now?'

He said nothing (though his face said it all) as he felt the impulse to run at her and . . .

'Really?' she said reading his expression, 'why don't you then? Just push me off – you'd be doing me a favour.' Running her fingers through her hair she continued, 'Perhaps it may help if I told you that everything I told you was a lie: that I have no husband or business, that I work for Babe TV; you probably had a wank over me, yes?' she said in a Swedish accent. 'Oh, and by the way: the one-night-stand with Mark never happened; just wanted to hurt you; but,' she added, 'I guess the biggest pain of all is knowing that I killed your Eve and that I enjoyed it. Your perfect Eve!'

'Stop!' he cried, wanting to throw a punch.

'Oh, you poor thing; you have emotions after all?' She knew her acid tongue had the better of him as she continued to pick away at the scab in front of her. 'You didn't even see me in the pub at Eve's wake; thought you were hearing things, you stared straight at me and you saw nothing,' she scoffed, her breathing heavier than before.

He saw it clearly as she spoke, the past catching up with him and kicking him at every opportunity. 'That was you?' It was all he could say, though his fists wanted to say more.

'Why would you see the dote?' She was angry now. 'You who used Anabelle and then slipped off outside with Miss Cute. What would you see?' she roared, 'but an insignificant girl who was happy with the scraps you might throw her way.'

'Is that it then: you got me back?' he said shifting uneasily, his left leg feeling as if it had gone to sleep.

'Oh, fuck no,' she laughed. 'Didn't Anabelle explain it to you? You're responsible for everything. It should have been the death of an innocent – the plump one with the glasses – and now,' she said staring just above his head, 'well, it's me. I'm going to jump because of you; you, Kev; it's you; you're the reason. Your selfishness killed Eve and now me.' The smile was back: Stella's kind face, her large expectant eyes looking deep into his as if trying to anticipate the next line. 'Maybe this might help?' she said, producing a photograph from her pocket and holding it up for him to examine.

'Where did you get it?' he snapped, examining the picture of himself and Eve standing deep in conversation on the deck of the disco boat as Waterloo Bridge loomed into view in the background.

'I was there, remember? You looked up from your posing as your foot slipped down the wall and the perfect one laughed. Oh, Kev, you really can't remember, can you?'

Of course he remembered: the people milling onto the deck just as they thought they were the only ones in the world; the only ones engaged in the magic and beauty of the black-ink Thames. 'Why would I remember?' he replied, because it was the only spiteful thing he could say.

Suddenly, the blimp which had been hovering out at sea was lifted by a freak gust, bouncing as it went higher and higher, before dropping like a lead weight as it was slowly blown in towards land. Remaining level with Stella, it appeared to pick up speed as if catapulted ferociously inland.

'But you will remember. For the rest of your life, and we will never end.'

Closing her eyes, she stiffened and let the weight of her body carry her backwards like a felled tree. She was gone, lifted gracefully on the returned wind. A gasp could be heard from the growing audience behind him as she was released without a sound.

Watching the soles of her shoes glide up and then drop like a kite, her trench coat flapping and ballooning as it was caught on the air, Kev wondered what she was thinking as her contented expression remained stolid and unflinching as she briefly opened her eyes to look at him. In that split second he only saw the Stella he'd loved. It was then that the blustering, out of control blimp violently smothered her, the banner from its tail wrapping around her ankles as it turned her upside down, carrying her off to sea, screaming and howling like a tormented animal. As she was swept away, tangled and twisted by her name, wriggling to set herself free, she gradually became silent and at last limp as Kev's name wrapped itself around her neck, the letters turning her blue. Soaring now at considerable speed, tied and trussed, a jettisoned comic character, she floated west, dead.

And so stood the man on the cliff: solitary, only the sky and ocean for company, swaying like a still Buddha arched back onto his heels, looking at and feeling nothing as the gulls shrieked and called out above his head, the horizon nothing more than a thin pencil line.

Chapter Thirty-one

365 days later

'It's a plague graveyard.'

'How do you know?'

'The graves are closer together; head to head.'

In truth he'd been looking further beyond the spire of St John's to the bank of the river where you could just make out the tip of the London Eye. 'Yeah, I was wondering about that.' Once a liar always a liar, he thought, smiling politely as the man who'd made the cheery chit-chat retreated back into his *History Today* magazine, casually adding that it was a department he'd once worked in for the City of London planning department in which his area of expertise had been no longer used cemeteries.

'Mausoleums: do people ask for them any more?' He'd surprised himself at his readiness to engage the man further.

'More wicker baskets these days,' said the man, placing the magazine on his knee. 'Though that said, Catholics still tend to go for the traditional casket and headstone.'

'Right.' He'd only been to one Catholic funeral and that had certainly been the case.

'You know that eventually most plots will just collapse; the ground cannot hold over time, especially when they're boxed one on top of the other.' He hesitated for a second before continuing. 'There I go again talking about work and death.'

'I know, it's catching.'

'We should know better,' smiled the man, nodding towards the door that led into the maternity ward, 'we should be talking about the miracle of life.'

'I suppose we should.'

'Section?' enquired the man in solidarity.

'Yeah, and you?'

'Same.'

Just then a middle-aged nurse with very red cheeks and flared nostrils opened the flappy, bendy door and called both the men's surnames. 'Mr Saunders, and . . .' she paused checking her clipboard, 'Mr Parker – your partners are prepped and waiting for you. Follow me into the gowning area and we'll get you ready.'

'Good luck,' they both said to each other awkwardly as they slipped into matching green gowns and the nurse plopped two hairnets on their heads.

'Anyone would think you were delivering the babies,' laughed the nurse, her nostrils expanding with every breath like a young bull's. She probably said the same thing to every expectant father, he reasoned, smiling limply. Whether it was their appearance or the terrified expressions on their faces she was remarking upon, he couldn't make out, but he was pleased to hear a voice rather than the oppressive silence that would otherwise have accompanied an uncomfortable situation. More out of embarrassment than comradeship he patted the graveyard expert on the shoulder as they both entered doors side by side each other into a world which they had only seen on TV dramas.

Was it a tent? he wondered, trying to make sense of the array of dark green sheets draped over a square frame and clamped tight above the netted head of the mother to be, obscuring the view of her yet to be cut open bulbous belly. Holding back the tears he tentatively stepped forward.

'Kev, hold my hand,' she said, her expression lost and scared, the words lost to him as he stared straight through her, before his dull eyes fell on the forever grease stain on the tip of his toe.

Clutching his hand tightly she pulled him in close, her sweaty clasp like a blacksmith's vice. He wanted to run, perhaps hide under a green sheet and curl up in a ball as if a bad dream had just begun, hoping that it would be forgotten and mean nothing when he awoke in a far-off snow-covered Narnia.

Sarah: her wondrous eyes and faint seductive smile beamed up at him. 'I can't believe it, we're having our own baby,' she croaked, her tone lower than usual because of the medication. He smiled back, flinching inside as he thought of their sordid second round of liaisons which had led to the conclusion below him beyond the drape. 'A new beginning,' she managed as she visibly jolted as the medical team at her belly cut, clamped, separated, clutched, wiggled and pulled. 'Ohh!' she groaned.

'Weird?' he asked.

'Yeah, feels like a lot of wriggling around down there.'

'Pain?'

'No pain.'

'Nearly there,' announced a new nurse he hadn't seen before. He noticed that the contours of her face, in particular her nose, cheekbones and forehead were the same as Stella's. Studying her closely, wishing the woman looked nothing like her, his mind turned to the darkness he'd been trying to avoid all these months as a heavy sweat formed under his arms and a cold shiver climbed the discs of his spine as he saw the woman he'd known as Stella being violently entangled and elevated to her death.

'A girl,' announced the surgeon as the nurse whisked the baby away to be cleaned and checked. Quickly returning to the mother's side of the tent she brought their daughter close to Sarah's cheek. A scrumpled-up, new face, a warm covering of brown fuzz on her head, her tiny pink fingers pumping in and out as if trying to grab an imaginary sweet, a missed speck of blood on her chin: she was a picture of new life.

'Oh, Kev, she's beautiful,' she cried, her shaky, drug induced hands cradling the child as best she could.

He closed his eyes like the closing chapter of a predictable novel. He knew, no, dreaded, what was coming next. *Please,* he pleaded to himself within the seconds of time he could not control or roll back, but only pray would pass and be bubble-wrapped, slung to a far off corner of the universe, a place which had no name, permanence or meaning. Like the sperm which had sprung free from the swimmers and gone it alone in pursuit of survival forty weeks past, its name had been celestially attached, branded and bound to infinity.

There had been no mention of names. He'd just convinced himself that it would be a boy. And there it was, hanging in the stillness of the sacred family triangle, uttered like a prayer, a hymn, an echo from the Garden of Eden. 'Eve, she's called Eve.'

The words reverberating through his mind, spiking every nerve in his body, he pulled open the shutters of his tear-drenched eyes. Sarah smiled warmly at the perceived tears of joy as she repeated the mantra, her joyous moment lost to him as he held tight the girl who wore flats and nestled a pen in her hair.

The End

Acknowledgements

Many thanks to my family and friends from Ireland, UK and further afield who have supported me as a writer, you know who you are. Bea Grabowska and all the team at Headline Publishing for their incredible input and believing in this book. My editor Greg Rees for his spot-on observations and insight. Thanks to Katrin Lloyd in Cardiff for her powers of discovery. To Sculptor Colin Grehan for the lend of his *inspiration overalls*. Ultimately, to my wife Teresa and son Louis who have had to endure years of me sitting in front a laptop and their unfailing, loving support throughout. I would like to remember my mother Pauline and a special mention to Karen and George. Thank you to the warm people of Claremorris, Co, Mayo and the West of Ireland.

To all the writers, artists, songwriters, musicians and creatives who have unknowingly inspired me.